C000109917

King Henry

Book 4 in the Struggle for a Crown Series

By

Griff Hosker

Published by Sword Books Ltd 2019

Copyright ©Griff Hosker First Edition

Cover by Design for Writers

List of important characters in the novel

(Fictional characters are italicized)

- *Sir William Strongstaff*
- King Henry IV formerly Henry Bolingbroke, Earl of Northampton
- Henry of Monmouth (Prince of Wales and Henry's son)
- George de Dunbar, 10th Earl of Dunbar and March (Dunbarre)
- Ralph Neville, 4th Baron Neville of Raby, and 1st earl of Westmorland
- Henry Percy (Harry Hotspur) the heir to the Earl of Northumberland
- Henry Percy, the Earl of Northumberland
- Thomas Percy, the Earl of Worcester and Hotspur's uncle.
- Sir Edmund Mortimer,
- Edmund Mortimer, 5th Earl of March (Nephew of Sir Edmund Mortimer and claimant to the English crown)
- Archibald Douglas, 4th Earl of Douglas
- Edmund, Earl of Stafford
- Owain Glyndŵr (Glendower), Rebel and pretender to the Welsh crown

Prologue

King Richard was dead. At one time I had been captain of his Guard and protected him and his wife. I had been there at the end and knew that he had not died at the hands of his cousin, the new King, Henry Bolingbroke, as was the rumour amongst King Henry's enemies. I did not like King Henry for I believed that he had inveigled himself on to the throne. His son, Henry Monmouth, I liked. He had been, as had King Richard and King Henry, trained by me but I saw the spirit of the Black Prince in Hal! That had been sadly lacking in both Richard and Henry. Despite King Richard's words on his deathbed, *'Prince Henry, when you are King keep this man as close to you as your armour. You will live. Listen to him and heed his words for they are sage. I did not and I pay the price.'* Henry Bolingbroke had sent his son north to Northumberland to continue his training with Henry Percy. The King was a clever and cunning man. He did not trust Percy and thought to use his own son to spy on him. At the same time, he took Hal away from me. It was yet another reason why I did not like him. The death of King Richard did nothing to bring peace to a troubled land. Even some of those who had toppled the former king from power now opposed King Henry.

As for myself, I was not only happy, for my days of having to protect a king were over, I was rich. When I had been a camp follower holding the horses of the Blue Company in Spain, I could never have imagined that I would own four manors. I had been given Stoney Stratford, Weedon and the rich manor of Dauentre by King Richard and the Earl of Northampton; my wife had bought the manor of Whittlebury. Eleanor knew how to make coin and had a head for both farming and business. We lived at Weedon for it suited us and Sir John, who had been my squire, watched over Dauentre for me.

I had nothing to do with politics and that meant I kept to myself. My manors were renowned as places where politics were left to others. Despite the fact that I did not like him, I was the King's man and would not involve myself in plots and conspiracies. I did not think that Henry Bolingbroke was a bad king but I had yet to see him be a better king than Richard. After Richard's Queen had died; it was only then he became a tyrant. Before then he had tried to do his best for England and Normandy but he had been badly advised and served. He had said as much on his deathbed. '*I want you as a witness. I forgive Henry Bolingbroke, my cousin. Despite what others wanted he did not have me killed. I forgive him for I wanted him to kill me. I understand why he did not. As for the others? None are forgiven. I hope they rot in hell for having abandoned me.*'

Now those who had abandoned him were plotting against Henry Bolingbroke who had barely attained the throne when they began their machinations! They were self-serving hypocrites and I wanted nothing to do with them.

Unlike many lords, I maintained good men at arms and good archers. It cost coins to feed them, arm them and provide their horses but it was an expense worth bearing for my family was safe and if England needed me again, I could protect England too. I had two good sons, Tom and Harry; both would be warriors and so I closed a wall around my home and I practised the art of war. I was unsure of my age but I know that I had seen more than forty summers. That meant I had been at war for thirty-five years. I knew that I would draw my sword again and that I would fight. When that day came then I would be ready as would my men and my sons.

I also had two daughters, Alice and Mary. Both were coming to the age when they would be married. That was a new land my wife and I had yet to explore.

Part One
Welsh Rebellion

Chapter 1

My wife used to count every penny when we were first married but now, we had so much money that she began to spend more than she saved for we had four manors and a healthy income. We did not have to be frugal and keep some money back for the disastrous harvest. We had chosen to live in our manor at Weedon. Although it was not the largest of the ones I owned it was the one we loved the most. When we had first gone to Dauentre we had been treated badly by the local burghers and vowed to show them that we deserved our position. We had visited Northampton Castle and seen the way it was decorated and furnished. She had tried to copy that which she had seen. She had spent money to have seamstresses sew rich fabric to make wall hangings so that there were no bare walls and the hall was rich with the hue of strong colours. It was mainly a rich blue, which was the colour of my standard, but there were also splashes of red. It was an effective design and visitors to my hall were impressed. In addition, she had the best furniture which was made by the craftsmen of Dauentre. It was made from the finest oak and was well finished. We even had beds for not only us but all of our children. I had enough contacts in Gascony to be able to have supplies of good wine, fine pots and glassware as well as spices from the east. We lived well although I knew there were many who still thought of us as common.

The armour my sons and I wore was also captured plate armour. Roger of Chester, my captain of sergeants, thought it a waste of money to buy new for, as squires, they would not be in the forefront of battle for some time yet but I knew the effect of bodkin arrows. When I had been growing up the needlepoint bodkin was efficient enough to pierce mail. Now that men wore plate, as well as mail, archers used the heavy war bodkin. It was not a cheap arrow but it could pierce plate armour and was worth the expense! Our horses were the best that money could buy and came from the horse farm of Red Ralph in Middleham. I never liked the destrier; it seemed too slow for me. I preferred the courser which was faster but still a warhorse! What had changed since I was a young man, was the way that we fought. Horses were used for a chevauchée but, generally, men fought on battlefields on foot. Shields were only used by the common men. Plate armour was better protection than a shield. Once armies joined battle then it was harder for archers to use their bows and so once archers had thinned out the opposition the two sets of mailed men closed and fought a bloody battle to see who would hold the field. We also used longer weapons which often required two hands although some skilled men used a weapon in each hand; that was my preferred method of fighting. My father would have enjoyed the new style of fighting for he had been a wild man in battle.

I had been at home in Weedon a bare eight months when we heard of the rebellion of Owain Glendower. It was Sir Henry of Stratford who brought me the news. I had trained Sir Henry to be a knight when I was just a gentleman. He was not a natural knight but he fought well enough. His grandparents, both now dead, had brought the boy up and they had not begun to train him for war early enough. He would never be the knight that Sir John had become. His manor was closer to Wales than we were and he and his squire rode in one late afternoon having travelled from the west. I liked Sir Henry but we were not close neighbours and a visit normally meant trouble and so I had men watching. We had a watch tower which I kept manned and we had seen him coming. I had looked at the sky and told my wife to prepare rooms. It was getting late and he would not be able to return home.

My men all knew him and liked him. As he and his squire rode through the outer gate, I said to them, "We will end the practice. Sir Henry's arrival has given you some extra hours to yourself."

They cheered. The archers moved the butts and the men at arms collected all of the wooden practice weapons. They called cheerily to Sir Henry. Many lords found my men at arms and archers informal to the point of insolence but Sir Henry was not one. The men had saved his life on more than one occasion and, but for their intervention, his grandparents might have suffered a truly terrible end.

"Tom, Harry, see to his lordship's horses." My sons were both my squires and hurried to do my bidding. The life of a squire was little better than that of a house servant.

I clasped Henry's arm as he walked over to me. He nodded towards my hall. "Each time I see it I see improvements. One day, my lord, I expect to see it become a castle."

"I do not think the King would sanction a castle. This suits me and we know how to defend it."

He nodded and, as we walked to my hall, he said, "War is here, my lord, and the Welsh have risen. A Welsh lord has gathered men and raised the people. He wishes to become King. His name is Owain Glendower."

I vaguely remembered an Owain although I had known him as Owain ap Griffith. He had been one of King Richard's squires. King Richard had had many squires. Owain was a political appointment to gain him favour in Wales. It had worked as the Welsh liked King Richard! I shook my head, "He is an obscure landowner. It is like my raising the standard of rebellion over Weedon!"

Sir Henry said, "And yet he claims to have ancestors who were Kings of Powys. He has many men flocking to his banner and they are causing mischief on the borders. You know as well as any, Sir William, that a few men can cause mayhem in a peaceful land."

We had reached my hall and my wife opened the door, "Welcome, Sir Henry. How is your good lady?"

"She is well and she sends her greetings to you."

"She is a fine lady. And your children?"

"They prosper."

"Then all is well. Shall I prepare rooms for you and your squire?"

"If you would not mind, my lady, for I have business to discuss with Sir William!"

Eleanor beamed, "You are always welcome here, lord. There are others I dread crossing my door but not you."

8

I sighed. My wife had a habit of speaking her mind, "My love, leave Sir Henry to tell me the purpose of his visit and we will speak further when we dine." I smiled to take the barb from my words. I had learned that the tone I used seemed as important to my wife as the words! I did not understand it!

She gave me a thin smile and disappeared. I would pay for the barb, albeit unintended, later. We entered the Great Hall. I paused for my wife had worked wonders since Sir Henry's last visit and he gasped at the rich colours and tapestries, "My lord but this is magnificent. I fear I will not bring my wife for the purchase of such hangings would bankrupt me!"

I laughed, "Aye, Lady Eleanor does nothing by halves." I walked him slowly to the table so that he could take in all the detail of the needlework and the clever use of contrast. We sat and I poured the wine. My servants had learned that I did not need them to hang on every command. I was not lacking a limb and I could pour wine. "So, war? And in September? Is this cunning or happenstance?"

"A mixture, lord. Lord Grey of Ruthin is Owain's lord. They had a dispute over land and it was submitted to King Henry."

I nodded, "Do not tell me; King Henry decided in favour of his friend, Lord Grey." This was typical of the knight I had known as Henry Bolingbroke.

He laughed, "You are prescient, my lord. And when this Glendower objected Lord Grey threw an accusation at him that he had been tardy in responding to King Henry's muster for the war against the Scots."

I had not been asked to join the war for King Henry knew that I did not get on with Sir Henry Percy and his father, the Earl of Northumberland. Percy had sent killers to hunt me down and kill me. There was an old-fashioned blood feud between us. Worse, King Henry had given Prince Hal to Percy to continue the training begun by me. I said nothing for I did not wish to embroil Sir Henry in my disputes.

"And?"

"You have been asked to bring your men to Chester."

The message would have come from the Earl of Chester and that was now King Henry. I understood his reasons. King Richard had been most popular in Cheshire. The King would mistrust his

Cheshire men but he knew he could rely on me. "He did not specify numbers?"

Henry of Stratford smiled, "No, lord. I think he just needs you to be there and your archers."

"You are summoned too?"

"Yes, Sir William and I have to bring twenty spears and twenty bows."

"Have you those numbers?"

"Aye, but they are not the equal of yours. I will bring farmers and drapers who will be warriors for the working day and when it is over return to their trades. Yours are the professionals. Compared with Baron William Strongstaff's men, we will be ill-equipped and ill-trained but they are good fellows and I would not lose a one!"

I smiled. Sir Henry had never changed. He was solid and reliable but that was all. He was not a warrior and would not have lasted long in the Blue Company! My sons entered with Peter who was Sir Henry's squire. He was older than they were but my sons had become men. Harry had only recently begun to shave but his size and his skills with both sword and shield showed he was a man. Harry would hold our horses in battle while Tom would hold my banner and guard my back. Sir Henry's news made me realise that this would be their first test in war.

I heard voices and I said, "Sir Henry, I pray leave all talk of war until the morrow. I would not have my wife distressed before the meal."

"Of course, Sir William."

As Eleanor came in, followed by servants with trays of titbits, I knew I would have a hard task explaining why we had to go to war. That would be for later. While the cook prepared the evening meal we sat and chatted about family and all the irrelevancies which would soon become the most important memories we took with us as we went to war.

That evening, as we climbed into our comfortable bed, I knew I would have to broach the subject of war. She snuggled in to me, "It is good that Sir Henry has not changed and he is still the boy you trained. I hope this war does not take him."

I started, "You knew?"

She laughed, in the dark, "Of course. As soon as he and Peter rode in I knew it was a summons to war but I am glad that you did not speak of it while we ate. The girls will be upset when they discover that their brothers go to fight. Is it the Scots?"

King Henry and Percy, Harry Hotspur, were in the north quelling an ever-aggressive Scottish rising in the borders. "No, the Welsh."

"Now I see why the King did not call you for that war. He was saving you for the threat from the West. I thought the Welsh were subdued? Is not Henry Monmouth, Prince of Wales?"

"Aye, but that means precious little to the Welsh. It is a local lord who has risen against King Henry."

I felt her relax in my arms, "Then this might be over quickly and the men can be at their farms at harvest time."

"Perhaps but this is the north of Wales. I take nothing for granted."

The next morning Sir Henry and Peter left us. We had discussed the muster; it would be at Chester. I estimated that it would take a week for me to gather my men and make the journey to Cheshire. I used my sons to summon my men. Some lived very close to the hall but most had farms and homes which were some distance away. They enjoyed a life which the men of the Blue Company would have envied. They had land and property but they were paid a stipend to be warriors. Most were farmers albeit on a small scale. They each had an income from the land which had been greater than the stipend paid to Red Ralph and the other members of the Blue Company. They still practised each day for they were warriors but war was no longer their whole life and they had wives and families.

The captain of my sergeants was Roger of Chester and my captain of archers was Alan of the Woods. Both had been with me for a long time and both lived closer to my hall than any other. When they arrived, we went to the stables so that I could tell them all while we examined and chose the horses we would take. We had many horses and some were the wrong type to take to the mountains of Wales. I had a horse master and he watched over our animals for us. They were a valuable commodity and it did not do to neglect them. When we had chosen the horses we would take, we went into the yard.

"The Welsh have damned good archers, lord, they are as good as we are."

"I know, Alan, but they are not as well armed. I do not think that they have many of the heavy war bodkin arrows and our men have, in the main, plate. I think this will not be a war of battles but of skirmish and chevauchée. I confess that I hope it will be a brief one." I sighed for Sir Henry had given me news which was both unwelcome and unpalatable. "Young Hal, Prince Henry, is now under the tutelage of Hotspur, Henry Percy."

I already knew that but it came as a surprise to them. It stopped them both in their examination of the horses, "But Lord Percy is your enemy and sent men to kill you." Roger did not mention that the attempt had also been on their lives. "I thought the Prince was a hope for the future for he knows how to war but if he is changed by that northern demon then it does not bode well for you, lord." My Captain of Arms neither liked nor trusted Sir Henry Percy!

I had to trust that the young man I had trained to be a warrior kept the heart I knew he had and had not been poisoned by Percy. "There may be difficulties, especially in this campaign, but I have to believe that Hal will not forget the time he spent amongst us. Perhaps this is a test of him; just as Christ was tempted by the devil, so it may be that Hotspur is his test."

They both made the sign of the cross and nodded.

We would be taking spare horses as well as tents and spare weapons. A campaign was demanding and it paid to be as prepared as possible. We had a small baggage train. We also took four servants. All had come to me as old soldiers seeking employment as warriors. I employed them but as servants. It meant that when we campaigned, I had four good guards for the camp and if we fought that most rare of things, a battle, then they could also act as horse holders.

King Henry had returned from Scotland when he heard of the revolt and was at Northampton where he mustered others of his lords. We would both share the same road, called Watling Street, to Chester for it had been built by the Romans. He was on the road ahead of us but, as with all armies led by a king, it moved slowly. King Henry, like other kings before him, carried his treasure with him. The Tower had been sacked in times past and a wise king kept his coin close to him. It meant we caught up with the baggage train. We moved faster than any army for I had just one knight, Sir John of Dauentre, and, between us, we led less than thirty men. We overtook the baggage train and then custom dictated that we stay behind lords who were of a higher standing than us. I was a baron and I found myself amongst other lords from the Midlands.

One of King Henry's squires, Sir Richard of Helmsley, rode back to me when my presence was made known to the King. "His Majesty would have you ride with him, Sir William. Your knight can command your men in your absence."

I nodded. John would not be put out. He had endured Henry Bolingbroke when we had been on a crusade and he knew him, warts and all!

The King looked careworn and that was not a surprise. He had been supported in his attempt to gain the crown by almost all of the nobility and now that he had it, he had most of the nobility trying to rid him of it. He had surrounded himself with young knights who were not affiliated to any of those with claims to the throne. That was a wise move. I was not seen as a threat for I had been King Richard's bodyguard and, for a while, I had guarded Henry Bolingbroke and his son. I had saved him from assassins on more than one occasion. For that reason, I was trusted more than any other knight. That was shown when he waved away the knights from around him. What he would say to me would be in private and for my ears only.

He gave me a wry smile, "This crown sits heavy on my head, Will."

"As it did your cousin, King Henry."

He nodded, "Aye, for you knew him as well as any and better than most. I feel more sympathy for him now than when I wished for the crown."

"The old, wise women always say '*be careful what you wish for*'!"

He laughed and was, briefly, the young knight I had first schooled in swordplay. "You are like the slave the Caesars had behind them in their chariots bringing them down to earth! It is good to have you at my side again, Will. It seems like a lifetime since the Baltic and now the Welsh raise their heads once again, and this is not even one with a true and legitimate claim to the throne! The men of Gwynedd support this Glendower as do the men of Powys! He has more support than King Llewellyn! I can do without this distraction. I have to be back at Eltham Castle by the end of November for the Emperor of the East, Manuel Palaiologos, comes to make a visit! I have enough domestic enemies without making foreign ones by dint of neglect. I would have you stay with my son while he deals with the threat."

I raised the subject which would be embarrassing for us both but had to be spoken aloud, "And what of Sir Henry Percy? I thought he was guiding the Prince and we both know that he and I enjoy less than cordial relations."

He laughed, "Sir Henry Percy is the only man I know could last more than a few swords thrusts in a bout with you, Will Strongstaff, but you need not fear. I will establish your position before I leave."

King Henry was not a great leader in battle. His father, John of Gaunt and his uncle, the Black Prince, had both been amongst the greatest generals of their age but King Richard and his cousin, whilst brave and able to defend themselves well, did not have the strategic ability of those great generals. Grudgingly I had to admit that Sir Henry Percy, Harry Hotspur, did and, I believed so did Prince Henry. My men believed that was because he had spent some time under my tutelage. All that I knew of strategy had been learned on the battlefield!

"My son will need you, Will."

"And will I be needed above the forty days service you are owed, King Henry?"

His face fell, "There is the rub, Will. You, of all people, know the problems brought about by money. When I was merely a Duke, I had coin to spare! Now I am King I have to go cap in hand to Parliament and beg for money to defend this land. Now I see the problems my cousin endured." He lowered his voice, "I cannot afford to pay an army and we both know that the Welsh are poor as church mice. The Scots are different, for they have ransoms and castles which are worth taking. My son is Prince of Wales and until Parliament funds him he will have to bear the cost. We defeat this Glendower quickly and go home but you, my friend, must keep in touch with my son. He is Prince of Wales and he will have to rule the land without me."

"And find the funds to do so, my lord."

"Aye. The pity of it is that Cheshire supported my cousin and they have a natural antipathy towards me and my family. My son has a poisoned chalice!" I saw his face break into a smile, "Talking to you makes me more hopeful, Will. You are one of the last men who fought with the Black Prince and all of France and Spain cowered when he shook his spear. You are a good luck charm and with you behind him, my son can become the Black Prince reborn!"

We chatted easily as we rode north and west. Thanks to my position at the head of the column I was able to secure good lodgings and stables for my men at each of our nightly halts. There was something to be said for having the ear of the King!

As we rode towards Chester the King looked behind him at one point, "You do not have enough knights, Strongstaff." I nodded. "Is your son ready yet?"

"No, King Henry, for he has too little experience."

"Then knight two of your men at arms; as I recall from the Baltic they are skilled enough." He saw the question on my face. "Are they good enough to be knights?"

"Of course."

"Then knight them! I would have you do so, sooner, rather than later."

"Yes, Your Majesty!"

I did not mind dubbing them but while Roger of Chester was an obvious choice, the selection of a second might cause dissension amongst my men. I would think about it before I rushed into the ceremony.

Chester was a vast camp. The Prince and Hotspur were within the castle when we arrived and King Henry thought it prudent if I stayed without so that he could speak with Percy and his son. I agreed and my men and I made camp by the old Roman ruins close to the river. Roger of Chester came from the city and it was his advice I took. It was good advice. There was good grazing as well as water. We were all seasoned campaigners and knew the value of both.

I had twenty archers and, while my men at arms and the rest of the archers made a good camp, I took Alan of the Woods to one side. "This will, hopefully, be a swift campaign. To ensure it is I want you to take my archers tomorrow and find the enemy. I hope that the Prince of Wales and his new mentor have already done so but I would prefer to have the opinion of an archer I trust."

"You do me great honour, my lord. Owen the Welshman and Geraint the Green both come from this part of Wales. When we rode north, they gave me an idea of where we would be likely to find the enemy."

"Good. I want one day's ride, no more. I dare say there will be a council of war tomorrow and we will have a better idea then of the problems we face."

Sir John and I sat on one of the barrels my men had brought from Weedon. It contained ale. All soldiers are mistrustful of what they deem to be foreign beer and we had brought four small barrels with us. One had been broached but the other two made functional stools for us. We looked south to the hills of Flintshire which gave way to the mountains of Gwynedd. Sir John shook his head, ruefully, "This is not horse country, lord."

I nodded, "I know and that is why King Edward built his castles around the edges to keep them penned. Harlech, Conwy, Caernarfon and Beaumaris, all are mighty fortresses. They will hold but you are right, Sir John, trying to hold the Welsh will be like trying to grasp a handful of quicksilver! The best we can hope is that they realise the futility of fighting men who are armoured and mounted. A few months of living on the side of a mountain might bring them to the table!"

I looked up as horsemen rode in from the south. They were led by two knights; I recognised one, Rhys ap Tudur, for he had been on campaign in Ireland with King Richard. King Richard had been so impressed with him that he had made him Sherriff of Anglesey. I took the other to be his brother, Gwilym ap Tudur. I was pleased to see them for they meant that not all of the Welsh were on the side of the rebels.

They reined in when they saw us and Rhys dismounted. He took off his gauntlets and held out his arm, "Sir William Strongstaff! Well met, my lord. Here, brother, is one of the mightiest knights you will ever see. He was good King Richard's protector." His face darkened, "His death was unnecessary."

I did not want to get into a debate which might embroil me in treachery. I merely nodded, "All deaths before a man has seen forty summers are unnecessary but I was with him at the end and he was hopeful of seeing his beloved wife in heaven."

They both made the sign of the cross, "It is to be hoped so. And you and your men are part of this campaign?"

"We are. Tell me, what do you know of this Glendower?"

"Glyndŵr," he corrected me with the pronunciation; I had used the English one. "He is a cousin and has assumed the title of Prince."

"Are you not thus conflicted?"

He shook his head, "Our fortunes are tied with those of England now but we hope to bring him to book by negotiation and not a force of arms. He has few knights with him but the people see him as a saviour."

His brother said, "Aye and he has the support of the best of Welsh warriors, the archers!"

"And that is why we are here, brother, to counsel the King!"

I pointed to the castle, "He is there with Henry Percy and the Prince of Wales."

"That is good for Owain Glyndŵr served with Sir Henry in the wars against Scotland. He was in the garrison at Berwick-on-Tweed. This is a hopeful gathering of English lords and may bring this rebellion to a swift conclusion. This is not the place to be in winter."

After they had left us, I felt more hopeful. With so many men on the side of King Henry, we might be able to bring the war to a swift conclusion and for that, I would offer prayers of thanks to God.

I was not summoned to the castle and we ate around my campfire. I did not mind, in fact, I preferred the company of ordinary men to that of nobles. Ralph, who was the son of Red Ralph a man with whom I had served in Gascony, brought me a platter. He was now Sir John's squire. I spoke to him as he ladled some stew onto my platter; squires cooked and served their masters.

"How is your mother now, Ralph?"

His mother, Mary, had been distraught when her husband had died. It had been exacerbated by the loss of Ralph who had become Sir John's squire. "She does not write much, my lord, but my brothers delivered some horses two months since and they said she prospers. Since my father's death, she has thrown herself into the running of the farm. The border should be quieter now although this war will create a great demand for horses."

"Aye, and it is right that your family should benefit. I intend to visit at Easter for the boys will need new horses. They ride palfreys, but Tom will soon need a courser."

"My father planned well, lord, and we have good bloodstock."

After he had gone, I reflected that only Old Tom and Peter the Priest remained out of the Blue Company. The others lived but only in my memory.

Chapter 2

I sent my archers off at first light. They had good horses and could ride eighteen miles before they would have to return. That would take them close to the Clwyd. The long valley marked a sort of unofficial boundary between the Welsh and the English. It was Prince Henry himself who came to fetch me for the council of war. He had two young squires with him and the three of them rode rather than walked.

"You had no need to trouble yourself, Prince Henry. You could have sent one of your men for me."

"None of this Prince nonsense when we are alone. It was Hal or Harry when I lived with you and your family and I still cherish those memories for I saw a family and that is something I have missed. Besides, I wished to speak with your men for they helped to make me the warrior I have become."

Roger and the others had seen him arrive at the gathering and they bowed.

Prince Henry spoke to them one by one and then, looking around, frowned, "And Captain Alan and the archers?"

"I sent them to scout this morning."

He laughed and turned to his squires, "This is what a true warrior does. While the rest of the lords lie abed, Sir William seeks out the men we would fight." He turned to Tom and Harry. Tom was slightly older than the Prince but he was much bigger. "And you Tom, where will they get the armour for you?"

"We have a good smith, my lord, and I hope to earn enough silver to pay for new armour when I am stopped growing." He had mail and plate but they were hand me downs and captured armour.

Shaking his head, the Prince said, "You will not make enough fighting against the Welsh but if any can make coins from this it will be your father's company! Come, Sir William, they await us.

I confess that I will be happier with you by my side for you, I know, I can trust."

Chester Castle had an enormous Great Hall which easily accommodated all of the barons and nobles who had been invited; they were standing around a huge table. As soon as I entered all eyes swivelled to view me. One pair burned with the fire of hatred and they belonged to Henry Percy. I saw he was standing next to the Tudur brothers but their eyes bore no enmity. It was just the knight of Northumberland who wished my death. There were others who wished it, I had no doubt, but none were in the hall.

King Henry beamed, "The champion of kings is now come and we may make a start." Prince Henry took me to stand next to his father and that was on the opposite side of the table from Percy. This would be an interesting experience. I wondered at Prince Henry's decision. Why had he not wished to stand next to his mentor? I had little time to ponder the matter for the King began to speak.

"These Welsh rebels are growing in number and we need to snuff out this game of insurrection before it begins. Sir Henry, you have managed to deal with the Scottish incursions well, how would you suggest we deal with these Welsh brigands?"

There was a map on the table and I expected him to point out their defences and suggest ways of defeating them. Instead, he assiduously avoided the map. "That is simple, King Henry, we take our army to the Cheshire plain and threaten Wrecsam and then, Powys. They are the only two strongholds worth worrying about. We force them to meet us on the battlefield and trounce them."

I was about to speak but there were other knights who spoke first. Sir Edmund Mortimer and his family had long fought the Welsh and he shook his head. "That might work in the north, on the borders, but here the Welsh will just melt away into the hills. They will use ambush and arrows to thin our numbers. They will sneak into our camp and hamstring our horses. These are not Scots! These do not use knights." He pointed to Rhys and Gwilym Tudur, "Those are the exception and it is no surprise that they fight with us."

Percy's eyes flared angrily despite the fact that he was married to Mortimer's sister; he was well named, "Then what do you suggest?"

Sir Edmund turned to me, "Sir William once served in Spain in a Free Company when the Black Prince took on the Castilian rebels. I believe that they had a similar country in which to hide. Tell us, Sir William, what did the Black Prince do?"

Many men would have been embarrassed to have their common roots brought up but I was proud of my past. I remembered when we had been split up into smaller companies and sent to forage in the hills and to defeat the enemy in smaller groups. It had not been a total success but then Spain was not Wales and there were differences.

With all eyes upon me, I began, "Your Majesty, soon it will be winter. In Spain, winter meant rain and a chill. Here winter will bring snow and blocked passes. If we want this to end quickly then we do not take this huge army into Wales, we divide it into self-contained companies and attack on every front. Drive them from before our castles and back to their homeland. Come the Spring then we might bring them to battle but, in my experience, the Welsh will avoid battle at all costs."

Sir Henry Percy snorted, "And there you have the advice of a mercenary! What you suggest, Sir William, is little more than a chevauchée."

I did not rise to the bait. If he thought calling me a mercenary was a slight on my honour then he did not know me, "Tell me, Sir Henry, do you know where the Welsh army is to be found?" I looked around, "Do any of you? Have any sent out scouts to ascertain their whereabouts?"

This time the embarrassment came from around the table. None knew. They were planning to fight an enemy and they knew not where they were to be found. Even the Tudur brothers remained silent.

Prince Henry gave a slight smile, "Do you know, Sir William?"

I shook my head, "Not yet," Sir Henry Percy's face lit up in a triumphant smile, "but by this evening I shall." Percy's face fell.

The King said, "How, Sir William?"

"Even as we speak my archers are searching the Flintshire borders for them. I am guessing that they will be wreaking their havoc around Ruthin." I saw Lord Grey flush. "If that is so then we drive them from the Clwyd valley. I agree with Sir Henry, if we can bring them to battle then that would be the perfect solution but the Clwyd valley will not suit our heavy horses and will suit their archers."

Prince Henry nodded, "Sir William is, as usual, correct; we need to have self-contained companies. I have followed his banner and know the value of his mounted archers, men at arms as well as his knights. We have less than a thousand men at our disposal. However, an attack on many fronts by smaller groups of men will prevent the Welsh from combining. When his archers return and we know where the enemy are to be found, we strike."

The Prince was clever. By taking my ideas and giving them his voice, he gave them his credibility. His father nodded, "And my son, the Prince of Wales, is correct. I bow to my son in this matter. Now all that remains is to divide the army into smaller battles."

The natural divisions of the lords dictated the organisation. Mine proved to be the smallest. The knights who followed Sir Henry of Stratford and his neighbours were allied with mine. It meant I would lead less than eighty men. I would only command eight knights but I was happy for battles such as Henry Percy's, which also included Prince Henry, were large and cumbersome. Even worse, they were made up, largely, of knights. King Henry seemed pleased with the plan and all of us were invited to dine with him. "Your archer can report directly to us as we eat, Sir William!"

I sent my sons back to the camp to warn Alan of the Woods of the ordeal he would have to endure and to bring him to us as soon as he arrived. Percy made a point of asking Prince Henry to join him and his knights so that they could plan their action. I knew it was just a way to take the Prince from me. The King had brought clerks with him and he had much business to conduct. I knew that he would be happy with the plan for he had managed to abdicate all responsibility and his son would have to prosecute the war. Any failure could be laid at his door. I had been around kings enough to know that they would do anything in their power to keep a tight rein on their reputation. Children could be sacrificed!

Edmund, Earl of Stafford came to speak with me when food was brought in the afternoon and we spoke apart. "I like your plan, Sir William, for it shows a great knowledge of our enemies." He nodded over to Percy, "Do you trust that one?"

I smiled, "The knight and I have our differences, my lord, and I fear that my judgement would be coloured. The King must value him for he has given Prince Henry into his care."

The Earl tapped the side of his nose, "Perhaps the King does not trust Percy either. He is an ambitious man! It is good that you are the King's man. Your loyalty to King Richard was truly inspiring and I hear that it was you he asked for at the end?"

I nodded, "He was a troubled man but he believed in what he did. I am sure that if the evil de Vere had not tainted him then things might have ended differently."

"And that is my fear for Prince Henry and Percy but it is good to know that you stand with us, King Henry will need his loyal knights."

I wondered what his words meant. Did he have intelligence of a plot? I would keep my eyes and ears open. I was no longer a king's bodyguard but I could still watch out for his family. The words of the Black Prince still rang in my ears. That his son had died without an heir meant that his nephew, Henry, was deserving of my loyalty.

It was many hours later and we were eating the fish course when Alan of the Woods and Tom, my son, entered. Alan had come directly from the camp. I saw noses wrinkling for he stank of horse and sweat. The King did not seem to mind. Prince Henry stood and pointed to a servant, "You, fellow, give the archer beer. Come, Alan of the Woods, we are all eager to hear what you have learned."

Alan looked at me somewhat nervously, although Prince Henry's words had done much to alleviate his worry. A servant brought a pint of ale which Alan quaffed in one. He grinned at the prince he had helped to teach, "Thank you, my lord. We rode across the Dee and as far as the Clwyd. The rebels have taken Ruthin but not yet fortified it. They are enjoying causing mischief. Farms are burned and many animals are being roasted on open fires. It seems to me, Your Majesty, that they are more like brigands than rebels."

The King nodded, "And how many men did you see?"

"There must be more than a thousand Welshmen in the Clwyd, Your Majesty, but we only saw knights towards the estuary end of the Clwyd. They were gathered there in some numbers.."

The King took a small bag of coins and threw them to Alan who deftly caught them, "Here is for your troubles, archer. You have done well."

Bowing, Alan walked backwards from the hall. Tom stayed where he was for he would serve me food and ale.

Percy was next to the King and I saw their heads together. I was with Walter Blount and Stafford. The Earl of Stafford shook his head, "Whatever that Percy is suggesting I do not like it!"

Walter Blount nodded, "I do not understand why he is here. Surely, he is needed on the border. One thing is sure, he will benefit from all of this with lands and manors for that is his way."

The King nodded to Percy and then stood, "Tomorrow I will return to London. Sir Henry Percy and my son, the Prince of Wales will advance to Ruthin and deliver that castle back into the hands of Lord Grey. Lord Stafford will take his men and clear the valley towards St. Asaph and the sea and Sir William Strongstaff will act as the stopper in the jar and secure the upper Clwyd. One more thing, I appoint Sir Henry as Lord of Anglesey and Lord of Conwy castle."

The Earl of Stafford nodded and said, "I told you!"

Conwy was one of the strongest castles and Anglesey the breadbasket of Wales. He had given the Northumbrian knight more money and power than any save his own son, Prince Henry. I saw Prince Henry's face. He did not look happy; those were his lands his father had so blithely given away.

Walter Blount pushed away his platter as though he had lost his appetite, "And Percy will have the knights to ransom while we just sweep up the poor who will fight hard and yield us nought!"

They were both right but we had to serve and I was happy with our task.

The King stood, "You may now withdraw, my lords, and prepare to take back that which this Glendower has stolen!"

Tom was disappointed as we headed back to the river and our camp, "There will be no treasure for us and Sir Henry will become richer."

"Fear not, Tom, for your mother can make more money from our manors. This will be well and is the first opportunity for you and your brother to test your skills. We will see if the armour you and your brother wear is good armour."

"And which horse will you ride?" As my squire, he needed to know.

"That is easy, Hart. A good palfrey is all any shall need and Caesar is too valuable to risk with the hillmen of Wales. I will speak with you and your brother tomorrow before we ride."

Alan and the archers were already eating when we reached the camp and they had told Roger of Chester what dangers the campaign held. Roger moved an empty barrel to make a seat for me. "It is good that not all of us have rid ourselves of our shields. Alan saw bodkins!"

The Welsh were good archers with strong backs and arms but they had fewer bodkins than my men. The new bodkins could pierce plate and certainly rip through mail. I nodded, "Alan, will we need to camp?"

"Aye, lord."

"Then we leave the servants here with our tents and we will use hovels. I would not slow us down. If the other lords wish to take a baggage train then that is their problem." They nodded, "Apart from that is all ready?"

"It is, my lord."

"Good then I have a pleasant duty to perform, Roger of Chester, take a knee."

He looked puzzled. "Lord?"

I took out my sword, "King Henry reminded me that I am a banneret and have obligations. You, Roger, are to be knighted. We have no spurs and we have yet to hold your vigil but this will do!" I touched him lightly on both shoulders. "Rise, Sir Roger of Flore, for there is small manor there which is mine to give!" My men cheered and I held out my arm which he clasped, "And now you will see the true expense of knighthood!"

He looked dumbfounded but the rest of my men gathered around him to pat him on the back and to congratulate him. I had begun to do that which the King had demanded. I would knight another before we returned home. It was much later that we had the opportunity to speak with one another.

"I was not expecting this, my lord."

"The King merely reminded me that which I should have done myself. You deserve the honour and it will not mean a great deal of difference to you, except that you will have your own livery and squire."

I saw his face fall, "I had not even thought of that."

"Do not worry, Harry can tend to your needs until you find one and Martin can make your spurs when we reach home. You are no longer a hired sword, Sir Roger, you have obligations just as I have. Life will change for you."

He laughed, "And I have to tell Mary that she is a lady!"

I knew that there would be more to it than that. In many ways, I had had an easier transition for I had been a gentleman before I was knighted. Eleanor had grown accustomed to the change from the wife of a farmer to a knight. The small farm Sir Roger ran would now be his manor. He would need to pay for a squire and horses. It would eat into the profits from the farm. Many knights had to go to tournaments to make the money to allow them to be knights. I suspected that, just as I had, Roger had squirrelled away money.

Unlike many of the other battles we were up well before dawn and by sunrise were approaching the Clwyd. The knights, like Sir Henry, who were with me would follow my rules and the way I fought. We had to close off the end of the Clwyd Valley. This was the hardest place to take horses and that was why I rode Hart. We had to cross the hills and ridge to the east of Ruthin. Hotspur and the Prince would have to negotiate the same route. When we reached the top, we rested and adjusted our girths. I waved off my archers to find the enemy and then I led my knights and men at arms towards the road which eventually led to Wrecsam. Here we were in the true Welsh borders. Ruthin was an English castle surrounded by a sea of Welsh. That the Welsh had no castles always struck me as strange for the land was made for hilltop forts which could easily defy an enemy.

It was just after noon when Much Longbow rode in, "My lord, Captain Alan said to tell you he has spied a column of men. They are heading down this road towards Ruthin."

The road we were on was lined with dry stone walls. I looked ahead and saw that there were two patches of hedgerow four hundred paces from us. They were not next to the road but lined a track which led to the high ground to the left of the road. The high ground was heavily forested. Had we been earlier we could have used that to ambush. The hidden track way was, at its closest, fifty paces from the main road and gradually lengthened until it was two hundred paces away from the road. The roads were not Roman and they twisted and turned to follow the contours of the land. Turning in my saddle I saw that there was a slope behind us. The fields had been cultivated but as the crops had been harvested sheep and cattle rooted around the remains of oats, barley and beans.

"Much," I pointed to the hedgerow, "have Captain Alan use that for cover. I will form up our horsemen up the road. I intend to draw them upon us and then our archers can attack them from their rear."

My men were well trained and I did not need to elaborate. He knuckled his head and grinning said, "Aye, lord. They are in for a shock."

When he had gone, I pointed up the slope, "Follow me. I wish to entice them on to us."

I waved the five knights I did not know to ride with me and I explained my plan as we rode. "You lords have sixteen archers between you and we have thirty-five men at arms. I would have your archers and your men at arms dismount and block the road. I wish the Welsh to think we are weak. Your men at arms can use their shields to protect the archers. My men have better armour and I intend for us to charge. We will use two wings. I will lead one and Sir Roger the other. I will divide my men at arms and you, gentlemen, can choose which side you will fight. I will sound the charge but only when the archers have sent a few flights at them."

We had reached a flat part of the road. It continued to climb but this would give the archers and dismounted men at arms the best place to fight. They would need shields for Welsh archers were good. As the horses were led away, I formed up on the east side of the road. I saw that the five knights had lined up behind me.

"Sir John, Sir Henry, form up behind Sir Roger."

I saw Sir John grin. He would happily follow Roger. I divided up the men at arms. As we waited, I turned to Tom. "Today you ride with a spear. It is not a replacement for me; you will use it. I have taught you the basics now comes the practice. When you strike do so firmly. If you break the spear so be it but you need to hurt whomsoever you strike. Look for flesh! I doubt that they will have plate."

I saw that the other knights had the helmets with a visor. They had them raised while we waited. I did not like them and I had my sallet basinet which had no visor. I risked an arrow but I would have better vision when the fighting began.

"They come!"

I turned. There were about a hundred and forty men. Six knights led them and I saw metal gleaming behind. They had a few mounted men at arms. As I had expected, as soon as they saw us, they stopped and conferred. They were just fifty paces from the trail which led to Alan and his archers. "Tom, unfurl our banner, my lords unfurl yours too. Let them see who we are."

As the wind caught the banners and made them flutter, I saw the Welsh leader wave forward his archers. There were fifty of them. Forty men armed with an assortment of weapons followed them. They hurried up the road and they were followed by the horsemen. When they passed the hedgerow, I breathed a sigh of relief. We could now spring the trap.

Wilfred of Loidis led the six men at arms with me. We must have looked pathetically few in numbers to the Welsh. They saw just twenty-odd mailed men on horses. They would dismiss our squires as a threat. "Wilfred, my intention is to hold the attention of the Welsh until Alan can drop arrows on them. We keep the speed steady!"

"Aye lord." He grinned. He knew that my words were for the knights with me. I was telling them what they would do!

A Welsh horn sounded and the archers and the men on foot all halted two hundred and forty paces from us. Their horsemen then formed a double line behind them.

28

I shouted to our men at arms and archers, "Your task is to hold them. Archers, when you think you can hit them then do so. Keep releasing so long as you have arrows!"

They chorused, "Aye, lord."

"Tom, use your shield!"

"Aye, lord!"

Then the Welsh horn sounded again and the archers ran forward to a line some one hundred and fifty paces from us. They drew back on their bows. We would see now if they had heavy war bodkins. There was no way for an archer to know if a knight wore mail or plate for we all had some mail beneath our surcoats and the linen could disguise a multitude of different types of armour. Our horses all wore thick caparisons, and they would be able to stop a war arrow or prevent it at least from penetrating too deeply. Alan would wait until he was certain that the Welsh warriors' attention was on us and he had heard my horn sound before he loosed his first arrow. We had to endure an arrow storm and then charge.

I said, quietly to Tom, "Avert your gaze from the enemy and fix it upon the ground and be ready with the horn."

"Aye, my lord."

A bodkin would be deflected by the top of a good helmet. The Welsh would be seeking shoulders and legs. The knights and the men at arms who followed me all had plate on their thighs as well as poleyn for their knees and greaves. I heard the whoosh as the fifty arrows came down towards us. We had higher ground which meant the arrows did not have the range they would have wished. There was a series of cracks as arrows hit metal. I felt at least three blows strike me. They hurt and I would be bruised. That was to be expected. My banner would draw arrows like flies to a horse. I had obeyed my own instructions and I saw that the Welsh were using a mixture of needle bodkins and war arrows. If we were closer to them then the needle bodkins could hurt us.

I heard the order from the side as my archers released their arrows. We were higher and the sixteen arrows were heading for men without helmets, shields or mail. Six archers fell and as the second and third flights flew another five joined them. The Welsh now switched their target to our archers and the men on foot moved forward. Now was the time.

"Tom, sound the charge! For God, King Henry and England!"
I spurred Hart and her legs opened. We all had lances and I
had gauntlets with metal plates sewn on to the back. My greatest
fear was that an archer would send an arrow at my face. It was a
small target but the Welsh archers were good! They saw their
danger and switched targets. At the same time, I saw the arrows
which fell upon the rear of the Welsh lines. Alan and my men
were there and they had sprung the trap. The Welsh horn sounded
three times and it caused confusion in the ranks of the foot
soldiers and archers. An arrow came directly for me. I knew that
it was not aimed at my face and I allowed it to strike my tunic. It
was not a bodkin for when it hit the missile fell from the surcoat. I
held my lance slightly behind me; I was never totally confident
with a lance but I knew that it would be more than effective
against men on foot. I saw another arrow come for me when I was
just forty paces from the Welsh archers. The foot soldiers were
beginning to break as our horses thundered towards them. This
time the arrow was aimed at my face and I flicked my hand up. I
managed to strike the arrow which flew up in the air. The
surprised archer was still nocking a second when my lance drove
into his chest. I allowed my hand to drop and his body slid from
the end. I was through the archers and I aimed Hart at the knights
who had turned to charge us. They had no spears! I glanced to my
right and saw lances striking the backs of archers as they tried to
flee. If they had had better bodkins then they might have slowed
or even stopped us but their inferior arrows were no match for
plate armour. We had spent well!

The nearest Welsh knight, for I was at the fore, had a full-face
helmet with a boar's snout. He galloped at me wielding a war
hammer. It was a deadly weapon. It could crush bones and the
beak could tear a hole in plate. His problem was that he was
riding uphill and I had Hart galloping. My horse had not been
impeded and was eating up the ground. I pulled back my arm and
punched my lance as he swung his war hammer. He was slightly
unsighted and the war hammer swept over the top of my lance
which punched into his plated shoulder. Normally the cantle holds
a rider in the saddle, even one stricken, but my blow had been so
powerful that he had slipped and, as he tumbled over the side of
the saddle, his weight pulled his horse over.

I saw that Alan of the Woods and his archers had won the battle. The survivors were fleeing south. Sir Roger and his cohort were sweeping around the side of the helpless knights and squires. I reined in and rested my lance at the knight's throat, "Yield!"

He raised his visor and said, "I yield."

Just at that moment, I caught a movement behind me. Two archers had feigned death and risen. They had their daggers and were trying to drag Tom from his saddle. Even as I wheeled my horse to go to his aid, I knew that I would not be in time. He tumbled from the saddle. He had the wit to throw the standard from him and kick his feet from his stirrups. I saw him draw his dagger. It would have ended badly for him but for Wilfred of Loidis who brought his sword over to split one archer's head in twain. As his brains and blood spattered the other Tom lunged up with his dagger and drove it into the thigh of the second archer. The arcing spray of blood told me that he would soon be dead.

I shouted, "Make sure all these bastards are dead!" To prove the point, I reared Hart and her hooves smashed into the skull of a foot soldier who lay nearby and showed signs of movement. I had almost forgotten that the Welsh liked to play dead and then leap up to gut a horse with the rider still upon his back.

It had the desired effect. Weapons were thrown to the ground and men lifted their arms in the air. I dismounted and went to Tom. His horse had stood and I helped him to his feet. Wilfred of Loidis dismounted, "How are you, Master Tom? That was bravely done!"

"I owe you my life!"

He laughed, "And how could I have gone back to Lady Eleanor and told her I had allowed you to die!"

I had seen this done before and this would be the right moment for such an act; I would knight my man on the battlefield. I shook my head, "You deserve a reward. Take a knee!"

He looked around and Sir Roger laughed, "Do it for it seems I am not the only man at arms to be elevated!"

He did as I asked and I used my bloody sword to dub him, "Arise Sir Wilfred of Norton!" Norton was a tiny manor between Weedon and Dauentre. I was sure it would suit Wilfred. I now had my two knights and I hoped that would satisfy the King. This knighthood had been truly earned. He had saved my son!

There was a derisory laugh from the Welsh knight. I turned to look at him. He was younger than I was. He shook his head, "If you are forced to knight swords for hire then Owain Glyndŵr will triumph and this land will all be ours."

His accent was not Welsh. He wore fine mail and he had a breastplate. The blow I had struck with my lance meant it would need work. "Know that I am Sir William Strongstaff and I was an urchin who followed the Blue Company behind the Black Prince and yet I rose to be the captain of King Richard's guard. What is your name, knight? Have I heard great things about you?"

I saw that he had heard of me and the confidence evaporated from his face like morning fog. "I am Sir Richard of Talacre and I have yet to achieve greatness."

"Well, I hope that your family has coin else you will be enjoying the hospitality of my hall in Dauentre!" I looked and saw that we had cleared the battlefield. "We make camp on the flat ground. Have men sent to the families of the knights for ransom and then pile the enemy dead together. We will burn them for we have no time to bury them!"

I watched my archers as they took the arrows and bowstrings from the dead archers. If there were bracers and arrow bags, they took them too. The arrows would be sorted and new heads fitted. We wasted nothing. Horses were gathered and weapons and mail taken from the dead men at arms. There were few of them. The fire lit the road as we camped and ate cold rations. We had done that which we were asked. Had the others done the same?

Chapter 3

I sent the prisoners back to Chester the next day. They were escorted by Sir Walther of Leamington. He had suffered a wound. Alan of the Woods had tended to him but he needed a surgeon. Six other men had also been wounded and they made up the guards. The Welsh knights had surrendered their swords and given their oath. They would not attempt to escape.

The smoke from the funeral pyre still burned as we viewed the land. Autumn was here and there was a damp feel to the air. There would soon be fogs, showers and winds from the west which would make the campaign unpleasant and I wanted it over as soon as possible for the men, even the ones with small holdings, had crops to harvest. I stood with Sir John and Sir Henry and spoke aloud my thoughts, "What to do now, eh? Our orders are to close this road while Prince Henry reduces Ruthin. There is little point heading further into Wales. What say you?"

Both of them had been my squires and were confident about making suggestions. Many lords would do as I had done merely to mock suggestions made by inferior knights. "There is a village just a mile away. We passed it yesterday. We could camp there."

"Aye John, and that would be a good suggestion except that it would be hard to defend if we were attacked but we could head there and use their water and grazing. I should have noted the road when we passed along it but I did not. Take the men and graze the animals, give them water. I will ride with Tom and my archers. We will find somewhere to defend."

Sir Henry ventured, "But perhaps we will not need to defend the road if the Prince is successful."

"He will be successful, of that, I have no doubt, but there will be those in the valley who are raiding even as we speak. We are too few in numbers to hunt them down and so we must stop them getting back to Powys." I pointed to the mountains to the south and west of us. "They can get home that way but it will be on foot. The ones led by knights will come down this road and we were charged with preventing any escaping. We have to be prepared to fight them."

I took just half of my archers and we rode back towards Ruthin. I knew that we were close to the manor of Owain Glendower, Glyndyfrdwy. Our enemies, when they were defeated, would try to get there. We came upon a small hamlet which lay just eight miles from Ruthin and ten miles, as the crow flies, from Glyndyfrdwy. It was a small, mean place but it had potential for there were woods on both sides of the road and it was at the crest of the rise in the road. It would do.

"Stephen the Tracker, fetch Sir John and the rest of our men. Here we will guard the road to Glyndyfrdwy."

"Aye, lord."

Stephen had once led my archers but, now, he was a solitary figure who enjoyed his own company. While many of my men had married, he lived in a small hut in the woods close to my home. Sending him alone on the road was a task he would enjoy.

"Owen, tell the people at the hamlet that we will be camping here and there may be fighting. If they wish to leave, they may do so and we will not take from their homes. Give them my word."

"Aye, lord."

I was not certain they would believe my word but I had to give them the opportunity to leave. They would not be harmed in any battle but the aftermath would be a different matter. Unlike my men, many other knights would be unconcerned what their men did after they had won. I had seen terrible things in Spain. Even in England, there had been acts which turned my stomach. When I had been without a title I had had to stand and watch. Now I was a baron I could take action.

None left and I took that as a good sign. Most of those in this part of the world would not worry who was their lord for the majority would have a hard life no matter who ruled. When my men arrived, they set up a camp in the woods. They had grazed our horses and here there was water and a little grazing, it would do.

The next day a rider came down the road from Ruthin. He had an escort of four men at arms. We had men in the woods watching the road in case they were Welsh but the livery was recognised. It was one of Prince Henry's pages. "My lord, the Prince sends his compliments. He hopes to enter Ruthin on the morrow and asks you to be vigilant for there are many bands of men fleeing up the valley. It is why the Prince sent me with an escort. The Earl of Stafford has closed the estuary."

I nodded for it meant we had succeeded and that meant we could all go home soon. "Tell the Prince that we had a skirmish and defeated a force of a hundred and twenty who were heading for Ruthin. Is there any news about Glendower?"

The page shook his head, "There is no sign of him in Ruthin, lord."

After he had gone, I wondered at that. I suspected that he had been warned of our attack and left Ruthin. There was a vast area to the south of Snowdon and he could gather men there. The knight I had captured had been confident that his leader would gather men. The capture of Ruthin would not end this rebellion but it would, at least, contain it to those parts of Wales which were desolate and bare.

For the next two days, we rode the trails which fed into the main road. Although the warriors whom we caught were defeated, it was to our benefit to capture them for it meant we could take away their means of making war. We had to kill those who fought against us but they were few and far between. When mounted archers, not to mention knights and men at arms appeared, the Welsh brigands surrendered. We took their arms, helmets and mail. There was precious little of the latter. Then we let them go. They were surprised at our humane treatment of them and I hoped it would encourage them to remain loyal. It did not.

Three days later came the news that Ruthin had fallen and the Prince had captured many knights. Our work was done and we headed back to Chester. We were the first to reach the castle and that meant we had accommodation in the warrior hall. As the autumn rains had started that was more important than anything else for the loop in the river where we camped would soon flood. Technically we were done with the campaign but protocol dictated that we await the return of our erstwhile commander, the Prince of Wales. For my part, I was happy to do so. I was anxious to talk to him about the campaign. I had high hopes of young Henry.

The ransom for our knights arrived the day after we did and we sent them on their way. Despite the fall of Ruthin, they all seemed arrogantly confident that their leader would prevail. I divided the ransom for the two knights we had captured between my men at arms. Sir Wilfred and Sir Roger were most grateful. They had more expense now and that was thanks to me therefore it was only right that they share in the bounty too. The Prince and Henry Percy, along with the Earl of Stafford reached us the following day. Lord Grey had his castle back and they had brought many knights who awaited ransom. It soon became evident that there would be too many men for the castle to house and so Prince Henry's steward, Sir John Stanley, spoke to us in the Great Hall.

"The Prince thanks all of you for your good work and tells you that you may return to your manors. The rebellion is over."

I heard a voice say, "And what of our pay?"

It was not one who had followed me and I guessed it was one of Mortimer's men.

Sir John frowned, "When the ransoms are delivered and the fines collected then the monies will be divided up."

There was grumbling as men left. In theory, we owed forty days a year to the King. However, as a result of problems which had begun in the reign of Edward III, pay was normally forthcoming at a rate of two shillings per knight and twelve pennies for a man at arms. I doubted that we would see that sort of money but the ransom and horses we had collected, not to mention the weapons and mail meant that we were all better off.

As men began to leave Sir John said, "Sir William, Prince Henry would have conference with you, in private."

I was led by a page to a small antechamber close to the Prince's quarters. He sent away the page and then spoke, "Sir William, know you that I did not wish you to be isolated at the head of the valley. The decision was not mine; Sir Henry does not like you and I am disappointed in him. He seems small-minded and vindictive. I regret my father's choice of him as my mentor."

"Then dismiss him, Prince Henry."

"Not as easily done as you might imagine. I dare not offend him for he now commands Anglesey and Conwy not to mention most of the land to the north of Cheshire. In addition, there are many men in Cheshire who have switched their allegiance from King Richard to the Percy family. We do not want another civil war."

The Prince, for all of his youth, was wise and I was pleased that he was aware of the danger the Percy family represented.

"Know, Prince Henry," I saw his frown and, smiling, said, "Hal, that all you need is to send to me and I will be at your side. When I am asked to train a young warrior that training is for life. I did not abandon King Richard, nor your father and I am ready to resume the training which your father interrupted any time you choose to avail yourself of my company."

"And I am glad about that but I must learn from this. I will keep Percy close. I smile at him for I can play the game of politics but I know, only too well, that there are few men I can truly trust and you, Will Strongstaff, are one of them."

We left after noon. It would take us three days to reach home. However, the delay in Chester meant that Sir Roger and Sir Wilfred were able to make some purchases. They both had wives and were sweetening the pill that they would have to swallow. As my wife had discovered becoming a lady was more than just acquiring a title; it involved all sorts of expense not to mention more servants. Both of their wives were of low birth and the climb up the social ladder was a hard one. The two new knights rode with Sir John and me.

"Sir William we are knighted and Wilfred and I are honoured but what else is our commitment both military and financial?"

"When I am called upon to muster men then you owe me forty days service. As you learned in Chester that does not guarantee payment. As a man at arms, I bore the cost for you were my familia. As for the rest," I shrugged, "that is up to you. The men who serve you on your farms may now be called upon by you as warriors. You need to ensure that your men can use the warbow. You are not barons and for that you should be grateful, for with my title comes the burden of taxes and the maintenance of law."

They nodded and both looked relieved. "We have been talking and we would ride to Red Ralph's farm for we need more horses and we have coin we had accumulated."

I saw Ralph look at Sir John who nodded, "Aye Ralph, you may go with them and see your family for it will be quiet now until Easter."

Red Ralph had died but we honoured his memory by using his name for his horse farm. His wife and sons still produced the finest horses. It was worth the long ride to Middleham for beasts which we knew were worth the high prices we paid for them.

"And do not forget your squires. I loaned Harry to you, Sir Roger but my son, Tom, will be ready for knighthood sooner rather than later and I want Harry trained by then."

"Do not worry, lord, I have spoken with Alan of the Wood. His eldest son, Abelard, is eight summers old. That is too young for war but the lad is keen to be a warrior and I can train him. I believe that the Blue Company trained you at about that age?"

I laughed, "I was younger. When I was eight summers, I had already sunk a blade into a man's flesh. The Blue Company was a hard school!"

Wilfred nodded and gestured back to Harold Four Fingers, "That lad he is raising as his son, Pyotr, is a handy lad with a sword. I will speak with Harold. I know he would be happy for his stepson to become a squire and I like the lad."

Pyotr and his mother, Magda, had been taken on by Harold when he had saved Pyotr's life in the harsh winter of a Baltic crusade. This felt right and I nodded my agreement.

My wife was pleased when I told her the news. "I will speak with their wives, husband, for the lessons I learned were harsh and I would make life easier for them."

"Thank you, wife. You are a good woman."

"And speaking of women, you have done all that you can for our sons and that is good but our daughter, Alice, is a woman grown and Mary is not far behind. Alice will need a husband for she is of an age to bear children. He will need to be of noble stock or from a family which is well off for you are a baron. She has grown up as a lady. I was a farmer's daughter who knew how to get her hands dirty but she will expect a better life."

I smiled but inwardly I groaned. I had not mentioned this to Roger and Wilfred but it was a fact of life. I would have to provide a dowry as well as ensuring that the young man was a suitable bridegroom. It would not be easy. Running four manors was hard enough without worrying about finding a suitable husband and I confess that I forgot about Alice and her needs as I held assizes, dealt with disputes, collected taxes, dispensed justice and trained men.

There was no longer an Earl of Northampton. The King was the last to hold that title. Northampton was, in effect, a royal castle. The constable of the castle was Sir Richard Knollys and he had begun the practice of having the lords who owed fealty to the Earl of Northampton, to meet once every three months. It allowed him to inform us of decisions made by the King which affected the lords of his manors whilst also enabling us to meet informally. When war came, we would all fight under the same banner. We had not met since the rebellion of Glendower and the next meeting was scheduled for the end of November. I took my two squires but my knights were not required to attend. We would normally stay overnight as the castle was well made with plenty of chambers. I had only attended two before the one in November but I enjoyed them. The other barons were good men and were loyal to King Henry. That made for an easier life.

There were twenty of us in the Great Hall. Our squires served us. Tom was one of the older squires but I saw another who looked a little older. Those two would be knights soon enough. Harry was learning by watching the other squires. He served us at home but here was different. Here were men who would not merely smile when a squire made a mistake but might make a comment which would reflect badly on his lord. I doubted that would happen amongst this company but Harry did not know that. The talk was of the tiny war we had fought in Wales. Only two of the knights had served under me for the other barons had greater manors than I did.

I had had the most success and so I was questioned by the others about the quality of men I had fought. "What do you think, Sir William? Is the war over in Wales? Will Glendower hide in his mountains or is there more to come?"

I shook my head, "No, Sir Richard. We have not brought this Glendower to book and Wales has many places he could hide and gather more men. But if we hold the ring of castles around Snowdon then I believe he will be contained."

Sir Henry Longchamp nodded, "There is no money to be made from a war against the Welsh! However, it is good practice for our squires eh?" He nodded to his son, who was the squire of an age with Tom, "My son, Richard, did well enough. He managed to kill two Welshmen. I shall knight him next year." I saw the grin on his son's face as he heard the news. Tom, too, was pleased for his friend.

"I am afraid that Tom will have to wait. He is blooded and he has unhorsed a man at arms but he is not quite ready yet."

Tom nodded. He was sensible and had heard the tales from my men at arms of other young knights who had been knighted too early and come to a bad end.

Another knight, Sir Humphrey Boyer asked, "And the Scots?"

"The Percy family regard the border as their own fiefdom." I heard the bitterness in the constable's voice. "I know that His Majesty is less than happy that he does not receive his share of ransom from them. I think that they believe that the distance from London makes them immune from our laws and customs. He has the cheek to demand money from the King for doing his duty and keeping the northern march safe. Still, now that he is in Wales with Prince Henry, that might change." I doubted that very much but I kept my own counsel.

When we returned home, the next day, I reflected that I had learned much. Tom and Harry also seemed in good humour, "It is good, father, to speak with other squires. If nothing else it tells us that our training with your men at arms is superior to the training some of the others receive. You know that Richard Longchamp cannot use a bow!" Both my sons could use a bow. They would never be archers for an archer had to be dedicated to the art but they could pull a warbow and it made them stronger, more importantly, it taught them the real value of archery. Harry hesitated, "I invited him to visit with us and then Alan of the Wood could teach him. He seemed quite keen."

"You should have asked me first but I can see no harm. When next we meet, I shall ask his father."

Harry gave me a sheepish look, "Harry and I already invited him. We asked him to visit for Christmas."

I shook my head, "What of his family?"

"He has many brothers and sisters. He will not be missed."

"And your mother? What of her? You know how she frets about entertaining guests."

Tom just grinned, "We thought you could speak with her!"

"I can see those games of chess have paid off for you have used a clever move to achieve your aim. I shall ask her but I am not hopeful that she will be happy about it."

In the event, I could not have been more wrong. She was delighted! I knew there was more to this than the simple answer I received from her. Of course, I had to endure the next weeks which involved much cleaning and preparation of my already immaculate hall but I put up with it all for she was happy and my life was better for it!

The reason for her happy mood became clear three days before the arrival of the squire from Piddington.

Alice was fitted out with a completely new set of expensive clothes. I cocked an eye at my wife, "A great deal has been spent on these clothes. Am I missing something?"

She shook her head, "This is an opportunity for Alice. We can show her off to an eligible bachelor. Richard Longchamp may not be the young man who will wed our daughter but she sees precious few young men as it is."

I looked over at Tom who was shamefaced and hurried out to the stables, "Don't tell me you put our son up to this!"

She smiled triumphantly, "Sons! You do not think I would leave it to you to find a young man for our daughter? I asked Tom and Harry to determine if any squires were looking for a bride and Richard Longchamp was one. Of course, Alice has to approve but I am hopeful."

"And what of me?"

She stood and kissed me on the cheek, "Why you do not matter, husband. You just pay the dowry if he pleases Alice and, of course, me!"

I actually felt sorry for Richard. He was entering a dragon's den. I would just sit back and enjoy the spectacle.

I know not if it was the fact that Alice had seen so few potential suitors or if it was meant to be but they got on well with each other from the moment they met. My wife liked him too for he was an affable young man. I think the reason it worked was because Richard was very similar to Tom and Harry. He seemed to fit in well with the house. When he left, after twelfth night, he asked if, when he had gained his spurs, he might be able to court my daughter. I could not say no. My hall was more peaceful and I was happy. I was hopeful about the coming year. The small, day to day events of the manor had now become as important, if not more, than the affairs of state to which I had been party for so many years.

It was Easter which brought potential disaster for both the King and the Kingdom. Conwy Castle, that mighty bastion holding back the Welsh had fallen!

Chapter 4

We heard about the disaster on the eighth of April, a week after it fell. I was summoned to Northampton to meet with the King. He was incandescent with rage. It emerged that Rhys and Gwilym Tudur had been working with the rebel leader and while the garrison was at church on Good Friday, the gates of the castle had been opened and the castle fell without a blow being struck! The handful of men in the garrison were now prisoners.

The King had the Earl of Stafford, Hugh le Despenser and his other advisers with him in the castle. "Hotspur! That Northumbrian cockerel has lost my strongest castle! I gave him the castle and instead of watching the Welsh he spends his time in Chester! My son should have known better than to rely on him!"

I thought that was a little unfair for it was the King himself who had appointed Percy and given him the castle but no one argued with the King when he was in this mood.

The Earl of Stafford said, "Your Majesty, what do we do?"

"Do? I would have thought that was obvious. We ride to my son's side and I punish Percy. We cannot afford a muster for the exchequer is empty and parliament is unwilling to negotiate with the Welsh. You gentlemen will bring your men at your own expense!"

I now saw why there were so few of us. He wanted those who were the most loyal to him and who would not refuse to join him.

"We ride immediately!"

I was annoyed for had he given us some warning I could have sent riders to Sir John and my other knights. I was luckier than some for Hugh le Despenser had to return to London first. At least my manors were on the march west. It also meant that I could speak with Sir Henry on the way west and we could discuss a dowry.

However, as we headed west, my mind was wrestling not with a potential marriage but with the fear that there was treachery involved. Rhys and Gwilym had made no secret of the fact that they were related to Glendower. What worried me was that they had also seemed close to Henry Percy. As they had managed to infiltrate his castle I wondered if there was collusion. It seemed a little convenient to me that they had taken over such a powerful castle so easily. What game was Hotspur playing?

This time our column moved faster for the King had brought fewer men. The finances must have been in a parlous position and he had had to cut his cloth accordingly. I saw that the Earl of Stafford was now one of his closest advisers and they spent most of the journey deep in conversation. I had seen many knights assume the position of confidante to the King. I was happy with the Earl of Stafford to do so for he was a good man and certainly no Robert de Vere. I knew that in his mind King Henry saw me as a bodyguard. My advice might be sought but only on military matters. That did not worry me. The poisonous world of politics and power had been the downfall of many men who thought they could change England.

I spoke at length to Richard's father. Our sons rode together behind us and their laughter lifted our mood. They were young and did not have the worries which we did. "My son is much taken with your Alice."

"And your son has charmed my whole family. When he is knighted it will be a good match."

"Aye, I would have knighted him already but for this campaign. His mother insists upon all of the pomp and ceremony which is due him."

I wondered if that was a criticism of the way I had knighted Roger and Wilfred. Perhaps Sir Henry thought I disparaged the act. I did not. For me, it was the title and responsibility which were more important rather than the vigil, the clothes and the ritual but then like Roger and Wilfred I had been brought up a commoner.

This time we did not head for Chester but the Clwyd Valley. I knew what King Henry intended. He rode to Glyndyfrdwy, the home of Glendower. Servants only were within the hall and the grounds. The King sent them packing and then we burned the hall to the ground. We wasted a day devastating the home of Owain Glendower. It was vindictive for the Welsh rebel was not there.

He was in the vastness of the heartland of Wales surrounded by mountains whence we could not pass easily.

We reached the siege lines at Conwy. It was lucky that the Welsh had taken only the castle and not the town or else it would have been the devil's own task to shift them from the town. We heard the hammering of siege engines as we rode through the town gates. It was Prince Henry himself who greeted us. We dismounted and Prince Henry dropped to a knee, "I am truly sorry that we lost the castle, father, but there was treachery!"

This was not the place for recriminations; we were in a very public place and King Henry was aware of that. "This was not of your doing. I gave this castle to Sir Henry. Where is he?"

"He and his men are prosecuting the siege. We have a hall for you. Idris, the merchant who owns it took shelter with the Welsh rebels in the castle. We believe he was part of the conspiracy. It was well planned."

"Come, take me to the hall and we can speak in private." He turned to me, "We may need you, Sir William, come with us."

I handed my reins and helmet to Tom and followed father and son and the Earl of Stafford. They did not speak until we were within the hall. Prince Henry had two of his own household on guard and they were detailed to guard the door. Once inside King Henry said, "Will, find us wine and some food."

By the time I returned the three of them were deep in conversation. "We have to assume that we cannot trust any knight who is Welsh."

"What of lords like Mortimer, father?"

"His family may have vast tracts of land in Wales but he is as English as any man! No, I speak of those like the Tudur brothers."

I had been brought for a purpose and I did not remain silent, "They were close to Lord Percy when we were at Chester, my lord."

They both looked at me, I saw the Earl of Stafford smile, and King Henry shook his head, "You are suggesting treachery which could cost Percy his head! Besides this was his castle."

"King Henry, it makes no sense to me either, however, I am just a common soldier and I do not play high stakes for crowns, thrones and power."

King Henry smiled, "And you talk of me, Will. You may be right but if he is playing a traitor's game, we must be cautious and careful. Who else is involved?"

Prince Henry was clever. When he had been Hal living in my hall and playing chess with my sons, I had seen that. He was astute and observant, "Perhaps Glendower himself?"

"Why, my son, what has he to gain?"

"From what I have seen, father, Wales is a rocky, mountainous country which is not worth much. If an enemy of the crown sought to take the crown from your head then he could happily give away all that King Edward took and return it to the Welsh."

The Earl of Stafford nodded, "It is true; the lands to the west of mine go to Shrewsbury and I know the Welsh would have the rich land of Shropshire back under their control."

The King sipped his wine and pondered. I knew that King Henry had a mind for plots and he showed it that day. "Glendower is not within the castle walls?"

"No, father, it is the Tudur brothers and their knights."

"Then Glendower is hiding in Wales. He will be gathering men, for while we are here at the siege we are tied to the land and I have brought precious few men with me. Sir William, I want you to take a battle of men. Use my knights from Northampton and your own. With your archers and men at arms, you have a fastmoving force. I want you to harry the Welsh and make it hard for Glendower to gather his forces. You need not fight battles. Use ambush." He smiled, "Do as you did in Lithuania. There you impressed even the Teutonic Knights."

He had given me a tall order for Wales was vast and the roads which criss-crossed it few and far between. "And where will he be?" I looked at the Prince.

"Machynlleth and Aberystwyth are the most powerful centres of Welsh resistance, my lord. They always have been."

I nodded, "And how long should I chase him, King Henry?"

"I charge you to take no more than two months. If we have not reduced the walls of Conwy by then we will have failed." I nodded. "I would have you lay waste to the heart of Wales. Make them hungry and they will sue for peace."

"It will be hard on the ordinary people, King Henry."

"You have your orders, Sir William, and I know that you will obey them." I nodded. "Do not tell your men nor your knights whence you ride until you are on the road. If Percy is the traitor you, my son and the Earl of Stafford believe him to be then let us not give him the opportunity to warn his ally, eh?" I saw once more that he had a mind which was like a steel trap. "And now we can let in our lords. Send for Percy, let us see what he has to say for himself."

I stood to the side when King Henry addressed the assembled lords. All eyes were on the King and the knight of Northumberland. "How did you lose the jewel that is Conwy, Lord Percy?"

I was able to watch Percy's face and I noticed that he had hooded eyes and he could mask what was going on behind them, "Your Majesty, we were betrayed. The garrison was in church. These Welsh are Godless creatures that they should use such devices."

"Just so." The King flicked an imaginary speck of dirt from his tunic, "And are you confident that you can affect the surrender of the castle without damaging its walls? This is a bastion against the Welsh and I would have it returned to its former position."

"I swear that I will do it before June, my lord!"

"Good! Then I will leave the Earl of Stafford to aid you. We return to London for I have pressing matters there which also demand my attention. I will take the knights of my household as I can see that you have no need of horses here."

I had to admire King Henry. We would leave the town together but while he would head home, I would lead my men south to find Glendower. My sons were disappointed that we would not be participating in the siege. I pointed out that sieges were the bane of knights. "The only way into a castle is over the walls. That means clambering up a ladder while those on the walls can rain death upon you. The castle of Conwy is well endowed with heavy war bodkins. I doubt that they will use knights to attack for if they did then they would die. The gates will be attacked and if men are to climb ladders and siege towers then it will be the men at arms!"

We left the next day and escorted the King as far as the Dee and he crossed to Chester. He took with him just his personal escort and we turned to head along the Dee into the heartland of Wales. I sent Alan of the Woods ahead to scout. I planned on reaching Glyndyfrdwy and camping there in the desolation of Glendower's home. The King had appointed me lord of the battle when he had left us but I saw, as we headed south and west, the questions on all of the faces of the knights who rode with me. I normally told all to those with whom I rode but I was silent.

It was almost dark when we reached the blackened earth of the Welsh manor and while our men made camp, I gathered the twenty knights I led around me, "We have been ordered by the King to find any Welsh rebels and destroy them. We are heading for Machynlleth and Aberystwyth. Regard this as a chevauchée. The Welsh think to fix our attention on Conwy while they raise an army. We are here to slow down or even stop that growth. We ride hard and we ride fast. There will be no battles and there will be little glory but what we do is by the command of King Henry and I will do all that I have been asked to do!"

The knights who knew me were not surprised by my tone but I saw that some of the other knights were taken aback. I softened my tone when I spoke with each one individually and explained what precisely we would do. We had twenty knights, forty archers and forty men at arms. With our squires and servants, we would be approaching a hundred and thirty men in total. We could not take any castles and so we had to destroy the Welsh halls which lay in the heartland of Wales. We had to take or kill their animals and make them hungry so that they could not fight. I was the one knight who had been in this part of Wales. When I had accompanied King Richard from Ireland I had travelled down the narrow roads and passes. I knew the difficulties which lay ahead.

We had some Welshmen amongst our men. Three were mine and I trusted them implicitly. I would use those as my scouts. Our horses would mark us as English but my men were good and knew how to hide. Their knowledge of the language could make the difference. We headed along the Dee Valley and then the Afon Dyfrddwy which led to the sea and Abermaw. My aim was to cut the lines of communication from the south. We reached the lake and the village of Bala in the early afternoon. This was too small a place to have a lord but there were rebels for, as we approached, they fled into the hills. We camped in their village and slaughtered their cattle. We would eat well, for one night at least.

The next day we rode hard down the road towards Dolgellau. There was a hall there for Owen the Welshman knew the place. We moved fast down the road but word travelled faster for we had to stop to collect animals and destroy buildings. The only people we saw were the very old or the very young. The rest hid as our company galloped through their villages and hamlets; we were not stopped. Dolgellau was different and there we saw a wall of spears and archers awaiting us. They had blocked the road into the town with carts and wagons from behind which they would loose arrows at us. My scouts had warned me of the barrier and we were prepared. The nature of the ride meant that we had not brought our horse armour which remained in Chester. For that reason, I was loath to risk our horses in a charge against bowmen. We dismounted.

"We will advance with our archers. The squires have shields and they will precede the archers. I do not think that they will have heavy war bodkins and, until we are close, our plate armour should protect us. This is our first test. I believe we will pass it."

We formed up. Many of the knights used long pole weapons including pikes and poleaxes. A couple had war hammers. I had my sword and a dagger for I had seen little evidence of mail and helmets. There were four standards which suggested four nobles and I intended to take my household knights to engage them. We marched down the road to within arrow range. I knew when we had reached it as they began to rain arrows upon us. Those men at arms who did not have plate still retained shields and they took the force of the arrows as they fell. We had no such protection and the war arrows and occasional needle bodkin rattled and cracked against our armour. It sounded terrifying but we were relatively safe from harm. The danger lay in an arrow loosed horizontally. A war arrow in the face could kill and certainly disfigure. Our own archers sent arrows at the enemy. Their arrows would thin out the Welsh archers who would try to eliminate the mailed men.

After the initial rain of arrows, I saw that my archers had hit twenty of their archers. Now was the time to attack, "Forward!"

I had a tightly fitted coif and my face was a small target; nonetheless, one Welsh archer sent an arrow at my face. I barely saw it but I had enough of a glimpse to move my head to the side. The war arrow slammed into my mail coif. The tip actually broke the skin on my cheek but I had had worse cuts shaving! Although we were not mounted, we still used the same commands and when I shouted "Charge!" we ran. We were twenty paces from them when I gave the order. It proved too much for the Welsh archers who broke and fled through the line of knights and spearmen. It was not a solid wall and I was able to deflect up the spear which was rammed at my throat by using my dagger. I sliced across the body of the Welshman and hacked him open. He tumbled to the ground and the knight who was behind him swung his war hammer at me. He brought it over his shoulder and tried to split open my skull. I held my dagger and sword up to make a v and I managed to hold his weapon. I had learned to fight in the mêlées of Spanish battles. There were no rules in such fights and I drove my poleyn up between his legs. He was a knight and had no protection there. His face contorted as his genitals were crushed and the strength went from his arms. I smashed the pommel of my sword and the hilt of my dagger on to the top of his helmet. The two blows, combined with the strike from my knee made him fall backwards. As he lay there, I drove my sword between the metal plates of his breastplate and the plates on his arm. I put my weight on the sword and it drove through the mail. He screamed as my sword tore through the tendons and muscles. He would never wield a sword again.

"Yield!" He nodded for he knew he was finished.

A spear was rammed at me and I was unable to deflect it. It smashed into my breastplate and forced me back. The man at arms, who wore an open helmet and had a mail hauberk thought that he had me for he pulled back to lunge again. This time I was ready and I swept my dagger up. The blade rang off the metal of the spearhead and I lunged at his face with my sword. My blade drove through his mouth and out of the back of his head. Tearing it to the side I let his body drop to the ground.

When Sir John slew another knight and Sir Roger captured a third the heart went from them and they broke. I turned and shouted, "Alan of the Woods, mount and pursue them. Kill as many as you can!"

"Aye, lord!"

It was brutal but any who survived would only return to fight us again. "Captain Edgar, search the bodies. Tom, see to our prisoner. His wound needs binding."

I took off my helmet and lowered my coif. It was hot. I saw that all of our knights had survived but a couple of the men at arms from some of the other companies had either been hurt or killed; the healer we had brought was tending to them. I sheathed my sword and Harry fetched my horse. I mounted and rode through the bodies towards the town. I saw that the door to the hall was open and I dismounted and went inside. They had left in a hurry for there was still food upon the table. I heard shouting from a back room and, drawing my sword, I headed for it. When I opened the door, I saw a bound man. He had been beaten.

"Who are you?"

"I am Dafydd Gam of Parc Llettis and I would be grateful if you would free me, Sir William Strongstaff."

I nodded and sliced through the bonds. When he stood, I saw that he had a bad leg, it explained his name for Owen the Welshman had told me that Gam was Welsh for lame. "What is your story, Dafydd and how do you know me?"

"My family have always supported the English kings. I served King Richard in Ireland and I led four archers. I saw you there. Owain Glyndŵr had me imprisoned for I would not support him and, in his eyes, I was a traitor."

"Then I will tell King Henry of your action. You can join us if you wish?"

He shook his head, "No, lord, for I can be of more use further south. I can rally those men who are loyal to King Henry!"

Just then I heard my knights as they entered the hall. Harry was one of the first in. "Harry, go to the stables and find a horse for Dafydd Gam here and fetch him weapons. He is proof that not all Welshmen fight us!"

We buried our own men in the churchyard and we spent the next day gathering animals and food. I rode with four archers and my squires towards Abermaw. It lay on the north bank of the estuary and looked a mean and desolate place. I decided that we

would head south, as I had originally planned and raid
Machynlleth and then Aberystwyth. I doubted that we would
actually reduce Aberystwyth for it had a castle which had been
improved twenty years earlier. It had been English but the Welsh
had managed to take it too. It would do no harm to ravage the
countryside around that bastion of the west.

The next day we headed towards the heartland of Wales.
Owen had already told us that the road twisted its way down a
narrow valley. The places we passed would be small, Corris,
Corris Uchaf, Ceinws and there would be little opposition but,
equally, there would be places where we could be ambushed and
some of those who had fled us at Dolgellau would have spread the
word about English raiders. I sent two men at arms to ride with
the scouts in case the opposition was in the form of mailed men.

It took two days to reach the Afon Dyfi and the bridge which
led to Machynlleth. Alan and the scouts waited at the edge of the
forest which stopped some two hundred paces from the bridge.
The road itself was hidden by the woods. They would see us but
have no idea of numbers. There were armed men at the bridge.
We reined in next to my scouts. Alan pointed to the two ends of
the bridge. At one end were archers behind their pavise and then
at the other were pavise, men at arms and archers. He said, "And
you can bet that they have bodkins. They know we are coming.
This will be bloody, lord."

I nodded, for I was already thinking of a way around it. I
looked towards the town and saw that they had improvised
barricades and had men defending there too. I stood in my stirrups
and looked upstream. I saw, just less than half a mile away, what
looked like a sandbank. I was guessing we could ford it.

"Alan, we have height on our side, do we not?"

"Aye, lord."

"And that means we can release when they cannot." He
nodded. "Then have all the archers brought here and we will do
what they expect and attack them but we shall use archers to do
so. Use your skill to probe for weaknesses. I will take the men
upstream and ford the river. We will cross and negate their
defences by attacking the rear of their lines."

He nodded, "Aye, lord, but I fear we will not hit many of
them."

"Just keep their attention fixed here."

Turning, I rode back to the column. "We will head through the woods and make our way half a mile to the river. We cross the river and then attack the men who are defending the bridge. Archers ride to Captain Alan. You have target practice."

We rode through the woods, each rider plotting their own course for there were no paths. I led as I knew where I was heading. I gradually descended the slope. I managed to bring us out beyond the bend in the river. I let Hart pick her own way towards the sandbank. The water came up to the top of my poleyns but no deeper. Once on the other side, I awaited my men. Once again there was neither path nor track on the other side. The ground looked to be rough grazing and seemed to me as though it was a flood plain of some sort.

When the men had all crossed, I said, "We charge the men on the town side of the bridge and we stop them getting into the town. Once Captain Alan joins us then we will take the town. I will lead the attack with the knights. Squires, remain at the rear. We will not need banners this day. When we strike then join us and send them from the field."

I saw the joy on the faces of the squires. They had thought they would be relegated to holding horses once again.

I spurred Hart and she rose up through the undergrowth. I saw the bridge; it was four hundred paces from us. As soon as we cleared the hedges and bushes, we were seen and I saw the consternation in the frantic gestures of the men on both the bridge and at the barricade. I began to gallop towards the road which led to the crossing as the archers there were already thinking about fleeing. Their indecision was fatal for Alan and his archers began to send arrows into them. That decided them and they ran. As soon as they did then those at the northern end of the bridge also broke ranks. They raced for the safety of the town. Most would not make it. I heard Alan give the command to mount. He and the archers would be just moments behind us. We were spread out in a line of steel. I pulled back my lance and rammed it into the side of the nearest mailed warrior. He had a shield and a helmet but, in his panic, neither was of any use to him. There is an art as well as a technique to the use of a lance when chasing down fleeing men. You twisted as you struck and as you retracted the lance. It made the tip slip out and allowed the rider to strike again. My knights and men at arms were masters of it. His body fell behind me and Tom's horse trampled it.

The barrier bristled with spears and archers but none could use their bows for fear of hitting their own men. We were travelling much faster than the men who were running. We struck the barrier together. The Welsh who had fled the bridge scrambled up over the hastily crafted defence and our spears rammed over the top into faces and chests which were unprotected. The sheer weight of men, mail and horses made the barrier break and men were crushed by the flailing hooves of mighty horses. With the barrier down all defence ceased and it became a mad rush to escape us. Ahead of us, I heard the screams of women as they realised that they could not stop us.

We were only stopped by the exhaustion of our horses. We were a mile on the other side of Machynlleth when I called a halt to the chase. We made our weary way back to the town. It was largely deserted. This time the children had fled with their parents and only the old and infirm remained. There were no prisoners for us to escort back to England. After setting sentries we began to collect all that we could from the town. This time there was not only a great quantity of grain and animals, but there was also treasure in the houses of the rich. We found wagons and we loaded them. It was late in the evening by the time we ate and I was able to speak with the senior knights to discuss our plans for Aberystwyth.

Sir Henry Longchamp was in an ebullient mood, "We have done all that King Henry could have wished and more. We could return to Conwy now and be seen as heroes!"

I shook my head, "No, Sir Henry, we have made a good start only."

"But Aberystwyth is an English castle; it is well made. They will have the walls manned!"

"Aye, they will and I have no intention of attacking the castle for we do not have enough men. I intend to do that which I was ordered. We will seal up the town and then we will raid the countryside. We take every animal and every piece of food we can find. We let our horses graze until they are gorged and then when I decide, we will cross over the Dyfi and the Mawddach rivers and do the same to the land between there and Conwy."

Sir Henry's eyes widened, "You are a hard man, Baron."

"I have served two kings of England and I have seen what they need to do to hold on to a crown. We are their servants and it is our duty to end this rebellion. It should have been quashed the last time. The fact that there has been treachery and a lack of vigilance means that they will be encouraged. The harder we are the less likely it is that they will rebel a third time."

I was wrong but at the time I had no way of knowing that. If I had to do the same again then I would do.

That evening I sat with Tom and Harry. Normally they sat with Richard and the other squires. Richard had done well in the skirmish and I think that he and his father were discussing when he would be knighted. I understood the young man's frustration. He wanted to lead and not just be a horse holder. If we fought in a battle then he would not be able to draw his sword in anger. I felt, in my bones, that there would be a battle. It might not be with the Welsh for they were reluctant to face us but the French might choose to do as they had with the Scots and use this rebellion to further their own ends. During the reign of King John, they had almost succeeded!

Harry was also in a chatty mood and he went over every detail of the skirmish. When he stopped, albeit briefly, I asked, "Tom, what is on your mind?"

"Richard is courting my sister and will soon be a knight. I am just a month or so younger and..."

"And you would be the same?"

He shook his head, "I know that I still have much to learn but there is no bride for me. How did you meet mother?"

I laughed, "By accident although I believe that it was Fate which sent us to meet each other. You cannot plan for these things, Tom. It just happened that Richard and Alice got on. You may find a bride that way too."

"But she needs to be a lady."

"Who says so?"

He looked confused, "Mother!"

"She wanted a good marriage for Alice as she does for Mary but you will be a knight. I care not whom you marry so long as you are happy." I thought back to my parents. My father's nature and, perhaps, the wrong choice of wife, had ruined his life and I would not have that for my son.

He brightened, "You mean that? Truly?"

"Aye son, for a good knight is never foresworn."

It was then that he began to talk about the skirmish. All was well.

We stayed in Machynlleth for two days and then made our way down the road to the coast and the castle of Aberystwyth.

Chapter 5

They were ready for us and there were no animals within a mile of the castle for they had taken everything of value within the walls of the castle. It was a foretaste of what we could expect in the future. I rode with Sir Henry and our squires to ask them to surrender. I knew they would not agree to it but it was part of the protocol of a siege. It would also give me the opportunity to gauge the resistance of the garrison.

I rode bareheaded save for my coif and my hands were empty. Tom carried my standard. We halted within hailing range and I shouted, "Ho, within the castle; I am Sir William Strongstaff sent by Prince Henry of Monmouth, the rightful Prince of Wales, and I am here to demand the surrender of this castle."

A face appeared above the gate. It was a younger face than I expected but he was flanked by two older knights, "I am Sir Rhodri of Machynlleth and we reject your offer. You have laid waste to our land, killed our warriors and taken our animals. Leave our land for in Owain Glyndŵr, we now have a leader who is capable of fighting you and your King."

"This will not end well, Sir Rhodri. As you have said we have already slain many warriors and we have suffered no hurts. Surrender now and save yourself the hardship of siege."

I saw a brief nervous glance from the young man towards one of the older men next to him. The older knight said something and Sir Rhodri returned his gaze to me, "Leave now Sir William for we have spoken enough."

As we rode back, I said to Sir Henry, "They have little food. We will spend a week besieging them and see if that makes them more amenable to talk. We form siege lines. Have the men hew down the largest trees that they are able. We will make them think that we intend to build war machines."

"And we do not?"

"No, Sir Henry. We use the branches for firewood and we spend a week raiding. We leave archers to clear their walls and ten men at arms on duty to deal with any attempt to leave. The rest will ride with us to lay waste to their land."

When we reached the camp, I put all in place. The sound of the axes would seem like the cracks of doom to those within. They would see our numbers and assume that we had more men coming. By the time they realised that we were all that there was it would be time for us to leave. I sent out four scouts to discover where we might raid. This was the largest place along the coast but there would be farms. Anywhere which was more than ten miles from the castle would be a ripe target. We cleared the town of all that was valuable. I contemplated burning it but I decided I would leave that until we left. We dug a ditch around our camp and embedded some of the branches we cut from the two oaks we had felled. They would not stop an enemy raid but they would slow it.

Four days later we had raided every farm, hamlet and village within fifteen miles of the castle. We had twenty head of cattle and forty sheep. We slaughtered the older beasts and cooked them. The smell would madden those within who were on rations. It meant we would have fewer animals to drive home and the ones we did drive would be faster.

Alan of the Woods and our archers had managed to hit ten defenders without loss. He and his archers had been sparing with their arrows. As we rose on the fifth day, I went with Edgar and Alan along with Tom, my squire, to view the walls. "We hit fewer men yesterday, lord, for they are becoming wise to us."

"Aye, and the grazing will deteriorate quickly now that we have so many animals."

"I know but I only intend to stay for two more days and then we will head north."

Sir John waved as he led my knights and some men at arms out for another ride to see what we had missed.

"This will be our last raid. Tomorrow we rest all of our animals and we leave the day after. Alan, have your archers collect all the arrows that they can." The Welsh had traded arrows with us.

"Aye lord, but it is only the shafts and the fletch we can use. The heads are largely hunting arrows. One hit Alf the Grim and it stuck in his leather jerkin."

"I am guessing that Glendower is still gathering his army elsewhere and that is where the best archers will be. I fear that we are limited with what we can do. If King Henry wants this land scouring of rebels then he must use the muster and bring a mighty army."

Tom said, "And why will he not do that, lord?"

"Money! King Richard emptied the treasury when he built the castles such as this one. I have heard that there were two thousand men working on Beaumaris alone. Masons and labourers cost money and that is another reason why the King is angry. If the money was spent wisely then the castles would be well defended!"

Sir John had found just two sheep when he returned. We had emptied the land and so we would spend the next day resting. Knights did not stand a watch but I had placed Edgar of Derby in command of the sentries. He knew his job and he had ensured that the men who watched were vigilant. That paid off for I was woken by him not long after midnight.

"Lord, there are men moving inside the castle."

"They mean to sally forth." I nodded. "They know how few men we have and the capture of the animals has angered them. Wake the men but do so silently." He left. Tom and Harry were already awake. "Come, help me dress and then prepare for a battle at night. It will not be pleasant!" I would use just my sword and a dagger.

It was hard to discriminate between friend and foe when fighting in the dark but I knew that we would be the ones with mail and armour. I hoped that the other knights were also attuned to the dangers of night fighting. I was the first to reach the sentries. It was Captain Jack from the company of Sir Hugh D'Arcy who commanded them.

He pointed to the side of the hill upon which the castle was built. "Lord there is a sally port there and I have seen shadows moving. They are coming."

"And the sentries are ready?"

"There are eight of us, lord." It sounded like criticism.

I smiled in the dark. "Soon there will be more but with my squires, there are eleven of us. Bring the sentries here and we will meet them in a block."

"Aye, lord."

The archers would be using their swords, hatchets and axes. I knew that my archers were more than a match for any enemy. Some knights took longer to dress than did my men. Thus it was, that only my knights, all three of them, were with me when the Welsh attacked. They had approached quietly and must have thought us all asleep. Edgar's vigilance and that of his sentries meant that we were partially ready. They had had time to spy out our defences and knew of the ditch and the stakes. We were waiting just beyond them. I did not know if they had been waiting for a cloudy and moonless night but they had found one. It meant we just saw shadows as they moved towards us. The movement from my men was behind us and they would just expect the sentries they had seen from their walls. Suddenly an arrow flew from the dark and struck me in the chest. My surcoat and plate stopped it. A flurry of other arrows followed and I heard a cry as one of my men was hit.

I roared, "Stand to!"

The Welsh also roared a challenge and ran at us. The nature of our defences meant that while we had a solid double line of men, they had to negotiate stakes and came at us piecemeal. A stocky Welshmen wielding an axe ran at me. He had powerful arms and, as he swung down at me, I used my sword to block his axe. My blade bit into the haft and locked the weapons together. As the Welshman tried to free it, I ripped my dagger across his throat. When his dying body fell backwards, I twisted my sword so that his hands, which were locked around the haft of the axe, tore the weapons apart. It was just in time for one of the greybeards I had seen on the walls rammed his poleaxe at my middle. Although I managed to slow it with my sword and my dagger, he still punched me hard enough to drive me back a step. He was encouraged by his success and pulled his axe back for a second strike. I was ready and I stepped forward and used my sword to push the head of his poleaxe to my right. I brought my dagger up under his arm. There was no plate there and my narrow-bladed dagger drove through the links and up into his shoulder. A poleaxe needs two hands to wield and he dropped it. He had with him, a squire, who bravely thrust a spear at me so that his lord could escape. I barely had time to strike at the spearhead and his spear hit me hard in the side. Tom brought his sword across the squire's neck. My son was strong and he severed both the mail links of the coif and also tore into the squire's neck. The brave youth perished. All along our line men were dying and they were mainly the Welsh. A horn sounded and they ran back.

I shouted, "Hold!" I did not want my men running into an ambush. Besides, we had thwarted them and that was victory enough.

The next morning, I sent Sir John to ask if the Welsh wished their dead to be returned to them. To be truthful it was easier for us to return them so that they could bury them and I wanted them to know that they had not harmed us. I had a feeling that the young lord of Machynlleth would try to disguise the numbers of their own dead. This way they would be even more disheartened. They wanted their dead and a truce was agreed. We took the mail, armour and weapons from the dead before we returned them.

Once back in camp I said, "We stay one more day in the hope that they might surrender."

"But you are not hopeful, lord?"

"No, Sir John, they will continue to hold out and we are needed at Conwy."

We left two days later. There had been no more attempts to attack us but, as the weather had deteriorated, I decided to leave and we headed back to Dolgellau and then Abermaw. We had many animals and we did not move quickly. If people had returned to Dolgellau then they hid as we rode through the town. We marched along the north bank of the river towards the little village of Abermaw. I guessed that they had seen us or else word had been sent of the English horsemen for we spied no one, but the fishing boats out at sea were all filled to capacity. We pushed on along the coast.

Abermaw was just eleven miles from Harlech. Before we left Abermaw I sent out my scouts who reported that the castle was being besieged by the Welsh. I knew that the garrison had but thirty-six men including a constable. It was, however, a well-made castle and one side was protected by the sea. It was kept supplied by ships from Chester. I held a council of war with my knights and captains. "We will try to relieve the siege. I am certain that the garrison might appreciate some of these animals and besides I do not like the thought of the Welsh besieging Englishmen. Alan of the Woods has told me that they have no siege engines but seek to starve the garrison into submission. I propose to march this afternoon and attack sometime in the dark of night when they least expect it."

Sir Raymond of Towcester asked, "How many men do we face, Baron?"

"Captain Alan counted six banners. They look to have more than two hundred men."

"Then they outnumber us."

Sir Roger had taken time to grow accustomed to his title. During the raids, he had become more confident. He spoke with authority, "Sir Raymond, I have seen very little thus far on this chevauchée which makes me fear a Welshman. We will be attacking at dawn, with the sun behind us and we are led by Sir William. I, for one, do not fear the Welsh, do you?"

He smiled, "No, Sir Roger, and you are right to chastise me."

We ate a hearty meal and then headed up towards Harlech. We made camp a mile or so north west of the castle. It was up a narrow track which led through a wood. I chose it, not because it was a good place to camp, but because it was close to the castle and we could be well hidden. If all went well, we would sleep in the castle and if not, we would be fleeing up the road to Caernarfon and hope that it still remained in our hands. Once in the woods, we prepared for battle. We would not be riding to battle. We would walk. The servants and the squires would guard the animals and the booty we had gathered. Before darkness fell, I went to the siege lines to inspect them. The Welsh had dug a ditch all the way around and placed a great number of pavise so that they could rain arrows upon the defenders. I could not imagine what it was like in the castle. They would have few men to guard the walls and would fear an attack each night. I saw the defenders as they patrolled the walls. At least our attack would give them better rest. The knights had their camp in the centre about three hundred paces from the main gate. The gatehouse at Harlech was one of the strongest of any castle and I could see why the Welsh had, thus far, been reluctant to assault it. The knights' horses and those of their squires appeared to be the only horses that the attackers had brought. This was a peasant army on foot. I saw little evidence of mail or armour. They were mainly bowman as was evidenced by the number of arrows sticking from the embrasures and gate. I saw that the Welsh were confident for I saw no sentries watching the road which passed beneath the castle walls.

When I returned to the woods, I told the men what I had seen. "Captain Alan, you will have the archers take their bows but I think that your swords will be handier. Captain Edgar, there are just six knights and we can deal with those," I waved a hand at my knights, "you and the men at arms will be better armed and mailed than any you fight."

"Do not worry, lord, we will chase them hence. We would like to sleep within walls the next time we lay down our heads." They, too, had gained in confidence; victory does that.

We moved up to their siege lines as darkness fell. The nights and the days were of an equal length and I wanted the Welsh asleep. The danger would be armour clanking. For that reason, I had my knights and men at arms spread out and walk behind the silent archers. Alan and I led. We stopped a hundred paces from the siege works and I held my hands up to stop the knights behind me. The archers joined Alan and me in a long line at the edge of the undergrowth. If we did not move then we would not be seen. The nature of the castle's position and elevation meant that the Welsh were on a low piece of ground which was overlooked by both the castle and by us. The Welsh were cooking and we heard some of them singing. They were in a good mood for they would be expecting the castle to fall soon. I guessed it would have been besieged since Conwy had been taken. Caernarfon would either be under siege or would have fallen.

I was used to waiting in the dark. When I had been in the Blue Company, I had stood many a watch at night but I sensed that the knights other than those of my household found the stillness difficult. I also knew that the squires, just a mile or so away would be listening for the moment the combat began; of course, they and the servants would have their hands full keeping the animals as quiet as possible. At night sound travelled. I peered into the camp. The food had been eaten and now men were finishing off their ale and moving to make water and empty their bowels. This was the critical time for they would come towards the undergrowth. I smiled, if Old Captain Tom had been in command of the siege, he would have had us dig toilets. He liked an ordered and orderly camp. These Welsh seemed happy to walk five paces from their hovel and drop their breeks! Eventually, they began to turn in for the night. I saw a sergeant at arms walking along the sentries who faced the castle. We saw the shadows as they moved. And then it was just the knights who were awake. Their voices carried to us. Owen would have understood their words but I did not.

When the words ceased, I tapped Alan on the shoulder and he and the archers with arrows nocked walked from the undergrowth. They would use their bows to slay the sentries and then they would drop them and lead the charge. I turned to lift my sword and wave the knights and men at arms forward. I was the one who knew exactly where the knights were sleeping. I had studied the ground and I moved quickly having chosen the flattest route for my attack. The sound which broke the silence was the whoosh of arrows as they flew through the night. Aiming at shadowy figures meant that my archers were not as accurate as they might have wished. Some men were wounded rather than killed and they cried out. That was the moment the attack began in earnest!

I was now one of the older knights but I had powerful legs and a gap opened between me and those behind me. That was good for they saw my path and did not encounter obstacles but it meant I reached the tents of the knights first as three of them emerged. They had thrown on mail hauberks and each had grabbed the nearest weapon they could. One swung an axe at my chest at the same time as a sword was brought over from on high. In that tiny moment of time, I realised that the sword blow represented the greatest danger for I had a breastplate covering my chest. I blocked the sword with my own and rammed my dagger into the eye of the knight. The axe hit my chest and was wielded with such force that I was knocked to the ground. The third knight saw his chance for he had a sword and he lunged at my face. Sir John had reached the axe-wielding knight and his sword struck the knight in the chest. He wore mail but the sword ripped through the links and sliced a long line across his chest. I swung my sword and held my dagger up to block the strike of the second knight. Even as the sword sparked against my dagger my sword had ripped across his leg and almost severed it.

Sir John lifted me to my feet. The other knights had now emerged from their tents as had their squires. The camp was a maelstrom of fighting and movement. Some of the Welsh commoners fought but more, having been woken from their beds by mailed, armed men, fled. While two of the knights Sir John and I had wounded were taken away to safety, other knights, slightly better prepared, came at us. Sir Wilfred and Sir Roger had joined Sir John and we now stood together. Two squires lunged at us with spears. Sir Wilfred was more ruthless than I was. He used his left hand to hold the spear and hacked his sword into the side of the squire's neck. The spear which came at me was easy to deflect with my dagger and I brought the flat of my sword against the side of the squire's head and rendered him unconscious.

Sir Roger said as he looked for another foe, "He will grow to be a knight, lord!"

"Aye, but he is younger than Harry!"

"Get your breath back, lord, that was a mighty blow you endured and besides, we have won!"

One of the knights had managed to break through Sir Raymond's defence and smashed his war hammer into the knight's chest. The beak broke the plate and Sir Raymond fell. Sir Henry and Sir John ran at the knight who roared, "It takes two English to fight one Welshman! You are cowardly English."

That enraged Sir Henry who flailed his sword wildly at the Welsh knight's head. The knight had mittens at the end of his hauberk and he knocked aside the sword and, one-handed began to swing his war hammer. Had it struck then Sir Henry would be a dead man. Luckily for him, it was Sir John who fought with him and I had trained Sir John. He knew that in combat you looked to win and you did so any way you could. He swung his sword across the arm of the Welsh knight. The Welshman was strong but he was wielding a two-handed weapon with one hand and when the arm was broken by the swinging sword, he was forced to drop the weapon. He had time to punch Sir John in the face before turning and running.

Sir Roger had been right, they were beaten. Four dead squires had bought the knights, wounded and whole, the time to flee. The one whose leg I had hacked was the only one who remained for he had bled to death before us.

Edgar of Derby ran up to me, "The camp is ours, lord." He saw that my surcoat was torn. "Are you hurt, lord?"

"No, but I hope they have a weaponsmith in the castle for I fear my armour is! Have your men search the dead and make sure none feign death. Have Alan of the Woods fetch the squires and the horses. Sir John, come with me and the rest of you secure the horses and the knight's camp. They ran so quickly they may have left valuables."

After sheathing my weapons, we walked through the charnel house of the Welsh camp, picking our way through the bodies and limbs. We reached the gate and I saw a line of faces above. I took off my helmet and slipped my coif around my shoulders, "I am Sir William Strongstaff sent by King Henry. Your siege is relieved."

An older man grinned and shouted, "Open the gates, they are friends! I am Henry of Nantwic and the constable here. I am right glad to see you. I will come down and join you."

The double gates took some time to open and I could hear the approach through the woods of our animals, squires and servants. The constable was a short squat warrior with flecks of grey in his hair and beard. He gave a slight bow, "I thank God that King Henry sent relief.

As I strode through the gates, I shook my head, "He sent us but our purpose was a chevauchée." Just then one of the cows lowed. "You will eat well for we captured animals. We are on our way to the siege of Conwy."

"Then you will have to negotiate the siege lines at Caernarfon first."

It was not unexpected news but it was unwelcome. I nodded, "With your permission, we will stay here for a couple of days for my men have hurts and if we have to fight again, I would have us fresher than we are. Have you a weaponsmith?"

"Aye, we have."

"Good for I have plate which needs to be repaired."

I discovered that the garrison was just thirty-two men. King Edward had built his castles well for Henry of Nantwic believed that they could have held out. "What concerns me is that we were not supplied by ship."

I nodded, "When I reach Conwy, I will put that to the Prince. He is young and he is learning but he will be a good Prince of Wales in the fullness of time."

We had lost seven men. None of them came from my company. Some of the lords of Northampton were not as experienced in such battles as my men. Sir Henry had been saved by his armour but it was ruined and he would need a new breastplate. Sir Raymond had the most serious wound. The beak had broken his skin and his breastbone. The castle doctor tended to him but he would not fight again on the raid. Luckily the Welsh knights had fled without taking their plate and it was replaced. We had taken twenty horses including eight coursers. There were also great quantities of coins. We buried the Welsh dead, noble and commoners alike, in the ditch they had dug for defence and the stakes they had planted were fashioned into crude crosses. Our men were buried in the castle close to the small chapel. I had no doubt that Harlech would have to endure other such sieges and I did not want our dead despoiled by vengeful Welshmen!

We ate well that first night in Harlech. There was a Great Hall and my knights and squires ate with the constable. The rest of our men ate well too and they shared the warrior hall. Our horses were stabled and the animals in the outer ward. We relaxed.

I learned that the constable of Caernarfon was also the Mayor of the town. His name was John Bolde. Henry of Nantwic was hopeful that the town would have held out. "They have good town walls and the castle is stronger than any save Conwy." But for the treachery of the Tudur brothers, this whole rebellion would never have ignited. "The townsfolk of Caernarfon are loyal to England for it is a prosperous town. Here we just guard the road from the south." He looked sad, "It is a lonely and thankless existence, lord." I felt sorry for the constable.

When we left, two days later, I felt nothing but admiration for the tiny garrison of Harlech. They had a thankless task for they were, as the constable had told us, forgotten and surrounded by a sea of enemies. I wondered at their choice of occupation. As we headed north, I realised that I had been in a similar position before the Black Prince had chosen me to train his son. But for that twist of fate, I might have been quite happy to serve my time in a castle in Wales.

I sent scouts out to look at the siege lines of Caernarfon. Alan came back and reported a similar situation to Harlech except that they had defences facing south too. The sun had just passed its zenith and I called a council of war. "We cannot do as we did at Harlech for we have fewer men and there are still those with hurts. We either abandon our horses and try to cross the mountains to get to Conwy or we try a trick."

Sir Henry asked, "A trick, lord?"

"I have no doubt that some of those who fled from Harlech will have come here and told them of the English who broke the siege. They will not know our numbers. The fact that they have defences looking south tells me that this is true. I propose to announce ourselves with horns and banners. We ride north as though we are a much bigger army. We have our squires don the plate we took from Harlech and ride the captured coursers so that they count our horsemen and assume we are a larger force than we actually are. We use our archers to rain death upon them and then we simulate a charge."

Sir Henry shook his head, "You risk all on one throw of the die?"

"It is a risk, I grant you, but the garrison at Harlech showed me the mettle of the men who defend these castles and the people are loyal. I hope that when we attack, the garrison will sortie. It is my decision, Sir Henry, and I will lead the charge."

Sir Henry laughed, "And I will follow you, my lord!"

Our squires were more than happy to don the helmets and plate we had taken from the Welsh knights and to mount their warhorses. They even fashioned gonfanon to place on their lances so that they looked like knights who led other knights. Our men at arms added to the illusion and, with horns blaring, we headed up the road to Caernarfon. The archers led and that meant they could dismount and nock their arrows as the rest of us marched up the road. We heard horns from ahead, most were from the Welsh but some were sounded from within the castle walls. The constable knew that we approached for he could see our banners. The Welsh began to form lines to fight against us. They had dug a ditch along both sides of the road but the road north was free from obstruction. The archers' horses were led away and my archers formed two long lines. Both sides were within arrow range but there was a protocol about such matters. I lined up my knights and men at arms. To add to the illusion of a greater army our servants sound horns. They were half a mile behind us and driving the cattle and sheep. My men turned in their saddles as though to encourage them to hurry to our aid. I rode to the fore and raising my sword shouted, "Loose!"

Our arrows flew first and the Welsh responded. I turned in my saddle and raised my sword. All of my men cheered. They made their horses rear; the action made it look as though we were going to charge. As a second flight flew from our archers and Welsh arrows clattered amongst my knights and men at arms, I heard Welsh horns and commands were given. The Welsh began to withdraw west away from this threat. It was crucial that they were not allowed to stop and watch for this imaginary army heading from the south and west.

I shouted, "Charge!"

My archers broke ranks and allowed us to charge through them. I had briefed my men about this eventuality. The charge was at the canter rather than the gallop, but it was realistic enough to deceive them about our intention. The orderly retreat became a rout as the Welsh raced away from the charge. A couple of foolhardy knights bravely counter charged us. The success of our trick was shown when they charged men at arms. The two knights were slain and that encouraged the rest to continue their flight. We followed them for half a mile and then I called a halt.

"My lord, I will dine off that ruse for many a month. They outnumbered us by more than three to one."

"Aye, Sir Henry, but not in knights. This Welsh rebellion is dangerous because the people are behind Glendower, but so long as he has few knights then they will always flee."

We entered the castle at Caernarfon as conquering heroes.

Chapter 6

When we reached Conwy, the siege was over but the Tudur brothers had escaped justice and they had fled. The Prince had lost men in the assault and there was little joy in his eyes when we spoke. However, he was delighted at our success and pleased that Harlech and Caernarfon had resisted the Welsh.

We were alone and so I could speak plainly, "The people are behind this rebellion, lord. I am not certain that the chevauchée I led will have done any good. I obeyed your father's orders but I fear it will harden the resistance to our rule. The only way we will succeed is if we destroy Glendower and that will require an army for he is able to slip away through the high passes. I do not think that your father will sanction such an expense."

"You are right. I must build up my own forces. First, I have to win over the men of Cheshire."

"And that will be easier said than done."

I looked around, "And there is something else, lord, do you not find it strange that the only castle they took was the castle which was Percy's and that the Tudur brothers were known associates of the Earl?"

He nodded, "And my father is of the same opinion. I have received, a few days ago, a missive from the King. I am to strip Lord Percy of Conwy and Anglesey."

"He will not be happy." I looked at Prince Henry, "And why have you not spoken of this yet? One day you will be King. You cannot fear men like Percy or they will use that fear to control you."

He coloured and I knew that I was close to the mark, "The castle fell the day I received the letter and we have had much to do." He smiled, "I confess, that when I saw your banners, I felt more confident. I would that you were with me when I tell him. I

70

do not fear him but you have witnessed the great and the good conduct their business for twenty years. I value you, your advice." He smiled, "I learned more from you in one week than in all the time I have been with Percy. I am still young, Sir William, but I am learning."

It was then I realised that Hal had only seen fourteen summers. He was still a boy. I had been unfair in my judgement of him. He waited until we had all dined in the Great Hall at Conwy and the heroism of the attackers praised. A singer made up a song about Prince Henry. Hal did not enjoy the attention and it was not a particularly good song. I saw Mark the Minstrel, one of my men, wrinkle his nose at some of the poor lines. The singer was a Northumbrian and the song made rather too much of the actions of Henry Percy. As the evening degenerated into a drinking contest Prince Henry waved over Henry Percy. The knight had been less than happy that Sir John and I flanked him while we ate. He took it as an insult.

"Lord Percy, I have to thank you for your advice during the siege. It was most informative." The faint praise from Prince Henry told me that Hotspur had done very little indeed! "However," he proffered a parchment from which the King's seal could be clearly seen, "my father has sent this." The Prince did not let him read it. "He is displeased with the loss of Conwy and, as a result, he has taken back from you that castle and the right to tax Anglesey."

Henry Percy did not look at the Prince but at me, "I can see that your father has been badly advised and I know who my enemies are. I am insulted, Prince Henry. Tomorrow I will take my men home to the north. There I know there are knights I can trust who keep their word. There they are not dissembling, fawning guttersnipes raised to be amongst their betters."

He was looking at me and I said, quietly, "Go carefully, Percy! Do not live up to your reputation. I will put this down to the drink but one more word and you and I will settle this with swords. I do not fight tournaments. I was brought up to fight to kill. Think on that before you choose to cross me!" His eyes narrowed. "Or is it that you prefer to have hired men do your dirty work as at Middleham?"

That proved too much. He shouted, "Knights of Northumberland, we have endured enough from these mewling southerners, pack our bags! We leave this castle now!"

I almost burst out laughing. By the time they had packed it would be almost dawn. He would be riding home with men still suffering from drink and he would have to beg accommodation on the way home. He had lived up to his name; he had acted rashly!

The Earl of Stafford was as concerned as I was about Percy. "I know not why King Henry allowed him to be your mentor. He may be a brave knight who holds back the northern barbarians but I do not trust either him or his nature." He smiled, "And I will also bid farewell, Prince Henry, but unlike Henry Percy, I will not do so with such bad grace. I have done as I was asked and now my men and I can go home. If you need me again then ask and I shall serve with you for I have seen great hope for England in your young body!"

I liked the Earl of Stafford. He was a true knight and gentleman. While he might not have Percy's skill, I would rather have one Stafford at my side in a battle than five Percys.

There was no need for us to rush home. We had mail and plate to divide and we had animals to sell. Prince Henry was returning to Chester and so we rode with him. The markets there would pay us more than in Wales although we did sell some of the animals to those who lived close by Conwy. The siege had taken all of the animals from the surrounding countryside. I rode with Prince Henry and we were now as we had been when I had trained him. We were easy with one another and the shadow of Percy no longer lay between us.

"I fear you may be right about Henry Percy, Sir William. Now that I think back, he was closeted with the Tudur brothers for long periods. He went hunting with them in the Welsh forests close by Snowdon."

"In which case, he could have had contact with Glendower. The attacks on Harlech and Caernarfon show planning and we found no sign of the rebel leader, Glendower. Perhaps he was warned that I had been sent."

The Prince's face was as though a thunderbolt had struck close by him, "Of course! He always had riders going hither and thither. I took them to be messengers going to his home but now I come to think about it they all returned too quickly for such a journey! I am a fool!"

I smiled, "No, Prince Henry, there was no reason for suspicion and you are young. Your father is King and he should shoulder some responsibility."

"Baron, some might construe that as treasonous talk!"

I laughed, "I know treasonous talk for I heard much of it when I guarded King Richard. I am William Strongstaff and I speak that which is in my heart. It is my way."

He nodded, "I have much to learn but first I must stand on my own two feet and begin to gather men around me whom I can trust."

"And you can trust me but I now have a family and lands to manage. More than that, I am getting old. When my son and young Richard Longchamp are knighted, they would be men you could trust and they are young. More, they are untainted by politics. That is the bane of the crown. There are too many men seeking power."

"Yet you do not; why is that?"

"My upbringing. I had to scramble around for food, shelter and clothes. Worrying if someone else felt differently was not even a thought and that is all politics is. That and a desire for a crown, a throne, or power. Choose men who are happy and content. Look for comfortable men who worry more about the ale they drink than which seat they occupy at table. Seek men who have genuine laughter and not the false laugh with hooded eyes!"

"That is wise advice and I will take you up on the offer of your young knights. Hopefully, we will be given time to prepare for the next rebellion."

I did not think the Welsh would grant him the time and I was proved correct. After selling our surplus in Chester we began the long ride to our home. I do not know if it had been the intention of King Henry but one effect of the campaign was to draw the men of Northampton closer together. There was easy banter as we rode home.

"So, Sir William, if you would still allow my son to marry your daughter then I intend to knight him at the time of the summer solstice."

I nodded, "And that would mean a summer wedding. I am agreeable but I will have to speak with my wife for the exact date, my lord."

He laughed, "Aye, fellows like us can beard the Welsh and not blanch but ask us to question our wives and we quiver and quake. I am the same." He nodded, "And your son? From what I have seen he is brave and ready to be given his spurs."

"He has said that he is not ready yet. He will be knighted before we go to war again."

"You see war on the horizon?"

"Did we extinguish the flames of Glendower's rebellion or did we merely dampen them?"

"Aye, you are right and that means, unless the King finds money from somewhere, that we will be footing the bill. Instead of ploughing money back into our land we throw it at Welsh and Scottish wars."

"I cannot complain, Sir Henry, for war made me what I am. If there had been no wars then I would not be a knight and have the lands I do. I can bear the financial cost but it is the human one I do not relish. I will thank God in my church that I lost none and there are no maimed warriors returning to my manors."

I parted from Sir John who took Ralph and his men to their home in Dauentre. Ralph had also excelled himself in battle but, like Tom, did not feel that he was ready for his spurs. I know that pleased Sir John for he liked his young squire and to train another would take time. I knew that I was lucky to have Harry almost trained as a squire already. Until Sir John's children grew, he would have to find young men who wished to serve as his squire. "Give my love to your wife, the Lady Blanche."

"I will, lord, but you should know that she is always grateful to you for she lives in the finest hall in Dauentre."

"Weedon is our home, Sir John, and Lady Eleanor is comfortable there."

I hurried home and this time our greeting was not only warm there was, for the first time, concern from my wife and Alice for another, "Father, how is Master Richard? Was he hurt?"

Tom could have a wicked sense of humour and he had the ability to keep a straight face when telling a tale. He shook his head, "It was terrible to behold, sister. He is whole and I am sure that the lack of a nose will not impair his looks too much!"

Alice screamed and put her hand to her mouth and my wife paled as she wrapped her arm around our daughter. I cuffed Tom none too gently on the back of his head, "Your brother teases you! Richard suffered no harm and acquitted himself well on the battlefield. He is to be knighted in June and we may arrange the marriage after that!"

In an instant, both changed. It was as though storm clouds had been blown away and the sun shone. Both my wife and Alice threw their arms around me.

Mary said, "And what of a husband for me, father?"

I put my arm around her. "When your sister is wed there will be many young men who will be at the wedding. They will see the jewel that is my Mary and they will all seek her hand! We shall choose you a good one"

I had said the words not knowing if I had chosen well but her reaction showed that I had. She threw her arms around my neck and kissed my stubbly face, "You are the best of fathers although you need to shave!"

My wife slipped her arm through mine, "Aye, you are husband but you need to beat some manners into our son! He is patently not ready to be knighted!"

It was another lesson for my son. He had become used to banter and the humour of the campaign. He had thought to do the same in our home. He now knew that a knight had two faces; he had one for war and the company of men and then a second when he was at home. Over the next days, while the women threw themselves into the seemingly unending plans for a summer wedding, we spoke of the changes Tom would need to make before he could become Sir Thomas of Weedon. His poor attempt at humour resulted in a different Tom. He became quieter around his mother and sisters and took more time to help train Harry. He also spent more time with the other squires and men at arms for there he could be himself. I had been brought up without siblings. My mother had other children and when I had visited her, I had seen them but I had not had to grow up with them. I had learned how to speak to women when I married Eleanor and I had been lucky that she had been a good teacher.

As lord of so many manors, the time I had spent on campaign had left many tasks which I needed to complete. I had stewards and reeves in my manors. As soon as I arrived home, they came to me with problems to solve and payments to authorise. The time between our arrival home and Richard's knighthood passed in the blink of an eye. The whole family were invited to Piddington for the ceremony of knighthood for once he was knighted, we would have to make the formal announcement of the marriage. Since I had been elevated my life had been changed. Eleanor and I had just had the priest and a couple of villagers at the church in Stoney Stratford when we had wed. Sir Henry and I were nobles and that meant we had to tell the King both as our King and liege lord. Sir George Dunbarre, a Scottish lord who had fought against the English and defeated them at Otterburn, had learned that to his cost. His daughter Elizabeth had been betrothed to the son of the King of Scotland. The Earl of Douglas had objected and the proposed marriage was annulled. The Scottish lord had come to England where King Henry had given him the manor of Somerton. He had now lost his homeland and was in exile. Life was not as simple for the nobility.

Sir Henry had no castle but a large and comfortable manor. Our wives got on and, on the night before the ceremony, while Richard held his vigil in the chapel, the wives and Alice gabbled on about the wedding. Sir Henry had a good cellar and I sat with him and spoke, as men do, of the state of the country.

"The Welsh still cause a problem for Prince Henry, Sir William."

"I have heard."

"It is good that he has knights such as Edmund Mortimer to help him control the main thoroughfares of Wales."

"Aye, but is not Mortimer Hotspur's brother in law?"

"He is but it is in Mortimer's interests to support the Prince of Wales."

I was not convinced. I did not like Percy and his tentacles appeared to be everywhere. I gave a guarded answer, "Perhaps."

Sir Henry had many visitors and knew much about the lie of the land. "Dunbarre is back in the north. He is aiding the Percy and Neville families to keep the border safe. The Scots are rattling their swords again."

"I do not mind Hotspur doing all that he can to keep the Scots at bay but I could never understand why he came to Wales to aid the Prince."

"His father was granted the Isle of Man by King Henry. Perhaps that was the reason. He gained the throne through the intervention of the Percy and Neville families. He owes them much."

I knew that for that had been the start of the friction between Hotspur and me. King Richard had lost his crown because of the Percy family.

The ceremony of knighthood went well. Richard had the simple white shift replaced with the coat of arms he would bear in battle. He was given his spurs and I gave him a sword. It was one I had taken in the Welsh campaign and was a good one. We left three days later with a wedding date in August decided. I had much to do myself. When we reached our home, I told my wife that I would need to ride to Middleham.

"But we have a wedding to plan!"

I nodded, "And you do not need me to do that. I need to go to Middleham to buy horses. War will come again and we will need better horses. Within the next year, we shall knight Thomas and Harry will then need a better horse. I thought to buy large numbers for we could sell them here at a profit."

As soon as I used the word profit then the attitude of my wife changed. She had lost all when she was young and knew the penance of poverty was not for her. She agreed. I took half of my archers and four men at arms, along with Harry and Tom. The men at arms and archers were for the simple reason that we were entering Neville and Percy country. I was the King's man and neither lord would dare to use their own men to harm me but the last time I had come north I had been attacked and had lost men. Consequently, we rode mailed and we rode good horses. We deviated to York for I wished to speak with Peter the Priest who ran an alms-house by the river. I regularly sent money to my old comrade in arms for he cared for old soldiers and that was a cause which was dear to my heart. He was getting old and when I saw him, I realised that he had aged considerably. Despite the few locks of wispy white hair, his eyes were bright and he still looked fit for a man who was over sixty.

He embraced me, "My lord, it is good to see you and your fine sons! I can see that they will be warriors like their father."

"Peter, it was always Will and it always shall be between us. You know that titles mean nothing." I handed him a bag of gold. It was made up of the coins I had taken from the men I had slain or captured in the Welsh campaign. Their horses, ransom and armour meant that I did not need them.

He gratefully took the purse. "You are too kind, Will. I shall meet you in the inn when my work is done."

I nodded. It was late in the afternoon yet he still toiled. We used the inn, 'The Saddle' when we stayed in York. It was close to the river and to Peter's alms-house, besides which the landlord was an old soldier and was honest. We were well served and we felt safe.

When Peter arrived, I ordered our food and ale. Peter would scrimp on his own food and I made sure that he had the largest meal which we could buy. While we ate my sons told him of our campaign. The old soldier in him was excited and his face lit up as Tom told of our chevauchée. He frowned when we mentioned Percy. I elaborated my suspicions and he nodded.

"We are close enough here to know of the Percy and Neville family. The old earl is a cunning man. He hitched his wagon to Henry Bolingbroke's wagon and has been richly rewarded. Many men would be satisfied with such a reward but the old earl has delusions of greater power. Be careful, Will."

"And the Nevilles?"

He sat back and drank some ale. "All is not well between the Neville and the Percy family. It has nothing to do with the north, I think that the Nevilles resent the rewards which Harry Hotspur has garnered. They were equal and now he sees the Percy family as pre-eminent. King Henry is a clever man but I sometimes wonder if he is too clever." Peter had known Henry when he was a young man. Like me, he preferred his cousin, Richard!

"Thank you for your information, old friend. I would invite you to my daughter's wedding but I know that you will not leave York."

He nodded, "So long as there are wars there will be men who are hurt and none cares for them but the likes of me. That is where I gain much of my knowledge, for Ralph Neville and Harry

Hotspur care only for their men so long as they can wield a sword. After Otterburn and the other battles of the north, I have many maimed men with no hope but for me. I give your daughter my blessing and best wishes."

I nodded, "And they will be as valuable as any pot of gold for you are a good man, Peter the Priest, and it is an honour to have served with you."

As we rode the short way to Middleham, the next day, Harry asked, "Why do not lords care for the men hurt fighting for them?"

"I know not. We do and I will continue to do so. Any man hurt fighting for me needs no alms-house. The family of our dead men will be cared for by us too."

They both nodded and Tom said, "When I am a knight I will do so, too, for it is only right and proper."

"Then remember that it costs. The Percy family like not only their fine castles but all that goes with that. They have the finest of armour and eat the finest of foods. We eat plainer fare and that pleases me for all else is vanity."

As we rode, I reflected on the change in Tom. He was more serious now. As we neared the horse farm he said, "Father I am no longer a boy and I would have my man's name. When I am introduced at Red Ralph's horse farm, I would be Thomas for that is my name. I shall be knighted as Sir Thomas and it is meet that is how people see me."

"Of course. That is your choice. And what of you, Harry? Would you be Henry?"

He shook his head and grinned, "No, for I am happy to be Harry! It is a cheerful name. I will change when I have to!"

My boys were both good warriors but they had different natures.

Mary, Red Ralph's wife, was a good woman and she was also as skilled as Ralph had been when it came to raising horses. She had gnarled and reddened hands which were as tough as any archer for she worked hard, but her heart was a soft one and made of gold. I saw her about to curtsy and I would have none of it. I swept her in my arms and hugged her, "That is how I greet the wife of the man who made me the warrior I am. It is good to see you. The farm prospers?"

"Aye, my…" she saw my face and she changed her words, "Will. We had a mild winter and the horses which were covered all had young. I assume that is why you came; to buy horses."

I felt guilty, "Aye, but it is good to speak with you and I thought to tell you of your son "

Her face beamed. She shouted to another of her sons, William, "Red Will, take the archers and the men at arms to the barn and then bring them to the kitchen. Mary, Maud," she waved over her daughters, "take the Baron's sons to their room!"

Red Ralph had not been a lord but he had used his money wisely and his hall was the equal of many a knight's. His kitchen had a table which could seat ten and he had a large room which could seat twelve. We would be comfortable.

"Well, how is he?"

"He does well. We fought against the Welsh and he acquitted himself as nobly as any squire could. Another year and he may well be knighted."

I thought she was going to burst into tears, "When he was taken as a squire, we had hopes but you say he is close? My son might be a noble?"

"Like my Thomas, he says he is not ready yet and that means that he is almost ready. I think both will be a knight next year."

"Heaven be praised! You are a good man, Sir William Strongstaff."

I sat and spoke with Mary, telling her of the wider world. Red Ralph's children took Thomas and Harry on a tour of the farm. There must have been much to see for they did not return until called for food. I confess that while my eyes are the best on any battlefield, often I miss glaring and obvious events before my eyes. I saw Mary and Maud as Red Ralph's daughters. I did not see them outside of the family. It took the girl's mother to point out the obvious.

"I see that young Thomas is now a man."

I nodded, absent-mindedly, "Aye, that he is."

She shook her head, "Have you not noticed how he looks at my Mary?"

I looked up and, as I wiped my mouth with my napkin said, "They talk and laugh; that is good is it not?"

"Mary has seen fifteen summers and is now a woman. They are flirting. You are a man! Did you not do the same with Lady Eleanor when you wooed her?" I gave a blank look. If I had flirted then I was unaware of it. She sighed, "I suppose my Ralph would have been the same. They like each other, my lord."

"Oh!" I looked again and saw she was right. My son had grown up, that much I knew but now he had taken one more step and it took me by surprise.

"Does it displease you?" I heard the fear in Mary's voice.

I shook my head for it truly did not, "No, Mistress Mary, it is just that it has come as a surprise to me." I saw her sigh. "What is amiss? Do you disapprove?" Women and their feelings confused me!

"No, lord, but it means another of my bairns will be leaving the nest. It is hard to bear."

"Not yet, surely?"

"Mary is a woman and soon she will wish a child of her own. It is inevitable."

I drank some more ale, "My daughter will be married in August."

"Then we will see if this is a sudden flaring which will die or if it is an inferno which cannot be resisted."

That night, as we made up our beds, I could hear the excitement in the voices of Harry and Thomas. I lay under the covers and said, when all had gone quiet, "Red Ralph's children have grown. I scarce recognised the girls."

It was as though a dam had burst and Thomas rattled on like hailstones on a wooden roof, "Mary is so funny, father, and clever too. Why she can read! How many children of farmers can read? She is a fine cook too. And…"

"And is there something else you would say to me, Thomas son of William, who is now a man?"

There was silence in the dark room. It was almost as if I could hear my son thinking. "I know not but I felt… I felt different tonight. I would normally have spoken with the boys but it seemed right that I spoke with Mary."

"And when we return home?"

There was another silence. It was longer this time. I think Harry had stopped breathing lest he disturb the moment. "I would find it hard to bear the absence." There was another silence. "Yet I know that I must."

"Aye, for you are now a man. I have spoken with Mary's mother. It was she who saw the flickering flames, not your half-blind father. Your sister is to be married in August. That gives you the distance to be apart. We will speak again after the wedding and you can tell me your thoughts. Until then remember that Mary is a maid."

"I know, father. I am a man but I have honour for I am your son."

We stayed for three days. Thomas and Harry spent some time with me for we were choosing horses for them but more often than not while Harry larked around with Red Ralph's two sons, Thomas and Mary would be off somewhere, alone. I completed the purchase of the horses and, as we prepared to leave spoke again with Mary.

"My son admitted to me that he has feelings for your eldest daughter. I have told him to give me an answer after his sister is wed. Does that satisfy you?"

"It does. Mary would run off now and marry him." She smiled, "Your son is very handsome! But she, too, has agreed to cast her eyes abroad to ensure she has made the correct choice."

"Then we will return in September with an answer, one way or another."

"Then I will prepare to say goodbye to my daughter for I have looked at them together. This is meant to be."

There were tears when we left from both mother and daughter. Edgar smiled at the red face of my son. He said, "Do not worry, Master Tom, she will wait for you."

For some reason that made him smile.

We were passing the Neville castle at Middleham when two riders emerged and rode towards us. I was not worried for there were just two of them but I remembered my last visit when we had been attacked not far from here. I saw that it was Ralph Neville, the first Earl of Westmoreland. He was about ten years younger than I was. I was surprised to see him here for his lands and castles in the west were of more importance.

"Sir William, may I have a word?"

I nodded, "We were on our way home but…"

He waved a hand dismissively, "I will ride a few miles with you but I would have privacy."

I nodded. I understood politics. "Thomas, Harry, give us space and keep others from us."

I spurred Hart and the Earl did the same with his mount. "I know, Sir William, that you have not always trusted me." I said nothing for he was now Earl Marshal, appointed by the King. He was the King's brother in law. "I do not blame you. I was King Richard's man and I changed sides. You were loyal to the end and the King knows that." Again, I said nothing. "I was at Carlisle when word came that you were in York. I knew that you would come to Middleham and I rode here directly." That told me much. He had spies. "The Percy family is up to something. There was a time when they included me in their discussions and plans but since before Glendower's rebellion, I have been kept out of all of his plans. Why, they even dispute my right to be Earl of Westmoreland. I have heard that Welsh emissaries have been in Alnwick."

"You have evidence?"

"No. My man who watches the castle saw Welshmen in the town and then they disappeared. When they returned, it was from within Alnwick's walls."

"Then tell the King. You are Earl Marshal and he is, as you say, his brother in law!"

"It is not as simple as that, Strongstaff. As I married his sister there are those who say I wish the crown."

"Percy!"

He nodded, "I do not but if I speak against the Percy family then it might rouse unsubstantiated suspicions."

I nodded, "But Baron Weedon who is known to be an enemy of the Percy family could risk his own position and tell the King." He had the good grace to blush. "I can see your dilemma. Fear not, Earl, I too harbour suspicions. The next time I speak with the King then I will tell him." I looked in his eyes. "I am pleased that you spoke with me for I have harboured doubts. I have looked in your eyes and I see no lie."

"Thank you."

"One favour I beg of you, my lord, Mistress Mary is a dear friend of mine. I would have her enjoy your protection for I fear my enemies may wish to do her harm."

"Gladly!"

We parted and I felt better for having given Mary and her family more security.

Chapter 7

The wedding was a spectacular affair for my wife wished to impress everyone who was invited. My steward had told me how much it had cost and I think he expected me to baulk at the expense but it was only money and I knew that when war came again, I would recoup all that was spent and more. I had invited the King. I did not think he would attend but he was my liege lord as well as my king. He surprised me for he attended, albeit briefly. I do not think he had the slightest interest in the wedding but he came. It caused my wife no end of trouble when the Pursuivant arrived to announce the imminent arrival of King Henry! I knew the Pursuivant; his name was Geoffrey and he had served King Richard too.

I was able to speak easily to him, "Geoffrey, does the King require accommodation?"

He smiled, "No, my lord, he will stay at Northampton." He leaned in. "He comes to make a gift to the couple and, I believe, to speak with you."

"Thank you." I turned to my wife. "He does us honour and that is all. The ceremony will go ahead as was planned and the King will fit in with it."

"He is King!" She was outraged that I would not change our plans.

"And this has a political reason, trust me. I will speak with the King. You just smile at him and curtsy. It will be enough."

The King arrived just moments before the ceremony began. I waited outside the church with the Pursuivant. King Henry came with four bodyguards only. He dismounted, "Have I missed it, Strongstaff? Or are they waiting for me?"

I smiled, "I told them they did not need to wait for you, Highness, and they are about to start."

He laughed, "King or commoner all receive the same from Will Strongstaff. You wait here. We will return to Northampton shortly." He smiled, "Let us go then!"

I was a little angry at the King. He had upset the day and I spent the whole of the wedding not enjoying the spectacle but worrying about the real purpose of the King's visit. As soon as the couple were wed and the service over the King hurried out to be there before the bride and groom. I know that it upset my wife for she had a thin, grim smile on her face.

The King beamed at the couple, "Congratulations. Sir Richard, I have high hopes for you and your children. They will come from the blood of William Strongstaff." He waved a hand and Geoffrey the Pursuivant stepped forward with a purse. "Here is a one-hundred-pound gift and there," he snapped his fingers again and Geoffrey handed him a parchment, "is the deed to Kislingbury manor." The manor was a small one but was close to both mine and his father's. For Henry Bolingbroke, this was quite thoughtful.

The crowds all cheered and Sir Richard dropped to one knee, "I cannot thank you enough, Your Majesty!"

"Just continue to serve me as your father and father in law and all will be well. And now I must take Sir William away, briefly, for I need to speak with him." As he led me away, by the elbow, he smiled, "It never hurts to show that a King can endure the mundane." We stopped in the churchyard amongst the gravestones. I saw that his four bodyguards had placed themselves so that we could not be overheard by any. He saw my look, "You taught me the value of bodyguards. These are not knights but they are in the Strongstaff mould. You visited the Earl of Westmoreland?"

"It would be more accurate to say that he accosted me upon the road. He spoke to me of the possible threat from Percy."

"And you did not think to visit with me to tell me of his news?"

"I knew not where you were, my lord, and I had a wedding to plan. Besides, I did warn you of Percy myself or is the Earl's word more trustworthy than mine?"

"Do not go too far, Will." He glared at me and then shook his head. "Our finances are still in dire straits. I cannot afford a war against the Percy clan. Luckily, I have heard that he seeks to make war on his neighbours, the Scots. That suits me. How do you feel about going to war with the Scots as well?"

"Me, lord? Would Henry Percy allow it?"

He smiled. Henry Bolingbroke knew how to plot and to plan. "Lord Dunbarre is back in the borders at his castle on the coast. You will serve with him. I do not need all of your men, just your banner." I wondered what he was up to. He saw my look and shook his head, "You are too clever for your own good, Sir William. I want Percy to know that you and Lord Dunbarre are raiding the Scots. Your presence will fix his eye. He would not wish to leave his northern strongholds with you and Dunbarre loose and he dare not attack those who attack our enemies. This will give my son the time to build up his forces to defeat Glendower and it will allow me the time to build up my war chest. Just spend the time between now and harvest time there. They do not fight in winter for it is too cold."

"And next year?"

"Next year? We shall see what we shall see." He saw the frown on my face. "The young couple will be happy in Kislingbury. It is a good manor and will yield a good income. Your grandchildren will prosper."

The look he gave me told me that the gift was to buy my services. He was ever manipulative. This way he had my skill and it cost him very little. Kislingbury had belonged to one of Robert de Vere's knights and the man had fled to France with his lord. It had cost the King nothing to give it to my family.

"I shall serve you as I have served you before, King Henry."

"Good. Enjoy the rest of the wedding and next time you have news for me, find me, Baron, for I do not like to be kept in the dark!"

After he had gone all wanted to know what had been said in the churchyard. I smiled and lied, "We were talking of the Welsh campaign. It was nothing of import." I forced myself to be happy and bright during the festivities. We had Sir Henry and his family as guests as well as the happy couple and I saw my wife and sons champing at the bit for they knew something was amiss. After Sir Henry had left us and Sir Richard and Alice had ridden to view their new home, I was confronted by my wife, sons and daughter.

"Well? It was bad enough that the King interrupted the wedding but for him to take you away, well, it does not speak well of him!" It was the bad manners which appalled my wife. She had expected better of a king.

"He wishes me to ride to Scotland and assist the Earl of March, Lord Dunbarre, until harvest time."

My wife looked puzzled, "And are we at war with Scotland?"

Thomas laughed, "We are always at war with Scotland!"

"Do not be facetious! Answer me, husband."

I sighed for I could not tell her what the King had told me. I gave her a version of the truth. "He is short of money and the Earl of March needs help to stop the Scottish raids. The manor he gave to Richard and Alice buys my time for a couple of months."

That, my wife could understand, "Then I suppose two months away is not so bad. I thought it something far more sinister!"

I decided that I would leave Sir Roger and Sir Wilfred at home. The King had not asked for them, neither had he asked for Sir John. He wanted me and I would take the minimum number of men that I had to. This was summer and we had a harvest to gather. I went, with my squires, to speak with Captain Edgar and Captain Alan. "I need men to come with me to the borders. I do not need all of our men. The ones who are single and the ones who do not have farms would be the ones I would choose. If you two have obligations here then…"

Edgar shook his head, "I am your Captain as is Alan. We are paid a higher rate and we will earn it. Besides, it has been some time since we fought the Scots. They have more coin than the Welsh and they are piss poor archers! When do we leave, lord?"

"Tomorrow!"

They both laughed and left me shaking their heads. I turned to look at Thomas, "And the haste of our departure is because of you. We promised a decision for Mary. We can call at Middleham on the way north if you have made up your mind?"

"Aye, father, I have. I have thought of little else since we returned and the look of joy on the face of Richard…"

I held up my hand, "Two things, you cannot marry until you are a knight and there may well not be a manor for you, yet."

He nodded, "I would not expect a manor and as for the knighthood? Perhaps I may have an opportunity to show that I deserve one whilst in Scotland."

"I will decide when you are ready. A squire can shelter in the rear and be safe. A knight cannot. I will not let you put your life in danger by fighting too soon. You can give your answer to Mary but it is on my terms."

"Aye, father, I am a man and I can live with those terms, harsh though they are."

That night, as my wife lay in my arms, I told her of Thomas' decision. I heard her sigh, "I knew it would come but this is different from Alice's situation. Mary is a good girl?"

"She is. She reminds me of you when I first met you!"

She laughed, in the dark, "Then our son had better watch out." My real fear is that you will knight him and then you will no longer be able to watch and protect him in battle."

"I will still do all in my power to keep him safe and he will fight under my banner."

"I suppose I should get used to this for Harry will follow soon enough."

"That he will."

The road north was pleasant; the days were long and the weather benign. Thomas kept urging us to travel faster for he was eager to see his would be betrothed. Mary was delighted with the news as was her daughter. When I told them that a wedding would not be imminent, they were not unhappy. Mary said, "I would that my daughter had a good wedding. We will need to save."

I shook my head, "We took your son from you. I will pay whatever is needed for this wedding."

"A fine offer, my lord, but would you have made the same offer had Ralph been alive?"

"I would."

"Then I will let you pay half for I would hold my head up. We do not seek charity."

"We leave on the morrow and when our work in Dunbarre is done we will call here on our way back to Weedon. It will be after harvest time."

"Be safe, my lord and keep your son safe for my Mary. I never had to watch Red Ralph go to war and I am not sure I would have enjoyed the parting, despite the rewards."

We negotiated the Percy lands by keeping to the higher ground closer to Westmoreland. I knew that I had a friend in the Earl, Ralph Neville. He had given me a token when he had spoken with me. It acted as a pass to ensure that his people knew me for a friend. It helped that my blue surcoat with the staff upon it was easily recognisable and so long as I kept clear of Percy land, we would be safe. We stayed in an inn which was south of the Tyne at a bend of the river close by the old Roman horse fort and then completed the rest of the journey to north of Bamburgh in one day. That way we avoided the castles of the Percy knights We stayed in the royal castle at Norham. Once it had been the northernmost outpost of England but now that honour was held by Berwick. I had been impressed by Bamburgh when we had passed it and Dunbarre, as a castle, was equally impressive. The Earl of March would take some shifting should an enemy come south. We were all weary when we arrived but the Earl made us welcome.

"Baron, you and your men are most welcome. We have fine fighting men up here in the borders but I have none who can compare with your archers. Douglas is in for a shock!"

"Good. Do we ride far?"

"No, East Lothian is where we will raid. I have to tell you that Hotspur and his men will be raiding in the region too. Our paths may cross."

The King had omitted to tell me that and his plan now became clear. While I was in the north Hotspur would entertain no thoughts of conspiring with the Welsh. He would be watching me and my banner would draw his eye thither.

The Earl saw my frown, "I know that you and he are on less than cordial terms but you should know that although we will both be raiding, we will not be together. You need have no contact with him."

"May I speak frankly, my lord?"

"Of course."

"What I fear is one of his men sending an arrow into my back during the heat of battle."

"He would do that?"

"He has sent men before to do me harm. If he is close to us then I will not fight. I am not afraid for myself but an assassin from behind us could harm my sons."

"As we will not fight on the same battlefield that is not a problem but your words disturb me. I may well have to reassess my opinion of the knight."

Dunbarre was now an English ally in a sea of Scots. All around lay enemies but the Earl of March's castle was the strongest except for Edinburgh in this part of Lothian and so dominated the land. The Scottish lords who lived close by had feared the English raids of the Percy family and now they feared raids from their own. I could see why King Henry had asked his new ally to return home. It also gave me hope that Percy might accept my presence. He had always wanted Scotland and now he had the opportunity to steal more of it.

The Earl had an old map and he used it to illustrate our raid. Traprain had been the site of an old hill fort which had been used for many years as a place where Scottish kings could be crowned. Since William the Conqueror had been on the island it had been raided so many times that the Scottish kings had moved the site of their coronations to a new site north of the Forth. It was, however, still a place worth raiding as it would lay a mark down to the lords and their king that we now ruled this land. The manor of Traprain lay below the mighty hillfort, now fallen into disrepair. Having been on the receiving end of many English raids, the Earl knew what the response of the locals would be.

As we headed west towards the high piece of ground which lay just eight miles away from the Scottish lord's stronghold, he explained his plan. "In itself Traprain is worthless but it has farms and the lords who live nearby would see it returned, once more, to its past prominence. Haddington lies close by and is a well-defended manor for it guards the eastern approach to Edinburgh. The village of Papple lies to the south-east and Morham to the east. With luck all the villagers from the three villages which lie close to Traprain Law will head for the mound, it will save us gathering animals. We will lay waste to the land around Traprain and that will draw Douglas' cousin, Jamie, to attack us. With Percy coming from the south towards Dalkeith we will spread

fear throughout the borders and fear means we can raid." He
smiled. "When we were in Wales, I wondered that King Henry
had made his son prince of such a poor place. I had thought these
borders poor until then."

I nodded, "And that is why his grandsire, Longshanks, built
those castles. Had not the Tudur brothers used deception then the
rebellion would have been confined to the mountains and the
Welsh can have those but you are wrong, my lord, about the
paucity of riches in Wales. The land in the south, towards
Pembroke, is rich! The locals call it England in Wales. If I was
King Henry then the Tywi Valley would be where I would fear a
Welsh rebellion."

We were nearing the hill fort and our banners and horses had
identified us. The Earl had expected us to be seen, indeed, he had
counted upon it and riders would be heading towards Haddington
to summon help. Lord Dunbarre had anticipated this. My men and
I were sent ahead, once we neared the town, for we were to take
the hill fort while he and the rest of his men took the manor.
Attacking the hill fort was not as daunting as it sounded for the
walls had been torn down by the English in previous attacks. The
ditches remained but we could dismount before them. As we
galloped across open fields in a race to reach the top of the hill
before the villagers, I shouted my instructions to my squires and
captains who galloped alongside me. We had discussed them in
the castle but now that I could see the hill, I modified them.

"Harry, you watch the horses, Captain Edgar, have our men
arrayed on the eastern side of the mound. If Lord Douglas sends
men then that will be the side they use to attack. Captain Alan,
once you have secured the animals then you will be ready to loose
above the heads of Captain Edgar and his men!"

The four of them chorused, "Aye, lord!"

I did not have many men but we were fast and we were the
best in this conroi. I was confident that we could hold the hill
until the Earl of March reached us. I saw people streaming up the
hill. They had done so since time immemorial. They were
hampered by the fact that they were driving animals and pulling
carts. I decided to ride further east before climbing the slope for I
believed we could reach the top before the people and their
beasts. I opened up Hart's legs and we began to eat up the ground.

I knew that I would be extending my line of men but that would help to panic the Scots. Panicking men made mistakes!

I saw a track which wound up the eastern side. Already there were people from the village of Papple heading for it. They would not reach it before we did. Once I reached the first of the ditches I dismounted. Harry reached me as my foot touched the ground and I handed him my reins. Thomas followed me and Harry held our three horses. Two other men would watch the horses of the men at arms and archers. Thomas took a wooden stake from Harry's saddle and using a hammer he drove the stake into the ground. Even as I hurried to the top Harry was tethering the animals and then he drew his sword to protect them.

The ditch was shallow. Over the years it had eroded and was not much of an obstacle. My helmet still hung on my saddle. I would not need it and I ran easily. However, by the time I had negotiated the other ditches and reached the top I was out of breath. Thomas, close behind me, was not.

The two of us were alone at the top for Edgar was heading for the ditches which faced east while Alan was scurrying towards the men driving animals towards us. I looked east and saw Haddington; it lay less than four miles away and I could see activity showing that they had been alerted. There was a tower there and I saw a wall. The Earl of March had planned well. I turned as I heard a noise behind me. There were three men and they had weapons.

Drawing my sword, I said, "I am Sir William Strongstaff and I have killed many knights. If you wish to die then approach my son and I. We will happily oblige you. If not then drop your weapons and return to your homes." The three men had two spears and an old sword between them. They saw two mailed men before them and they realised the futility of fighting. When there was a wail from below them, as my archers reached the bulk of the refugees, they did as I commanded and ran.

"Thomas, collect the weapons and bring them here."

I turned my gaze to the east and saw that Edgar had his nine men at arms in a thin line. It did not look much but once Alan of the Woods brought his nine archers it would be. We were bait. I saw horsemen forming up outside Haddington. I knew how long it took to arm. They would not leave for a short while. My archers drove the animals to the top of the mound. There were few of them and they would not move. They had grazing.

Alan shouted to his archers, "Form up behind Captain Edgar." He turned to me, "Most of the villagers stopped when they saw us and left their animals. They have fled back down to the village."

I nodded, "We have time yet. Have four of your archers go to the horses and bring them up. The ditches were not the obstacle I thought they would be."

Thomas and I watched the horsemen from Haddington as they moved slowly west. Thomas said, "Can we hold them? There look to be almost a hundred of them."

"More like a hundred and ten." I had seen four banners but only twenty or so mounted men. The rest were on foot. The men on foot were running to keep up with the horses but they would take at least half an hour to reach us. "Sir George will bring the men from the south-west to attack their flank. We just have to hold them. We can do that!"

I saw that Sir George and his men had finished with the village. He had brought men on foot who would occupy it and clear all of value. The sheep and cattle were with us but the villagers would have left fowl, sacks of grain, beans, pots and all sorts of other goods which the Earl could distribute amongst his people. It would keep them loyal!

"Thomas, unfurl the banner and plant it on the top of the hill. That should annoy the Scots and when they see so few of us it will encourage them to come to teach us a lesson!"

I heard the horses as they were brought up. The men who had been watching them could now be put to better use. I would have two squires to watch my back too. Both Thomas and Harry had long spears. We had not brought lances. I was still an old-fashioned knight and I would use my sword. I missed having a shield but I accepted that it was unnecessary. When arrows flew, however, I still raised my left hand. It had been ingrained into me by Peter the Priest and Red Ralph. Such lessons were hard to forget.

The Scots were approaching the bottom of the hill. They were strung out over, perhaps, half a mile. When the four knights dismounted their squires held their horses. The sergeants dismounted and I saw a leader, I guessed it was the cousin of

Lord Douglas, begin to form them up. They might be keen to get at us but the Scots would need their archers and crossbows to enable them to close with us. The mob on foot would merely add to their numbers. It was the thirty men who formed up who would make the attack. The twenty-odd archers and crossbows were chivvied into line and then they began to ascend. One of the squires carried a standard. The blue and white banner with the rampant lions and hearts was the sign of the Douglas clan. As they ascended, I had time to assess their fighting potential. The four knights all carried war hammers. The Scots like the weapon. The men at arms carried pikes and spears. I heard Captain Alan tell his archers, "War arrows and we take out the archers and crossbows. They are releasing uphill and we will have the range. Listen for my command and be ready to switch to heavy war bodkins. These knights wear plate. We can recover any heads after the skirmish."

I smiled for my men were totally confident that despite the odds we would win. I would not need to give the command for Alan knew what he was doing. He would release when the men with crossbows knelt. You did not use a crossbow standing up; it was a waste of a bolt. It was one of the many weakness of using a crossbow in the field. They were intended for use behind walls where they were a more useful weapon. The ill-armed men of Haddington had now reached the foot of the hill and were ascending. The Scots stopped when they were one hundred and eighty paces from us. Their bows were not the longbows my men used. They were a shorter warbow more akin to a hunting bow. We were close enough for me to see the heads on the bows. They were war arrows. As the men knelt Alan shouted, "Draw!" then "Loose!" He would not give a second command. Each archer would nock, draw and release in his own time. They were all masters of their craft. Six crossbowmen and an archer fell with the first shower of flights. I heard arrows and bolts clang off the mail and plate of my men at arms. Each of them had a breastplate. Our wars and battles had enabled us to take them from captured and dead knights. A second flight finished off the crossbows for the three survivors ran.

The Douglas knight who led the Scots realised that he had to close with us as quickly as possible. The squire with the standard took a horn and gave three blasts and they ran up the hill.

It was time for the three of us to join our men. "Come, let us join our men at arms. Remember to stay behind me and protect our backs. Use your spears over our shoulders." We made our way down. "Coming through!"

My archers parted and Edgar and Natty Longjack parted to let me in. Edgar spat, "They would have been better giving those crossbowmen a spear. They would have been of more use." The Scottish archers were still loosing and they showed that they had skill for one sent an arrow into the left arm of Ulf the Swede. The huge man grunted. The Scots would pay for the wound. It would not impair him for his left arm merely supported the pike he was holding.

The Douglas knight came for me. I had heard of a Douglas called, James, and Sir George had called this one, Jamie. He was a younger member of the family whose strongholds were in Annandale and the west. Perhaps he came here to make a name for himself for it explained his reckless charge up the hill. Running uphill in plate sapped energy not only from legs but, strangely, from arms too. He came directly for me as I was the one with the lord's coat of arms and I had squires. The other knights had boars' snout basinets and they flanked their lord. Edgar and Natty, along with my other sergeants, would deal with them. Some of the men who followed the four lords were patently unfit or, perhaps a little nervous for Alan and his archers had switched to bodkins and four sergeants lay writhing on the ground with arrows protruding from their mail hauberks. I ignored everything else as the war hammer swept from behind Douglas to strike me in the chest. If it had connected then I would have had a mortal wound. However, it was easy enough to take a step back up the hill. The beak of the hammer embedded itself in the ground. I stepped forward and brought my sword over to smash into his right shoulder. He wore plate, a mail hauberk and a jupon but my sword was like an iron bar and the blow was delivered from above. I thought I heard a crack and then there was a feral scream. I had broken a bone. I swung my left leg sideways and it connected behind his right knee. He dropped to the ground and my sword was at his throat in a flash.

"Yield, Douglas, for you cannot raise your weapon."

I saw him glance to the side as Edgar hacked into the helmet of the knight next to him. The knight fell backwards and Lord Jamie Douglas nodded, "I yield!"

His squire still held the standard aloft, "Louder!"

"I yield!"

The standard came down and the Scots stopped fighting. It was too late for ten of the men coming up the hill who were caught by the men of Dunbarre as the Earl of March charged into their flank.

I turned to see if any other than Ulf had been hurt, they had not. Already my sergeant's comrades were tending to his wound. Alan of the Woods and his men were scouring the field for arrows and flights. I slipped my coif from around my head. The knight who had surrendered was helped to his feet by his squire. He scowled at me. "My uncle, the Lord Douglas, will have your head for this."

I smiled, "He may try but only after he pays the ransom and, as you are a close relative, it should be substantial. I fear that your days of fighting well are long gone. Captain Edgar, see to this knight until the Earl's healers arrive." My men knew how to stop bleeding and clean a wound but not mend a broken bone. The knight would not die. My men knew that they would share in the ransom. "Thomas and Harry, fetch those horses before the Earl's men think to get them."

The men of Dunbarre were chasing the survivors of the Scottish attack back to Haddington. We had taken the risk and we would reap the reward.

Chapter 8

We were so close to the Earl's castle that we headed back as soon as we saw him return from his pursuit of the enemy at Haddington. He and his men led ten horses. They had captured mail, plate and weapons but the only knights for ransom had been taken by my men. We were already approaching Dunbarre when he caught up with us.

"You did well, Strongstaff. James Douglas has won tournaments in Burgundy."

I shrugged, "I have never yet fought in a tournament."

"You should, you would do well."

I nodded but I would not take part for it meant travelling around France, Germany and Burgundy. My family and my men were more important than the money I would make.

We sent Douglas' squire for the ransom the next day. It would take some time for he had to reach the west coast. Already Sir George was planning his next raid. "We attack Musselburgh! There is no castle besides which the port is filled with the ships which are waiting to get into Leith. We will be close to Edinburgh but I hope that Percy draws that garrison towards him. When that is done, we will mop up the smaller manors and your work will be done."

I was seated with Sir George and I spoke to him quietly, "My lord, what is your purpose in all of this?" He gave me a strange look as though I was speaking a foreign language and so I elaborated. "You are a Scottish lord from a noble family yet you fight against your own country."

"I do not fight against my King. I am a loyal Scotsman but my honour and that of my family has been impugned. I fight Douglas. When he stopped my daughter marrying the heir to the throne so that his son could do so, I knew I had to do something to stop this monster taking over my country. He has ambitions to be King or for his sons, at least, to rule. This is a drastic move I grant you but in the long run, Douglas will be defeated and Scotland will be stronger. I am old, Strongstaff. I do not do this for me but for my children! I wish them to have a Scotland which is ruled by their kings and not by a self-serving noble who cares not for his own land."

I nodded for I understood him. I had felt the same about de Vere when he had wormed his way into King Richard's life. I also began to wonder at Percy's motives. Could he be doing the same thing? We did not ride for a few days. The horses needed recovery time and some of Sir George's men had hurts. During the time that elapsed, we heard that Henry Percy had also had success further south. The Scots in Edinburgh had withdrawn behind their walls and were watching for our next move. I now saw the cleverness of Sir George's strategy. I had wondered at the two-pronged assault but now it made sense to me. Perhaps the squire who was heading for Annandale would bring back Lord Douglas and his army. That would be the only way to stop us. We did not have vast numbers of men but the ones we had were professionals. Our archers and men at arms were superior to anything the Scots had. Their knights were good but no better than us. They could stop the two raids but only by bringing greater numbers than we had and this was coming up to harvest time and their men were working in the fields.

Musselburgh was north of Haddington and east of Edinburgh. They must have expected some sort of attack but what they did not know was the direction nor the timing. The Earl of March was a wily old campaigner. He had been the cause of the defeat of the English at Otterburn fourteen years earlier. We left Dunbarre as the sun was setting and headed for the small port. It was really a large fishing town but it had been made a burgh before Edinburgh and was prosperous. As it was just five miles from the centre of Edinburgh it would frighten the burghers of that town.

We reached the outskirts of Musselburgh while it was still dark. Sir George had sent men to silence the dogs and to secure the main roads into the town. There were three roads into the town. An east-west road ran through it and crossed the River Esk. A third road, the one we used, came from the south and joined it

99

close to the bridge. The plan was a simple one: one-third of our men would approach the town from the east while the rest would ride up the road which joined the east-west road. I would lead my men to take the bridge and to secure the road from Edinburgh. Essentially, we would be doing what we had done at Traprain Law. Earl George would take the town and, after emptying the ships, burn them. As we followed the Scottish scouts, Thomas spoke, "We seem to be given the harder task, father. If we take the bridge then any reinforcements from Edinburgh will attack us."

"You are wrong son for ours is the easier task. The Earl and his men will know not who is a warrior and who is a civilian. I would not do what he does. I have never minded fighting and killing a soldier for I am one and it is what we are paid to do. But killing honest men who are just defending their land has never sat well with me. The men who try to shift us will be knights and men at arms."

Behind me, Captain Edgar said, "Besides, Master Thomas, there is more profit from knights than burghers and your father harvests knights like farmers scythe barley and oats!" I heard my men at arms chuckle.

This time we knew that the alarm would be given. The two recent attacks from ourselves and Percy meant that the Scots were alerted and kept guards, even at night. We were less than half a mile from the bridge when there was a cry in the night. I spurred Hart as I shouted, "Strongstaff! With me!"

Sir George would know what I was doing and the men before us parted as we galloped down the road. I was holding a spear, rather than a lance. I rode with Edgar next to me and Stephen of Stockton and Mark the Minstrel rode behind us. As it was not yet dawn, the archers and my two squires brought up the rear. Ahead of me, I heard the cries of alarm and I saw torches at the bridge. This time I was wearing my helmet. I couched my lance and lowered my head but I still missed my shield for I liked the extra protection it afforded. There were mailed men waiting on the bridge. The light from the torches flickered off their helmets and spear but I also saw men kneeling down. They were crossbowmen and a crossbow could hurt the horses of my men at arms. My horse had a cloth caparison and a metal plate between her eyes but a bolt could easily penetrate the cloth. I dug in my spurs. Our best tactic was to terrify the men on the bridge with the speed of our horses and the thundering of their hooves. I began to edge ahead of Edgar and I knew he would not be happy. Two bolts flew towards me. I saw neither of them until the last moment but one struck my helmet a glancing blow and the other smacked into my plate armour. A handspan closer and the one aimed at my head would have torn into my cheek or eye.

And then I rammed my spear into the chest of the crossbowman who was busy trying to reload his cumbersome weapon. He would have died quickly for he had no armour at all and the force of my strike aided by my horse threw him over the parapet and into the river. The second man suffered a similar fate. There were spearmen with shields but a spear could not harm my plate armour and my spear haft struck one spearman a glancing blow on the side of the head rendering him unconscious. He fell beneath the hooves of Mark the Minstrel's horse. The survivors ran down the bridge which had originally been built by the Romans. The bridge was only fifty paces long but eight men fell in that time. Those without armour threw themselves in the river and just three survivors escaped.

We reined in and I shouted, "Captain Alan!"

He rode up, "Aye lord?"

"Cut down stakes and small trees. We hold them here."

I dismounted and handed my reins to Harry, "Take Hart back across the river and tether her with the other horses. I think I saw some grazing, tie her close to it. Then return here. I shall need you and your brother."

One man in three took the horses back and I took my helmet off for the sun was rising behind us and the cool air would help me think as I assessed our position. The river ran north and I could see that it was lined with ships. That was Sir George's worry. There were half a dozen houses close to us. "Edgar, clear the houses and fire them. We do not need places behind which the enemy can shelter."

I rammed my spear into the soft soil of the river bank and looked closely at my helmet. I examined the dent from the bolt and saw that the helmet could be repaired. I ran my fingers over the breastplate and felt the indentation from that bolt. Hitting me straight on it had almost broken the plate. Martin would have more work to repair the damage. I heard the sounds of battle behind us but, for us, all was peaceful. The silence ahead was broken when Edgar shifted those who lived in the houses. I heard raised voices and then Captain Edgar's stentorian tone silenced all of the Scots, "You have your lives. Now move or I will take those too!"

The sun was rising when the flames began to lick the rooves of the houses. My men had fires lit across the river and the fowl we had taken from the houses, as well as the food we had liberated, were being prepared. We lit the fires on the Musselburgh side of the bridge on the same side as our horses. Men would come from Edinburgh but not yet!

It was a good hour after we had captured the bridge and we had begun to eat the food we had cooked when one of the archers we had sent down the road reported the column of men marching from Edinburgh. "They will be here within the hour, my lord."

I nodded, "Then fetch back the other scouts and have them eat. We have time."

The fowl we had slaughtered were still cooking but we had bread, cheese, pickled fish and some ham we had taken from the houses. My men liked ham cooked on a fire and we had that with the eggs we had taken while the ducks and chicken pieces cooked. The houses had been made of wood and they had burned quickly. Even as we were eating the last flames had died leaving a smouldering pile of black marking their place. My sons brought food for Edgar and me and as we ate we heard the sound of fighting in the town and now we could smell the ships as they burned. That meant the Earl had emptied them and was now preparing to leave.

Harry asked, "If the Earl has the cargoes from the ships, father, then why do we stay here?"

Thomas answered his brother. He had grown of late; perhaps it was the thought of his impending knighthood or his marriage, "The Earl does not wish to be caught on the road. We slow them down." He looked at me. "We will burn the bridge?"

"It has stone foundations but there is wood upon it which will burn. It will slow them up but there will be fords upstream which they will use. This raid is a nuisance raid; there will be profit but

102

Sir George Dunbarre wishes to punish those who support his rival, Archibald Douglas. When we have eaten, I will have men place kindling along the bridge. We will need to buy the Earl some time."

The small piles of kindling were ready by the time the men from Edinburgh marched down the road. I saw no mounted men and knew that the knights and men at arms would be fording the river; they would find it easier than men on foot. We would not have as much time as I had hoped for we risked being flanked. Jamie, one of Sir George's pages galloped along the bridge, "My lord, the Earl's compliments. He has cleared the town. He needs an hour to be down the road. Can you give him an hour?"

I nodded, "Aye, but warn him that mounted men are fording the river and they may be upon him sooner than he might like."

"Aye lord." He looked enviously at Thomas and Henry, "May you wet your blades today!"

Harry grinned, "We can only hope we get the chance and do not merely hold the reins of horses." Such was the optimism of youth.

Captain Edgar commanded, "Stand to!" The archers returned to the bridge and formed two lines behind my men at arms. We blocked the end of the bridge. Thirty paces before us were the embedded stakes my archers had put on the side of the road. They had also dug up some of the cobbles from the road. It would make an approach by the enemy difficult for them; anything which would slow them down would help us.

The mob which marched down the road were led by men with mail and shields. I could not tell but I guessed that there were lords who led them. They halted when they were two hundred paces from the bridge. The lord who led them waved his sword to his left and right. The warriors spread out in long lines on either side and that allowed me to estimate their numbers. There looked to be more than two hundred of them. The middle thirty were all mailed and bore shields. The poorly armed and protected ones were well to the flanks. Whoever led them knew their business as they were protecting, as best they could, those who had no shields. He raised his sword and with shields before them, a horn was sounded and they marched.

"Alan, do not waste your bodkin arrows yet. Wait until the ones without shields are close enough and thin their ranks."

"Aye lord."

I had too few archers and their arrows were valuable. If we sent them at mailed men protected by shields then they would merely slow them and not hurt them. The Scots moved cautiously. English raiders used mounted archers and they knew the effect of arrows. Perhaps this was why they had taken as long to come as they had; they were preparing!

Alan said, "Loose!"

As the handful of arrows were sent to two sides of the mailed men, they seemed inconsequential but each one found a mark. Not all who were hit died but it slowed the ones at the side as it demoralized them and made them look for protection. By the time four more flights had been sent the Scottish formation resembled an old-fashioned wedge as the men on the flanks slowed while the mailed men with shields forged on. They were now approaching the stakes and I said, "Now, Alan!"

When they tried to negotiate the stakes and cross the damaged road, they would be vulnerable. They would not have the cohesion of interlocked shields and they would be watching their feet. This time there was no command but I saw bodkin arrows fly towards the Scots. These were tough men. I saw an arrow drive into the left shoulder of a mailed Scot who continued moving as though nothing had happened. I saw the blood dripping down his surcoat. He was a sergeant at arms and bore the mark of the Edinburgh garrison. One man, at least, fell. The arrow found a gap and he fell forcing the ones around him to move aside and two more fell as shields were moved. And then they were just ten paces from us and Alan would have to switch to the targets at the side. I had a spear in my hand and I held it above my head to strike down above the shields. The Scots had had the advantage of shields and now they were an encumbrance for their right arms had carried their spears, war hammers and pikes one-handed. As the leading lord rammed his spear at my middle, I drove my own spear down over his shield. His spear struck my breastplate while mine found the mail around his neck. He wore no gorget and when I withdrew it and his body fell, I saw the blood on the end.

Thomas and Harry had their spears held lower and they poked, probed and jabbed at the advancing Scots. The men who came at us had hauberks beneath their surcoats but their knees and legs were unprotected. Harry and Thomas found flesh. It was when the bulk of their men negotiated the stakes that the pressure began to tell as the ones at the fore had comrades pushing into their backs. Even when a man was wounded his body was still pushed like a human shield. My spearhead was hacked in two. I threw the stump at the man who eagerly came towards me. He raised his shield to block the improvised weapon and it gave me time to draw my sword and dagger. This reminded me of the day Sir John Chandos had died at the bridge in Spain. That day I had been of an age with Thomas and it seemed a lifetime ago.

"Alan, start the fires! Thomas, Harry, get to the horses."

I did not need to shout the order to step back for my men at arms knew from my commands what I intended. As we stepped back on to the bridge, so the parapets began to protect our flanks. The kindling and piles of firewood were placed in the embrasures which were on the bridge. The Scots had the weight of numbers but that did not help them that much for they found it hard to wield their weapons one-handed in the confines of the bridge.

I heard a shout, "Fires are lit, lord."

I continued to work my dagger and sword; I blocked blows with my sword and used my dagger to winkle between plate and mail. My men at arms had two-handed weapons and they brought them over their heads to strike at the Scots. The confined space meant that the ineffective Scottish blows and the armour of my men kept them safe. Then arrows flew over our heads to fall, vertically, on the men pushing their mailed men at us. Suddenly the press was not as great as it had been for men fell and I was able to swing my sword diagonally. I hit a Scottish lord on the side of the neck; his blood spurted and sprayed those close to him. At the same time, I stabbed with my dagger and tore through the cheek of another. We had space and I said, "Back!"

I could hear the fires crackling as the kindling burned and ignited the firewood; soon the wooden timbers on the bridge would catch. I could see that we were halfway across the bridge. The fires would suddenly erupt and we needed to be on the other bank when that happened.

Alan's voice sounded, "Now, lord, we have arrows ready!"
I knew, without looking, that my archers had mounted their
horses. Loosing from the back of a horse was rarely as effective
as from the ground but at a range of less than forty paces, it would
cause casualties. I swung my sword in an arc and the Scots
brought up their shields. I turned and ran. I saw that Mark the
Minstrel was bloody and that he had been wounded. The flames
had begun to send smoke across the bridge and that was our
friend. The parapets were made of wood and as they caught so the
smoke increased. Henry and Thomas each held the reins of three
horses. I sheathed my weapons and pulled myself into the saddle
of Hart. Edgar helped Mark into his saddle. Alan and his archers
sent another flight of arrows into the smoke of the bridge and then
I shouted, "We have done enough. Ride!"

Our wounded man was protected by two of his comrades for
he was placed in the middle of them. Alan had half of his archers
at the fore and the other half at the rear. As we rode through the
town it was like riding through the fog for the smoke from the
burning buildings and ships filled the air. I rode behind the
archers and I was flanked by Thomas and Harry. Edgar would
stay at the rear.

"We have won?"

Thomas shook his head, "Not yet, little brother. When we are
back in Dunbarre then we can think of such things. We have
many miles to go."

"But the Scots are on foot."

I turned and pointed to the south, "We saw no horsemen and
they may have crossed fords. They might be ahead of us or
approaching our line of retreat. Your brother is right. You count
your treasure when you have taken your mail from your body and
you enjoy a beaker of ale!"

We had twenty-five miles to ride. The Earl would avoid
Haddington and that meant taking the coastal road. It also took us
further from any who had forded the Esk south of the bridge. We
halted at Longniddry to tend to Mark's wounds and to rest the
horses. A spear had managed to stab Mark in the left shoulder. He
would not fight again in this campaign and I knew, as I looked at
the wound, that it was the kind which would ache in the winter or

when there was damp weather. Mark the Minstrel would have a permanent reminder of the battle of Musselburgh Bridge.

We had seen little sign of the Earl's progress save the horse dung before Longniddry. When, some miles later, we found some still warm, we knew that we were catching him. We were eight miles from Dunbarre approaching Aethelstaneford when we saw the Scots attacking the rear of the Earl's column. He had been caught. The skirmish was less than half a mile away. I drew my sword and shouted, "Harry, watch Mark the Minstrel! Charge!" I spurred Hart as we tried to catch the archers. Once again Alan and his men would get as close as they could to make each arrow count as they would be loosing from the backs of their horses.

Enemy numbers were hard to estimate as they milled around with the Earl's rearguard. When we were closer, we would see the Earl's livery; a rampant red lion surrounded by eight roses but, until then all would be guesswork. The skirmish disappeared when Alan and his archers stopped to loose arrows. We split into two and rode around them. The arrows had made the riders turn and, seeing us, they tried to urge their horses towards us. Their horses were weary, as were ours, and the charge was not at full speed. The Scottish spears had shattered and so their riders used swords and hand weapons. I saw one knight wielding a mace and I rode at him.

There was an art to fighting on the back of a horse. A good rider used his horse as a weapon. Hart was neither a stallion nor a war horse but she was clever and she was quick. My sword was longer than the mace and I feinted to ride at his right side. At the last moment, I used my knees and left hand to ride at the knight's left. Standing in my stirrups I brought my sword down hard and hit him across his shoulders. Shoulders were protected only by mail and not plate and when my sword came away bloody, I knew that I had hurt him and he wheeled away to his right. Before I could either make him yield or finish him off a spear was rammed into my side. One of the squires had not broken his lance. Perhaps he was the squire of the knight I had hurt, I know not. He, too, had found mail and not plate. I felt the spearhead slide into flesh. Before he could twist it and penetrate to something vital Thomas' spear was rammed up under his chin to drive into his skull. The squire fell dead.

"Thank you, my son!"

"You are hurt!"

"It is nothing!"

I turned and saw that our sudden appearance and attack had broken the enemy who were now streaming back to Haddington and Edinburgh. I dismounted while our men collected the loose horses and took mail, weapons and coins from the Scottish dead. Thomas placed some linen beneath my mail to staunch the bleeding. It was not gushing but I would need either stitches or the wound cauterizing. I smiled at Thomas as we remounted, "Now you are ready to be a knight if you choose."

He nodded, "Six months ago I would have said I was not ready. I had no reason to be knighted and thought I did not have the skill. Six months ago, I would have hesitated before driving my spear into the skull of a squire little older than me to end his life. I have changed."

"Then you are ready. We will make the preparations when we return from this." I pointed to the squire's horse, hauberk, helmet and sword. "And now you accrue your own wealth. It is good." We remounted and followed the others into the castle.

The Earl was delighted with the raid for it had cost him fewer men than he had expected and brought him greater rewards. He was generous and we all profited. His doctor sewed my wound and used small stitches. Mark's wound required fire and he almost did not make it back to the castle for he had lost a great deal of blood. He would take no more part in the raids but he was philosophical about it. "I will have the chance to compose more songs now for the air around this castle is both sweet and pleasant with the wind from the east. It will make the words flow for I have many songs in my head."

We spent another three weeks raiding but none of them was on the scale of Musselburgh. We ravaged the country which lay within twenty miles of Haddington taking animals and burning halls and the Earl was happy. The night before we left, he brought me our share of the profits as the ransoms from Douglas had arrived. My wife would be pleased for we had more than two hundred pounds not to mention all the booty we had taken. Even Harry had profited.

"You are a good man to fight alongside, Sir William. I would be happy for you to join me again."

"And it has been profitable. We shall see."

"Think about it over winter. I resume my raids when the new grass is here and we will seek land which has yet to be plundered."

We rode home with a wagon we had taken. It meant our journey was slower but we did not have to burden our horses. The weather was changing by the time we reached Middleham. Autumn was coming and it came sooner the further north you lived. Thomas and I had spoken of his dubbing. I would need to tell the King and so we decided to use the Winter Solstice. That meant the earliest he could wed would be the spring. We decided on Lady Day, the twenty-fifth of March. It was significant for many reasons, not least the fact that it was the first day of the new year and also the day of the Virgin Mary. Thomas liked the symbolism of the day.

As we approached Middleham I said, "Of course, your bride may have some say in the matter."

He nodded, "So long as we are wed then I am content."

Mary and her mother were delighted with the news and more than happy to fit in with the plans Thomas and I had made. Red Ralph's widow said, "It shows great sensitivity, my lord, for my daughter and I are named Mary and the day you have chosen commemorates the Annunciation of the Blessed Virgin Mary. I hope my home does it justice."

"If you wish you could use my hall although I would understand if you wished it to be here in the hall built by Red Ralph."

"That is a kind offer and I will take you up on it, lord." She held out her hands, "My daughter will be a lady. These are not the hands of a lady nor is this the hall of one. The sooner she sees the change the better. I have good people who can watch my land for me."

I nodded, "Then I will send you an escort to bring you south for you and your family are now mine and I will protect them as I would my own."

We had a tearful parting for Mary could now almost see her wedding and could not bear to be parted from my son. My wife was delighted with all the news I brought. She began to plan a new wing which would be built to accommodate our guests and the money I had planned on using for more men was now diverted to building work. I did not mind. I informed the King of the ceremony of knighthood and the wedding but I had a feeling that he would not attend but, if he did, then I would fear the worst. I knew that I was a tool which the King used. I had been used as such by King Richard but the difference was that I believed that King Richard had been fond of me. I doubted that Henry Bolingbroke was fond of anyone save himself.

Chapter 9

My men would have been happy to build the new wing but my wife wished it all to be done properly. "What if the King should come? I would not have a hall built by sergeants. I will hire a mason and I will hire men. It will be money well spent and besides, husband, it has been a good harvest. There may have been wars in Wales and Scotland but around these parts there was peace and the unrest on the borders merely means we are paid more for our crops and animals. You are a good husband." She pointed to my side, "But you need to take more care on the battlefield for you are no longer a young man."

She was right. Red Ralph and the others had given up the sword when they were about my age. The ones who had not had all died in wars fighting men who were younger and fitter than they were. Despite the fact that my wife had taken the bulk of the money from the chevauchée, I still had enough to hire two more men at arms and two more archers. I went with Alan and Edgar as well as Thomas to visit with Old Captain Tom. He was ancient now but his mind was still sharp and he had a good tavern. I did not know when we visited with him, on a wet and windy October afternoon, that it would be the last time I would speak with him. Had I known that I might have spent less time speaking of me and my needs and more about him. It is ever thus. We always think that we have all the time in the world and that there will be a tomorrow. It is not true. However, that was in the future when the pestilence struck his village.

He was delighted with the news about Thomas and he was more than happy to supply us with more men. My son showed that he was ready for knighthood. He asked Captain Tom to find him an archer and a man at arms. He had coin and he had two spare horses. My son was changing before my eyes.

Captain Tom was a veritable mine of information about our land for travellers used his inn. "There is now great opposition to Glendower. If the King chose to finance a war to defeat him then I believe that Parliament would back his request."

I shook my head, "He wants money but he sees Wales as his son's problem. If he asked for the money then he would be in Parliament's debt."

"I never liked him as a young man and he has not improved as a King."

"Speak softly, friend, he is vindictive."

Old Tom laughed, "I am past worrying about kings! I have lived longer than any man I know and besides, here I am amongst friends." He leaned in, "However, I have to say that I have heard that Hotspur seeks to broker a peace or a deal of some sort with Glendower. He would make concessions!"

I was confused, "But why?"

"If land is conceded to Wales then it weakens Prince Henry and the King. They lose income. Hotspur raids the Scots and that is like his personal bank. He needs no Jews for coins for he has the Scots. He grows richer and if Glendower wins then the King grows poorer. Hotspur has ambitions." Captain Tom had lived in the murky world of politics longer than I had; I respected his opinion.

I had much to think on as we headed north with my new men at arms, Rafe Red Beard and Kit Warhammer and my two archers Egbert Longbow and Will Straight Shaft. My son Thomas was followed by his two men, Harold of Derby and Will of Corby. Our new men were not riding with Thomas and I but with our two captains. They would discover all there was to know about my manors and my particular ways of leading. I spoke, instead, with my son. "So, you have had an early lesson in being a lord."

He laughed, "I already knew about the expense. When Richard was knighted, he could not believe his new costs. I have told Harry already that he should begin to make a war chest. I hope that the Earl of Dunbarre asks for us again. It was lucrative."

It was my turn to laugh, "And there is a word I did not expect you to use. But remember we are the King's men. It may be he wishes to use us against the Welsh."

"Perhaps the rebellion is over."

Shaking my head, I said, "I can guarantee it is not. Winter approaches and only a fool fights in winter. Glendower was not hurt in our raids and he has the support of the Welsh."

"Yet you fought in winter in the Baltic."

"They have adapted there to fight in winter. They have such thick snow that it hardens to become almost as good a surface as a Roman Road. Here we endure rain and mud!"

When we reached my home, I inspected the work on the new wing. As I had expected, with my wife supervising, it was on time and under budget. I had to admit that it was a good investment. It made the hall stronger and showed me how we could make it even bigger if we wished. After the children had retired, I spoke with my wife and told her the news I had heard. "Then we had better invest our extra money wisely, husband. When there is rebellion you can pick up land cheap on the borders. Cheshire would be a good place to look. Next time you are on campaign keep your eyes open for properties which have lost their owners. The King and his son think highly of you. We should use that!"

"Is that not a little cold, my love?"

My wife was a practical woman and a realist, "Probably, but that is the way of the world. We do charitable work and there are neither poor nor beggars in any of our manors. You support Peter the Priest and the alms-house in York. God sees our good deeds and when St Michael judges us I will be content. You wish to continue to do this and so we need to make money. If we did not buy the land then some other, less worthy, would. Keep your eyes open. We have another daughter and a son to find a manor. We owe it to them."

I had been lucky to marry my wife. She complimented me so well and we worked well together. Other men were not as lucky.

The days became much shorter as December approached and the work on the new wing became more frenetic. Even as the work was progressing, I saw my wife looking to the other side of the hall where we had the space to build a second wing. I knew her well enough to know that she saw a grander house at Weedon. The poor reception we had received at Dauentre meant we would never live there and her aim was to make Weedon an even more impressive hall. The tiny manor I had been given had grown immeasurably since we had first come. That had been inevitable as we had parcelled land for my men at arms and archers. There were, however, other incomers. We would never be large enough to justify a market but we had men living in the village who made things which we needed.

As well as a new wing I had had an extension built to the stables. This was not mason's work. My men and I toiled at this. The new horses we had bought on our visit to Middleham and our success on the field meant we now had twenty good horses which needed to be housed. The sumpters and lesser palfreys spent all but the worst of days outside. If we had winter snow which was particularly cold then we brought them into the barn. Hitherto we had not needed it. With such a stable we needed a horse master and James was a good horse master. He had come to us some time ago. He had formerly been a man at arms who served in Poitou. He had been badly wounded and his left leg became lame. He had been lucky in that his company had not let him leave penniless and he had enough money to make it back to England with his wife and young son. They had worked in inns where he had been ostler and his wife had tended customers but, as their son grew, they knew it was not the life for him and so they left London and I had met him in Northampton at the market where he had been with the other men seeking a master.

I knew as soon as I met James that I had to find a place for him. His faded tunic had told me all that I needed to know. He had served in a company and, despite my title, that made us brothers in arms. His son also reminded me of me. He had seen nine summers and was his parent's only child. He accepted my offer immediately. As we had headed home, he told me that he had heard of the urchin from the Blue Company who had been elevated so high. It had given him hope. Now, as the stable extension was complete, I walked through the building with James and his son, John.

Caesar was the head of my herd and he had the largest stall and received the greatest attention. The other horses were placed in their natural order. "Will you be extending the stables any further, my lord?"

"Perhaps, but we have enough land. Why do you ask?"

"I do not mind hard work but, even with John to help me, it is difficult to give all of these horses and the others the attention they deserve. I am not complaining but…"

We had reached Hart's stall and I fed her a windfall apple I had taken from our orchard. James was right. Thomas and Henry helped groom my war horse but horses demanded much attention. If they did not receive it then they could suffer and horses were the way we rode to war. "You are right. We have to visit Northampton soon to buy that which we need for the ceremony of knighthood; bring your son and we will see if there are any old soldiers in need of employment."

My policy was always to take those who had been warriors. That meant that most of the men I employed had some sort of disability but it did not impair their ability to work. In fact, the reverse was true; they all worked harder for they knew they were lucky to be employed at all. James was a case in point. He could not run but his lame leg was no impediment in the stable.

The night before we were due to ride to the market we heard the rain as it thundered down on the roof. My wife shook her head, "I will not come to the market on the morrow, husband, I will give you a list of all that I need."

I saw Thomas and Harry exchange a smile. That meant that we would be able to visit an alehouse. They both liked such places but my wife would not cross the threshold.

My wife saw the look and her eyes narrowed, "And you, Thomas son of Will Strongstaff will need to buy the bolt of cloth for your surcoat so do not think you will spend all the day in the alehouse while your father hires men and makes purchases for your day! Remember, this will be your last winter as a single man. Come Lady Day you will no longer be a bachelor. Then will your life change and you will have responsibilities."

Thomas knew that but I saw, from his face, that he had not quite realised the other changes that would follow.

"Aye, son, you and Mary will have your own quarters here in the hall. You will not need them yet but you will need servants. It is not just a squire that you will require. Tomorrow you will need a clear head and sharp eyes to watch how I engage new men." That hit home. He had known he would have to have a squire but while his squire would wait on him while he was at home, when he was away there would have to be servants for his wife.

We huddled beneath oiled cloaks as the five of us rode to Northampton. There were other travellers heading for the market but most trudged afoot. I used a few coins to stable the horses in the alehouse. The Lamb and the Lion was close to the west gate of the town and was quieter than the ones closer to the market. It helped that I knew the innkeeper who was an old soldier too. Old Will had not been wounded like Captain Tom; he had made enough money from war to buy the inn and he was still hale and hearty. His large belly showed that he had bought the ale house for a love of beer.

"First, Thomas, we buy the bolt of cloth and send it to the alehouse. That is a task which has to be done or you risk the wrath of your mother and, besides, those seeking employment are still making their way here." We had arrived early, having left before dawn. The shorter days meant you used every moment of the thin light of winter. By the time Thomas had paid for the bolt of pale blue cloth the market had filled up and we wandered, with the list from my wife, making the rest of our purchases. Poor John and Harry were laden. When we reached the hiring market, we sent them back to the Lamb and Lion. Their grins told me that they would tarry on their way back. It did not matter for it would take time to choose good men.

After they had left us I turned to Thomas, "Do not forget that you need to see what sort of men and women are available. You will need them come March."

"Women?"

I saw the look of surprise upon his face. "Do you think that Mary will be able to manage without a woman to help her."

"She has no servant now!"

"Now she is not the wife of a knight! The tap of the sword on the shoulder means even greater responsibility. And remember that you will need a squire. I know you have given little thought to that but a squire is even more important than a servant. I was lucky with Sir John. You may have to seek yours!"

The hiring market was off to the side of the main market. There were thirty or so people there. Some had chosen to seek work while others had been forced, by changing circumstances, to seek employment. The women and girls tended to be gathered together. There were just three of them and I would not be hiring any. That was my wife's domain.. House servants also gathered together. They were markedly different from those who did physical toil. They tended to be smaller and thinner. This was a bad time of year for them. Those who laboured outside were used to the harsh conditions of winter. The house servants were not.

We stood and studied them. We could not tell yet what skills they might have. Other men were there hiring too but I was the only lord and I saw eyes looking expectantly at us. There was a hierarchy in their places. There was an awning above them and the bigger and stronger men were close to the wall where it was drier. James said, "There is little choice today, lord. We can always wait."

I shook my head, "When we dub Thomas, we will have guests and they will bring horses. You and John will need help. There will be fewer at the next market and by January almost none. See, already men are being hired." As we watched a merchant took two youths, they looked like brothers.

I put my hands on my hips and raised my voice, "I seek ostlers! Who has experience with horses?" Hands were raised and I nodded to James to speak with them. I saw one man, off alone at the side, who began to raise his right hand and then changed it for his left. He had a split nose which told me that the man had been an outlaw.

John and Harry had rejoined us by the time James had spoken with the potential ostlers. He shook his head, "None of them know a sumpter from an ass! They are all desperate for work and will be foresworn to get a job."

"What was his tale?" I pointed to the former outlaw.

James shook his head, "I did not speak with him for he was an outlaw!"

"Would you judge a man before you heard his tale? Go fetch him, Harry, and we will speak with him."

The man was in his thirties. He had a few flecks of grey in his beard. He was also emaciated but I saw from his frame that he had been a powerful man once. He had fallen on hard times. He kept his right hand hidden as he knuckled his forehead with his left hand, "Yes my lord? Can you offer me work? I am a hard worker that I swear."

"What is your name?" I saw his eyes and they told me that he was considering making a name up. "The truth!"

"Harold of Lincoln."

I held out my hand, "Show me your right hand." He reluctantly held it out and I saw that he had lost the middle three fingers from the knuckle. "You were an archer?" He nodded. I pointed to his nose, "And an outlaw."

He withdrew his hand and began to turn, "I am sorry to have wasted your time, my lord."

I pulled his arm back, "I have not yet done with you and do not presume to tell me when my time is wasted. It is my time so indulge me. Tell me your tale."

He sighed as though he had told this before and it had not helped his cause. "I fought in France, lord, and was caught. The French took my fingers. When I returned to England, I sought employment close to my home town. The lord I served was not a pleasant man. I had some skill with horses and cared for his animals. I like horses for they are not as cruel as men. He beat a horse when he fell from its back. It was his fault for the man was a poor rider, lord. I made the mistake of telling him that he should not have punished the beast for his error; it was a foolish thing to say. I was whipped and thrown from his land with no pay. I went to the forests there and lived with those who eke out a living in the green wood. It was a hard life but I survived. Then, in the spring, some lords came hunting for us. They said that deer had been hunted and that was a crime." He held up his maimed fingers, "How could I hunt with these?" He shook his head and hid his fingers. "They marked me as an outlaw and we were driven from the forest. That was last spring and I have been moving south trying to find work ever since. After this, I will head to London."

"What was the name of this lord?"

"He is a powerful lord, my lord. Sir Richard de Ros is a relative of the Percy family."

I smiled, "I am familiar with the family. So, Harold of Lincoln, could you work under James the Horse Master here at my manor of Weedon?"

He looked shocked. James looked surprised but Thomas smiled for he knew me better than the others. "You would take me on despite my mark?"

"As you spoke, I looked in your eyes, Harold of Lincoln, and I saw no lie. I was a member of the Blue Company and know that some lords are less than honest and many are mean and cruel men. I hope you find that I am not. What say you?"

He dropped to one knee, "That I will gladly serve you, lord."

"Good, then get your belongings and let us retire to the Lamb and Lion for ale and hot food." As we left, I saw the envious looks from the ones who had yet to find a master. Many would end up heading for London where there would be many more opportunities but life would be far crueller. I heard James speaking with Harold. My horse master wished to discover if I had hired a liability or an asset. The rain had stopped but the air still had a damp feel. It felt good to walk into the warm fuggy alehouse.

Old Will beamed a smile as we entered, "Ah, my lord, a successful day?"

"Aye, it was. A jug of your best ale and what hot fare do you have this day?"

"The wife has baked some fine rabbit pies." His face became serious, "Taken legally, my lord." I nodded and smiled. "And some good, freshly baked bread for the gravy."

"That will do. Have you a table?"

"Aye lord, I kept one for you." He lowered his voice and gestured with his head towards an angry looking man who was standing with a thin and emaciated youth of about twelve summers. "That streak of misery wanted it but there are just the two of them. I would have thrown him out but the boy looks like he needs the warmth."

I saw that, while the man was eating, the boy was just standing looking hungrily at the ever-emptying platter. I wondered at their story. The man had a sword and looked to be a sergeant at arms although I saw no mail. I might need men at arms but he looked to be the wrong sort. He would find a master but not one I would wish to associate with. We sat around the table as a serving wench brought over the jug and some beakers. She was of an age with Thomas and Harry and she grinned at them flirtatiously. Thomas just smiled but Harry blushed. He was still coming to terms with his manhood. Will snapped, "Enough of that Marie, let the young lords alone. They come here to eat and not to enjoy your company."

As she went Thomas grinned, "I don't know, I think Harry took a shine to the wench."

"Thomas, enough."

Even though he was present James said, "Harold here seems to know his horses, my lord."

I shook my head, "I am pleased you approve of my choice, James." I lifted my beaker, "Here is to my new company, welcome Harold!"

"Welcome, Harold." As we all chorused the toast, I saw the angry looking man scowl in our direction. It seemed we had disturbed him in some way.

Harold almost finished the beaker in one. He looked at it guiltily, "Sorry, lord, it has been a long time since I enjoyed an ale." Thomas topped him up. "When I was in France, I heard of a sergeant who was knighted. Is that you, lord?" I nodded. "And you were King Richard's bodyguard?" Again, I nodded. He shook his head, "I had put that down to campfire talk. You know the dreams men have of a future beyond the battlefield."

"I was lucky, Harold, and it has made me have a different view of the world. The Black Prince changed my life. When I am able I like to change the lives of others."

We all enjoyed the ale and the food was welcome too. Harold worked his way steadily through the pie and bread. When all was gone, I waved over Marie and asked for another loaf. Harold used it to mop up every particle of the pie from his platter. He had been hungry. I remembered Spain. I had endured such hunger.

I was about to pay the bill when the angry man suddenly backhanded the emaciated youth across the room, "You fool! You spilt my beer!" I noticed that he had an accent.

I stood as the man raised his hand again, "Hold your hand!"

The man faced up to me. He was as tall as I was and he had a long scar which ran from his eye to his mouth. I doubted that he would ever be able to smile. "This is my servant and I do with him as I like." As if to prove the point he punched the boy so hard in the face that he burst his nose and the boy fell to the ground. The man grinned. It was a challenge.

I stepped close to him. "You are not a man. I am Baron William Strongstaff and not without influence in this town. I command you to cease hurting the boy!"

He laughed, "I care not for lordlings. I am Jean of Caen and I do as I wish to my servants. Gilles, get to your feet."

I turned and held out my hand to help the dazed youth to his feet. "Gilles, would you leave this man's service?" I saw the frightened eyes flicker from me to the Norman and back. "If you wish I can take you from him and make you safe."

I sensed rather than saw the right hand as it swept towards my head. I heard shouts of warning but I needed them not. When I was a child, I had learned to duck the blows from my father. I blocked the blow with my left hand and then brought my right hand hard into the ribs of the Norman. I heard bones crack. I pulled it back and hit him again to make certain that I had hurt him. Then I pulled back my left and hit him hard in the stomach. He dropped to his knees, winded.

Thomas had jumped to his feet and stood next to me, "Thomas, guard the boy."

Will the innkeeper shouted, "Shall I send for the watch, my lord?"

I shook my head, "I need no watch to deal with scum like this. Is he staying here?"

Will shook his head, "He has a horse which is in the stable. The boy walked."

The Norman was still trying to get his breath, with broken ribs it was hard. I turned to Gilles, "Answer me, boy. I can offer you safety. Will you take it?"

The boy looked frightened but he said, "My master will not let me go."

Thomas said, "Did you not hear my father? He is never foresworn. If you come with us then you will be as safe as though you were the King's jewels."

The boy nodded. I asked, "Has this man anything that you need?"

"My blanket."

I smiled, "That you will not need."

121

The man rose, "Get here boy! I have not done with you."

"You have! Pay your bill and leave. Quit the land around here or I will have you brought before the assizes."

"He is my property!"

I turned to Gilles, "Did he buy you?"

The boy shook his head, "He killed my father and took me when our farm was raided. He and the others used my mother and she died."

"In Normandy?"

He shook his head, "Poitou, my lord."

"Pay your bill and leave!"

Harold, James, John and Harry had all stood in solidarity with me. I did not need them. The man glared at me. "This is not over and one day you will pay." He threw a handful of coins on the counter.

I said, "James, Harold, go and make sure he does leave."

Thomas said, "I will go with them for I do not trust him."

When they had gone, I said, "Gilles, sit. Landlord, ale and a pie for the boy. He looks as though he needs it."

My men returned. "It is a good job we watched him, lord. I think he might have hurt our horses else."

"Which direction did he take?"

"He went out of the west gate."

Gilles smiled and said, "He is heading north, lord, to Lincoln. He seeks work."

While he ate, he told us his tale. He had been with the sword for hire for two years. Jean of Caen was angry in every way and his company had tired of him. Gilles had been taken as a servant and dogsbody. He had seen thirteen summers but was so thin that his body looked younger.

Thomas asked, "Gilles, what did you do for this Jean of Caen?"

"Cared for his horse, cleaned and sharpened his weapons and cooked and fetched his food."

Thomas gave me a curious look. He leaned back and, sipping his ale, said, "When Ulf the Swede was wounded, he spoke to me of some strange beings who wove together the threads of men's lives. I thought it was a fairy story yet Ulf believed in them. I now see something in the story. This Gilles was sent here for a purpose. If it had not been such inclement weather my mother would have been here and we would not have visited this inn. We were meant to intervene and to save this boy. Gilles, I am to be knighted soon and I have need for a squire. Would you be my squire?"

"But I know not what to do."

"Do that which you did for Jean of Caen except that you will not be beaten and you will enjoy good food and be dressed in finer clothes. What you do not know then I will teach you." He turned to me, "This is good is it not?"

I put my hand on his shoulder for I could not have been prouder, "Aye, my son, it is."

"Well, Gilles?"

The youth's eyes widened and his face beamed, "Aye, my lord. I will!"

Thomas smiled, "Not a lord yet but soon!"

The new ostler was as hard a working man as I had ever seen. His maimed hand did not impair his work and he was so grateful to have employment that he sang as he worked. He endeared himself to all in the household, including my wife! We needed as many hardworking people as we could as we had a ceremony of knighthood and a wedding to plan. The King had not replied and I assumed he would not be attending but, on the off chance that he would, my wife made certain that the guest quarters for Mary and her family were fit for a king!

Chapter 10

My wife liked Gilles the moment she laid eyes upon him and when she heard his tale she burst into tears. "We have raised a good son."

"Aye, that we have."

My wife had Gilles and Harold deloused and cleaned as soon as they arrived. The boy and the old soldier appreciated it. Their old clothes were burned and they were dressed in good quality garments. The two waifs and strays soon began to show the effect of clean clothes, good food and a bed. As my son and I schooled our horses I spoke to him of his new squire, "It was a noble gesture but if you have second thoughts, we can find a place for Gilles. You need not have him as a squire if you do not wish to."

"I know but I think of the stories you tell of the Blue Company. Who knows what Gilles might achieve? He has few skills yet but, father, think what he endured. There is potential there. I have had an easy time as your squire; perhaps this is my quest to do as Red Ralph and the others did with you and turn you into a gentleman."

I knew he was right but he was beginning his life as a knight with many obstacles in his way. What it meant was that, instead of preparing for the ceremony and learning what he ought, my son spent every waking hour teaching Gilles how to behave as a squire. The boy had been badly treated and abused; he needed lessons in the simplest of tasks. My son was patient and Harry, surprisingly, helped his elder brother. Perhaps he saw what he might need to do when he became a knight.

Although it was winter the Great North Road was kept open and I used Sir John's squire, Ralph, to ride to Middleham a week before the ceremony just to ensure that the preparations for the wedding were proceeding apace. It also afforded Ralph the opportunity to speak with his family. I had promised when Ralph had joined my service that I would do. I left Ralph with his family for a few days and Harry and I returned home first. After I returned from the north I did not see Ralph to speak to until after the ceremony for I had much to do.

We had no chapel at my hall for Weedon was a small manor and so we used the church of St Peter and Paul in the village. Monks had owned the village until it was given to me and they had built a fine church. Dressed in his white shift Thomas spent the night before the ceremony knelt before the altar with his sword. One disadvantage of the timing was that it was incredibly cold in the church but Thomas was philosophical about that and felt it would make him a stronger knight. Two of my men at arms, along with Harry, volunteered to guard the door. The next morning, which heralded a cold and cheerless day, he was brought back to the hall. Guests like Sir John and Ralph arrived as dawn was breaking. My daughter, Alice, now with child and Sir Richard stayed in the new and almost completed wing. My men at arms and archers were also invited to the hall and so it was cosy. Sir Richard asked me, later on, why I had invited hired swords and bowmen. I had given him the truth; they were part of my family and it bound us all closer together.

As soon as Thomas rose Harry and Ralph slipped his new surcoat over his shoulders. I handed him his spurs and Sir John strapped on his sword. As we all stepped back there was a huge cheer and my wife was the first to rush to him and embrace him. I allowed others to offer their congratulations before I did. As Eleanor and Mary rushed off to organise the food and the drink Thomas came over to me. "I thank you for this, father."

"It is no more than you deserve. You could have been knighted on the field of battle but this, I think, is better."

"It is for I am surrounded by a sea of warmth which fills me with joy."

I nodded and Harry joined us, "Aye, family is all." I meant each word for I had had little family when I had been growing up.

Harry said, "Sir Thomas of Weedon!" I could see that Harry was delighted for his brother. There was not a hint of jealousy.

I saw a question forming on Thomas' lips. The ale and the food had been brought in and that created space around us so that we could talk. "Father, I know that mother has built the guest wing and Mary and I will use that but…"

"But you would like your own hall." He nodded. "I will be blunt, my son, you have not enough coin to pay for a hall."

"Mary's mother is giving us a dowry. Ralph told me that."

"It will still not be enough. I have the land for you already marked out but there is nothing there but fields." We had discussed the land he would have as an income. I owned and farmed the best land in Weedon. Some of my men at arms and archers farmed small plots and the result was that there were a number of fields separated from my land by these plots. Eleanor and I had decided to give one as a wedding gift to Thomas and his bride but it was bare earth. Some of the fields were bean fields while he had a field for animals and three fields for cereal.

Thomas smiled, "I am not afraid of hard work and I have two men who serve me as well as my squire. I still need someone to manage the land for me but I thought when the new grass comes to erect a small hall on the land so that we can live there."

"But your mother has had a wing built for you!"

"And it will take some time for me to make my home fit for my bride. We will use it but you see why I need to be my own man. My home will be Lower Weedon, eh?"

I smiled, "Aye, it is well and now, young Harry, you are my only squire so about your duties! You have gossiped enough! There is ale and food to be served."

His face fell, "I had forgotten. I cannot wait to be knighted, brother."

"And that will not be for some time, my son, now go and join the other squires in their work."

Sir John, Sir Roger and Sir Wilfred came over. I could see that they wished to speak with my son and I gave them space. I wandered over to the fire. I was aware that I had no ale. As I turned to shout over Harry, Ralph appeared with an ale, "Lord, I told Harry I would fetch it for I need to speak with you."

I saw that his face was serious. I feared there was something wrong with his sister or his mother.

"After you had gone and I was riding the pastures one of the Earl of Westmoreland's knights came to speak with me. He had a message for you. He said that the Earl did not wish to commit it to paper and so I had to memorise it."

I feared treachery. The Earl had not spoken with Ralph, it had been an intermediary. Even before I heard the message, I was suspicious. "Did you know the man?"

He nodded, "Aye lord, it was Sir William Neville, the Earl's nephew. He had spoken with Sir John on a number of occasions when we campaigned in Wales. I believe that he can be trusted."

"Go on."

"He said to tell you that Sir Henry Percy is recruiting men. He said that this is not the campaign season and most lords are letting men go. Sir Henry is filling the newly refurbished castle of Warkworth with men. He thought you should know."

I nodded. I knew that I had to make the time to speak with the King. "Thank you, Ralph." He looked relieved to have unburdened himself. "And the preparations for the marriage are still moving well?"

He grinned, "Aye, my lord. My sister is excited and cannot wait to come south. I know that my mother will be upset but she has other children who are not like Mary and myself. They will stay by the farm. She will enjoy their children."

"And you, are you ready for knighthood yet?"

"Perhaps, my lord. Sir John has suggested that I might be dubbed but I know that I do not have enough coin…"

"Your mother has promised a large dowry to my son."

He nodded, "And that is right but I am no catch and there will be no dowry from the woman I marry. I will have to hope that we go to war and I am rewarded. I am a patient man, my lord. I have risen beyond expectations already and if I rise no further I have done well for myself."

His father had grown a family late in life and he had been happy. I hoped that Ralph would be too.

The day ended well and our guests departed. We now had preparations for Christmas but this would be a quieter time. Alice and her husband were at their hall and Thomas' head was filled with his new manor and forthcoming marriage. Mary, my daughter, had attracted the eye of Sir Richard's squire, his brother, James and was distracted. It suited me as I had much to think on. I knew that King Henry liked to spend his winter at

Windsor. Once he would have been happy with his estates in Monmouth but since the Glendower rebellion, there was too much danger. Eltham Palace, which had been a favourite of King Richard, was too close to the fickle London mob and so he stayed in the huge castle of Windsor which was surrounded by a great park which could be used for riding and hunting. More importantly, he was safe there from those who wished him harm.

I spoke with my wife on St Stephen's Day. I had already told her what the Earl of Westmoreland had told me. "Harry and I will need to ride to Windsor to speak with the King."

"But it is winter!"

"And the last time I was not prompt with news I was chastised. I have to go and you know it."

My wife was a realist who knew that our prosperity was dependent upon King Henry, "You are right. The King does not deserve such a loyal and faithful knight as you, husband."

I laughed, "Of course he does for I am his subject and, despite his many faults, he does try to do the best for the Kingdom."

I saw the doubt in the eyes of my wife but she said nothing.

I took two of my new men with me, Rafe and Kit. They were single and the other men at arms either had wives or liaisons. This was a chance for me to get to know them and we would not be away long. It was just two days to the castle and two days back. We would be away for no more than six days.

Ralph had brought back a new horse for me. Hawk was a stallion and a courser. He was a present from Mary. I would pay her for him when she came to the wedding. I did not need charity and he was a fine horse. This seemed a good opportunity to get to know him. There would be no danger and we would be using a good road. I allowed Harry to ride Hart. The new men were nervous for they knew the responsibility they had. To make it easier for them I rode between them so that we could speak. I learned of the lords they had served and the wars in which they had fought. I already knew, from their mail and lack of plate armour, that they had not had great success before they came to me. I would not judge them on that for if they had a poor lord then they could not be expected to prosper. The fact that they had survived without wounds or scars wearing only mail hauberks spoke well of them. We stayed in an inn in Aylesbury. This was a royal manor and I was known here having stayed in the town when Richard was King of England. Although we paid a fair price, I knew that I would not be robbed. The landlord knew of my connection with King Henry and his son. My new men questioned my spending the money for beds for them. I learned that both their previous lords would have expected their men to sleep in the stables.

I smiled, "I began life as a common soldier. When I am able I make life easier but I have slept, quite recently, beneath the greenwood. This is better." I was also confident that King Henry would reward me for the news I brought.

The King had lost his wife some time ago giving birth to his last child. He had not remarried. I knew that he would but it would be a political marriage. When he had married Mary de Bohun, he had not been King nor even close to the crown. Now he would marry one who was related to a royal house in France, Spain or Portugal. He had sons enough. That had been the downfall of King Richard as he and his wife had failed to produce an heir either male or female. Although it was December, we had had no snow yet. That did not mean it was good weather, far from it but it did mean that the King was not abroad hunting or hawking. He was in his Great Hall, for once not engrossed in papers. Harry had taken the two men to the warrior hall as he knew his way around the castle and, after leaving my cloak and helmet with Harry, one of King Henry's pages, Paul, took me to speak with the King.

He did not smile but frowned, "This is most unexpected, Strongstaff. Does your visit herald trouble?"

I shook my head, "No, King Henry, although I was asked by you to fetch any news which came my way as soon as I received it. I have such news."

He waved a hand at the lords who were gathered around him, "Leave us and put a sentry upon the door." When the doors banged shut, he waved me to a seat by the fire. I was chilled to the bone for the cold and damp day made my bones and old wounds ache. "So, what have you heard?"

I told him the news from Westmoreland. He nodded, "It may be that Percy plans to hammer the Scots once more and if he does then I shall not worry overmuch but your news about a possible liaison between him and Glendower may not be groundless. Since you spoke I, too, have heard disquieting rumours of messages sent from Wales to lords in England." He leaned forward, "You know that there are rumours about King Richard and me?"

I could not deny it and I nodded, "Aye, King Henry, but they are groundless."

He stood and struck his right fist into his left palm, "Of course they are!" Then he smiled at me, "You, of all people, know that. My cousin was a troubled man! Know that the Archbishop of York, Richard le Scrope, plots against me and spreads the rumour that Richard is still alive! And there are others who say I had him killed. Are they all fools?"

"It is not my place, lord, but why not have the Archbishop questioned?"

"Do not think I have not thought of that already but he is related to the Percys through his brother who married the widow of a Percy and he has powerful friends in the north. It may well be that this is a plot to make me the tyrant poor Richard became at the end. I will not fall into that trap, Strongstaff! I will not release my grip on the crown so easily."

I now saw the dilemma in which the King found himself. King Richard had lost the crown because he saw plots everywhere and had men arrested. King Henry could not do that.

"I think that I may have to offer Percy some sweetmeat to keep him on my side." The King was a clever man and far more complicated than his son. He stared at the fire and then stood. "Is there more news?"

"No, Your Majesty."

"Then let the others back in lest they think we plot!"

This was a strange world in which the King lived.

When they all entered, along with Harry, the King said, "You did well in Scotland. The Earl of March has asked for you to return in the spring." I gave him a surprised look. The King smiled, "The Earl visited with me and told me of your valour. I approve and it may well increase your war chest. Hire more men! I need the steel of Strongstaff behind me and my son. In an uncertain world, you are a constant."

When we returned home it was with twenty pounds in silver to hire more men. I would need more men, for now I had another possible enemy, the Archbishop of York. I had not known of his involvement with the Percys and I had been open in my visits to York. Now I would have to take care for all knew that I was the King's man.

Lady Day came around remarkably quickly. Riders rode up and down the road to Middleham on a weekly basis. How my wife managed to organise the wedding as well as running the farms of four manors I have no idea. She was, indeed, a wonder. I sent some of my men to help Thomas build his hall. His labours impressed me. I paid for my wife's mason to offer advice to him once the wing was finished. The result was a hall with two floors rather than the simple one-storied building Thomas had planned. By the time we reached the start of March, he had a roof and the exterior was finished. He knew he would have to make do with improvised furniture but he had a hall for his bride and they had a bed.

When the guests arrived for the wedding it felt as though my hall would crumble beneath the weight of people. I feared for my daughter, Alice, who was within a month or so of giving birth. The mood was, however, joyous. The day was seen as propitious and everyone in the manor saw it as a sign that we would all prosper. Such superstitions were a throwback to the time of the Vikings and Saxons. I did not believe it would hurt.

Once the wedding was over and the guests had left my life could settle into a more comfortable routine. Mary and her sons and other daughter stayed for a week. She and my wife got on well. After they departed, I prepared to ride to Dunbarre again. When Easter had been and gone, I would take my men and any knights who chose to come with me and we would ride to Dunbarre. All four of them chose to do so. My son's wife, Mary, was a practical woman. Thomas had hired good servants and she planned on making the hall a home. The crudely fashioned furniture would not do for Mary and Thomas had an even greater need for coin. I used the money given to me by the King to hire more archers and men at arms. My name was enough to attract men from all across the county. This was the King's land; he had been Earl of Northampton and every soldier knew that I was not only skilled, I was lucky and soldiers knew the importance of luck.

Chapter 11

It was May when we headed north. I had bought a new breastplate from Martin who would use the metal from the old one to make a breastplate for Gilles. This time I led a much greater force of men and we required more rooms and stables for my retinue. I had a Royal Warrant from King Henry which he had given to me when I had seen him in Windsor. It meant we could stay in royal castles such as Lincoln. It was not just the financial benefits which I enjoyed, there was greater security. I was now wary of such places as York! We did visit with Mary. She was delighted for she got to see her son again and I was able to speak with Sir William Neville who was acting as constable for his uncle.

When he heard that I was travelling north he nodded approvingly, "That is good, my lord, for we have heard of Scottish lords gathering armies. They feel that Percy and Lord Dunbarre impugned their honour with their raids last year. We have men watching for Scottish raiders."

"Will they risk the Tyne and the Tees?"

"I fear so. We live on the hospitable part of the Pennines. There are trails through the forests and less accessible areas which the Scots can use. If they can avoid the men of Barnard Castle and Raby then they can ravage the Tyne, the Wear and the Tees with impunity. There is just the castle at Stockton to bar their way and the river can be crossed in many places."

"I had hoped just for a month of campaigning and then to return home."

"You may be required for longer, my lord."

The Earl of March was more than delighted to see me and the increased number of men I had brought. I gave him the news I had from Neville although I did not quote the source. The Earl nodded and said, "Percy is not in the north. The King has made him Royal Lieutenant of North Wales and he is there now inspecting the castles." The King had, indeed, offered Percy a sweetmeat! I wondered at the wisdom of such a move; the King was playing a dangerous game. "The absence of Hotspur may well encourage the Scots and from what you told me there is good reason for the muster of the men of the borders."

Over the next days, I rode with my knights and the Earl to inspect his borders. His lords now had a tight grip on this part of Scotland and the borders. It was when we rode to Jedburgh and the Tweed that I saw the issue. Norham and Berwick barred the river but to the south and west were thick forests which could easily be negotiated by what amounted to warbands. The Scots had been doing this since before the time of the Romans. The routes and passages were passed from father to son almost as family heirlooms. England was their larder! "I fear that the first we will hear of a raid is when messengers come from the south! Still, it cannot be helped. King Henry must have good reasons to take Percy away from the north although for the life of me I cannot see what they are." I knew he was playing a game of chess but the pieces were real ones. He had sacrificed a castle to win the game!

I felt like a fraud for we had little to do for a week or so except to ride to the borders of the Earl's land. He treated us well with good food and fine grazing for our animals. I began to wonder if the rumour was just that, a rumour, when messengers arrived a few days before the summer solstice to tell us that a force of over twelve thousand Scots were raiding Cumberland and Northumberland. Carlisle and the west were too far away from us to allow us to intervene there and the Earl of Westmoreland would have to deal with them, but Northumberland was a different matter.

Sir George rubbed his hands, "Now we have them. When they head north, they will avoid Norham and Berwick. That limits the number of places they can cross the Tweed and their route there will be predictable. They will use the Jedburgh crossing and we can catch them north of there. We do not have to travel far; we can let them come to us!"

I was dubious about the timing, "You can be certain?" He nodded confidently and I believed him. He was the poacher turned gamekeeper. "And the numbers, my lord? If there are twelve thousand Scotsmen on the rampage then we will be seriously outnumbered."

"I can see how you think that way but I have raided in England and I know how the raiders' minds work. There will be knights who keep their men in good order but there will be chiefs and other lesser leaders for whom the raid is just an opportunity to get rich quick. In addition, the twelve thousand will be spread across the north. I fear that Westmoreland will have more raiders for Bowness and Craven are both fertile places and worth raiding. We will catch them!"

We left to intercept them immediately. We had fewer than two hundred men all told and I thought it would be doomed to failure. I grew more confident when, after receiving a summons from Sir George, ten knights and their retinue arrived from Berwick. We now had thirty knights and all of us were well armed. With the archers from Berwick and those I had brought, we had fifty archers. It was not as many as I would have liked but Sir George seemed convinced that they would prove to be decisive. We headed for Duns which lay just north of Blackadder Water. One of Sir George's lords, Sir John Swinton, had a manor there, Kimmerghame House. It meant that we had kitchens to cook our food and some of the lords had a roof over their head. I shared the outdoors with my men. The nights were so short that there was not even a chill in the air. Sir John Swinton had scouts out and it was they who reported warbands heading north. It appeared that Sir George was correct. Some of the knights had kept their men together. There was one such group with over four hundred men. There were other bands of thirty or forty. They were driving cattle, captives and booty and all of them were moving slowly.

I knew how to fight but Sir George was the master of border wars. He knew just how and where to array our men. He had the archers and some dismounted men at arms form a long double line to the north of the beck. He knew their line of march for he had used it himself when he had raided Northumberland. He had the knights and the mounted men at arms form up in two wings. He commanded one and I the other. Mine was the smaller wing and consisted of just my own household knights and men at arms. Our banners would tell the enemy that we had fewer knights and I knew that it would encourage them to attack us. I did not mind. Sir George commanded and he seemed to know his business.

We rose at dawn with the expectation of a battle later in the morning. The animals they had captured must have slowed the raiders down more than they had expected and the bulk of the raiders did not reach us until the middle of the afternoon. That does not mean to say that we were not kept busy. Smaller groups of men, as Sir George had predicted, made their way north towards the Blackadder Water. I saw why they chose this route. The river was no wider than fifteen paces anywhere and could be forded by all but the shortest of men. By the same token that was why Sir George had chosen it. The Scots would have to cross the Water to reach us. We captured or killed almost forty men before the main raiding party returned. My men at arms and I had little to do. It was the archers who did the bulk of the work. I have no doubt that the raiders had been warned of our presence by those we failed to see as they headed north. Our numbers would have been reported so that when the banners of their knights appeared, they were advancing in battle formation. They had organised themselves into a larger warband to force the crossing and their knights led. We recognised some of their banners; they were led by Lord Hepburn, with de Lawedre, Sir John Cockburn and the Haliburton brothers. There were other knights but we did not recognise their banners. We would be outnumbered on the field but we had more knights than they did.

As they formed up, I turned to my sons. Thomas would be riding at the fore and Harry would not merely be watching our horses, he would be fighting. "Thomas, when you strike then strike to kill. Forget ransom."

"Aye, my lord!"

"And Harry, you are a squire and not a knight; just survive eh?"

"Yes, my lord," he sounded cheerful about such a potentially deadly encounter.

"Gilles, the advice to you is to watch Sir Thomas' back! No heroics!"

"No, my lord."

We had had little to do thus far. It had been the dismounted men at arms and archers who had both slain and captured the riders. We had yet to cross the Blackadder Water. It meant that the ground between us and the enemy was not churned up. The archers and dismounted men at arms now had the advantage of slippery and muddy ground before them and it would slow down the enemy before they entered the water. I saw the Scottish knights with banners holding a counsel of war. They were looking for a trick. They outnumbered us and, in theory, would easily win. When they turned their horses and began to shout orders, I knew that they had made their decision to attack. Their crossbows and archers formed up and began to move in a long thin line towards our men. The men at arms had shields as well as plate armour. The Scots had parity of numbers with our archers but I knew who I would back. Alan of the Woods was the senior archer and it was he who gave the command to release. He gave the order when the crossbowmen knelt. Once again, I saw the futility of using crossbows in the open. It was obvious when they would release their bolts. Their archers, using an inferior weapon, sent a ragged shower of arrows back across the beck. After four flights they were broken and they retired. Then the Scots sent forward their dismounted men who carried shields. There were well over one hundred and forty of them. Behind them came another hundred and odd men without shields. Their knights formed up across the Water from us.

Sir Roger chuckled, "Very obliging of them, my lord. We do not have to seek our treasure, it will gallop towards us."

My men all laughed. I saw the reasoning behind the Scottish decision. Our deadly archers would have to send their arrows at the men on foot. In addition, the Scottish knights outnumbered my battle. They believed that they would defeat me and then sweep around to take the archers in the rear.

Harry asked, "What will Sir George do, my lord?"

"Simple, he will cross the river and attack the flank of their men on foot. The decision of the Scottish leader has cost him the battle but he hopes to defeat us and cut his losses." I stood in my stirrups, "Spears and lances at the ready. We hit them when they rise from the water!"

The arrows of our archers smacked into shields and rattled off helmets. They also drove through mail and into flesh. I saw an arrow, obviously a heavy war bodkin, drive through a helmet and kill a man at arms instantly. The men with shields began to fall. They were not being reaped but they were being hurt. The twenty knights and their attendant men at arms and squires closed with the Blackadder Water. I raised my lance. We would not get to gallop. We would get as fast as *'Poignez, spur on'* and trot. That would ensure that our front line of five knights and my best five men at arms would hit together while the Scottish horsemen were trying to clamber from the stream. I heard a horn from my left and knew that Sir George was beginning his attack.

I concentrated on the banner of Robert de Lawedre of Edrington. From their angle of approach, I saw that it was he I would face. The Scottish line was more ragged than ours for they had been travelling all day. There were gaps. Sir John's boot touched my right leg and Thomas, my son's, my left. Timing was all and I slowed down Hawk, my warhorse who was keen for battle. This would be his first battle and he snorted in his eagerness to get to grips with the enemy. He would fight as hard as any knight. He would bite and kick. He would use his head and hooves as weapons. The first knight out of the water was Sir Patrick Hepburn the Younger of Hailes. He had the misfortune to face Sir Roger. Sir Roger cared not a jot for ransom. I suspect he thought to settle for the fine courser the knight rode. Whatever was going through his mind his action was clear. As Sir Patrick urged his horse from the water, Sir Roger pulled back his arm and smashed the knight in the chest with his lance. Sir Patrick was held in place by his cantle but he dropped his own spear. Sir Roger pulled back his spear and rammed it towards the leg of the knight. The tip broke off as it skewered the leg and Sir Roger threw away the stump as the Scot's horse finally found purchase on the bank and scrambled up. The knight was badly wounded but brave. He drew his war axe and swung it at Sir Roger. A knight with lesser skill might have been caught by the blow but Sir Roger merely rolled back from the arc of the head and used his left hand to grab the haft. A knight without a wounded leg and one who had not been hit by a spear might have torn the axe from

Sir Roger's grip. Sir Roger raised his sword and shouted, "Yield, my lord! You are wounded!"

"Damn you, English mercenary! I fight on!"

Sir Roger swung his sword and the Scot raised his left arm to fend off the blow. He merely slowed it and the blade tore through the coif and into his neck.

Even as the knight was falling to his death, I had to concentrate on my foe for the others had used the distraction of Sir Patrick's fight to solidify their line and five of them rode at us. The knight who fought me, Robert de Lawedre, had the disadvantage of striking upwards towards me. My spear was aimed down and both lances struck at the same time. I was able to use my hand to deflect the tip a little while mine hit him hard in the right shoulder. I hurled the broken haft at him as he reeled and then drew my sword. The knight wasted valuable time trying to pull back his arm for another strike but his horse was flailing in the mud as it tried to clamber up the bank. It was not helped by Hawk's snapping jaws. I swung my sword at the Scot's left shoulder. He too had a war hammer hanging from his cantle. Used two-handed it could cause terrible wounds even to knights protected by plate. His hand dropped his lance as my sword hit him. I pulled back on Hawk's reins and his mighty hooves flailed in the air. One struck the knight in the chest. Even plate could not endure such damage and the knight slid into the beck.

"Yield!"

He lifted his visor and nodded, "I yield for I cannot lift my arm! You have hurt me most severely!" As a second knight with a yellow surcoat and blue lions galloped at me I saw that my son was engaged with Sir John Cockburn. Sir John had a reputation as a good tourney knight and I hoped that my son would err on the side of caution in his first battle. Then I was struck in the chest by the Scottish knight's lance. It hurt but it also angered me. I had been careless for I had been watching my son instead of my enemy. My new plate had held and I swung my sword at the wooden lance. I hacked a chunk from it, making it useless as a weapon. The two lines of knights were now engaged and their standards still flew for their squires were yet to be engaged. Sir George and his horsemen were ploughing into the right flank of the Scottish foot and, already, the Scots were trying to flee. That would be hard to do with Sir George and his horsemen hard upon their heels.

I had my own battle to fight. I raised my sword and shouted, "Squires, now is your chance for glory! Take those banners!"

If the banners fell then we had won. Ralph shouted, "At them! For Sir William!" I leapt Hawk into the stream for it was time to end this battle. My mighty horse was so powerful that it made the young knight's horse reel and I was able to bring my sword down to smash the rider's right hand. He had a mail glove but it still numbed the hand. I backhanded the knight across the chest with my sword and he tried to raise his hand to fend off another blow. I did not give him the opportunity and I stood in my stirrups and swept my sword at the side of his head. His hand was still numb and he failed to lift it high enough. The blade rang against the visored sallet basinet denting it. I lifted my left leg and pushed him into the water. His horse, freed from its burden, galloped up the bank towards the safety of our lines. There was no fighting there. The knight sank beneath the water and then popped up. He pulled his helmet from his head which I saw was bleeding. I spurred Hawk and had my sword close to his eye, "Yield for you cannot fight on!"

He looked around. My son had unhorsed and captured Sir John Cockburn and Sir John had Sir John Haliburton nursing a broken arm. He too had yielded and he nodded.

"Your name, sir?"

"Sir Thomas Haliburton."

Just then I heard a cheer and saw that Harry, Gilles and Ralph had captured three standards and the squires and remaining knights had yielded. It was not just down to their skill, for Sir George and his men had routed the rest of the Scottish raiders and his light horsemen were now chasing down and butchering those who had fled.

"Well done! Fetch the prisoners to our side of the river. Alan of the Wood, have some men gather the spare animals! Sir George's men can recover the captives and the animals. We have earned our rest!"

We had had the harder fight. One Scottish knight lay dead but we had another twelve prisoners. Sir George would have a share of each of the ransoms, a tenth, but the rest would go to my men.

Even Ralph, Gilles and Harry would receive coin for they had captured standards and they were as valuable as knights. The Battle of Nesbit Moor was a great victory and we were all richer for it.

We discovered that the raiders had reached the River Wear. Durham had been threatened. The west had seen the Scots surround Carlisle before the Earl of Westmoreland drove them back. The losses were not as bad as they might have been. Had the Earl of March still been on the Scottish side then things would have gone ill. We sent riders for the ransom and to tell King Henry, now in Wales, and Henry Percy, of the raids.

It was the last day of June when we heard of the disaster of Bryn Glas. The Welsh had brought men towards England and Mortimer had led the men of Hereford to throw them back. The Welsh had not only defeated Edmund Mortimer, but they had also taken him prisoner. All the joy of victory and our low losses evaporated in an instant. All of us had expected that with Hotspur, the King and Prince Henry in Wales that the Welsh rebellion would be quashed. It seemed that was not the case. Edmund was the brother in law of Henry Hotspur and something did not seem quite right about the loss. The Welsh had yet to defeat the English in a battle and for a lord like Mortimer to be defeated seemed, to me, to be odd, to say the least.

"Sir George, when the ransoms have come, I must take my leave of you. I think that the King and Prince Henry will have need of me and my men. This border is secure; the Welsh one appears to be in a parlous state."

"Aye, you are right but I will be sorry to see you go. You are few in number yet you fight like a mighty host."

Most of the ransoms had come by the first week in July and we rode home. Sir George would send the rest when it arrived. We had mail, horses, weapons and coin. My sons had profited. Pyotr and Abelard both felt guilty because they alone out of the squires had not covered themselves in glory. Harry showed his maturity by telling them of the times he had been forced to watch others fight and be rewarded. As we rode south, I was proud of my sons as they both counselled the young squires.

"This was the first time you have faced an enemy. Harry here held horses prior to this battle."

I heard Harry laugh, "Aye, if I did not have to gather coin to become a knight then I might have stayed on our side of the river. I think I had a rush of blood! Fear, not. It will get easier and Ralph, Gilles and I will be here to help you. You are part of our company now and we look after each other."

I took Sir John and Ralph to one side, "That was bravely done, Ralph." He nodded. "Sir John, I would find another squire for I have a mind to dub Ralph here. I need more knights to follow my banner and Ralph has shown, this day, that he has what it takes."

I saw that Ralph was delighted with my words and Sir John nodded, "You are right, Sir William, although I will be loath to lose such a good friend."

"And you will not be losing him. He would still live in Dauentre. I know the value of such bonds as you enjoy with Ralph!"

By the time we reached Weedon, we had discovered that the country was on a knife-edge. A defeat by the Welsh was unheard of and Wales seemed much closer than remote Scotland. Only the Severn was a barrier. Cereals and food prices rose. My wife had something to be pleased about but she too was worried and, for once, did not object when I said I would be riding west to speak with the King. I left my knights at home. They would not be needed. I took half of my archers and men at arms and I rode Hart. As we rode I confided, for the first time, in Harry. His courage at Nesbit Moor had impressed me and he seemed to have grown since his brother had been given his spurs. He listened as I spoke my fears out loud.

"But it is just one battle. We have won many more."

"Aye, but we have lost a powerful lord. His nephew, also called Edmund Mortimer, has a claim to the crown. His claim is the equal of King Henry's. The fact that one so close to the crown has been captured is not a good sign."

I saw realisation dawn on my son's face. He now understood that it was more than just a battle lost. It was a shift in the political landscape. I needed to speak with the King and the Prince as soon as possible. As for Percy? I would speak with him if I had to.

The King was at Caernarfon Castle along with Prince Henry when I eventually found him. I had gone to Chester first. The battle had occurred on the border with Herefordshire and I wondered why the King and his son were so far from the scene of the battle. The King looked relieved to see me, "Baron, you bring good news about the Scots?"

"We defeated them but only after they had raided England. Families suffered, Your Majesty."

He sank back into his chair and rested his chin on his hands. He was deep in thought.

Prince Henry looked to have grown since I had last seen him. It had been more than a year ago. It was he who spoke to me, "My father has much on his mind. I am something of a failure, Baron. If I had defeated Glendower at the start instead of heeding the advice of Henry Percy then the Scots would not have grown so bold and tried to imitate Welsh."

I looked at the King. I was a father and I knew that Henry was asking his father to tell him that he was wrong but the King did not. "Speaking of Hotspur, where is he?"

"When he heard of the attacks on his lands he left and took with him all of his men."

I looked at the King. He shrugged, "I made a mistake, it seems I was too clever. I made him lieutenant of North Wales and it afforded me nothing!" He leaned forward. "There is a plot and I see it clearly now. Mortimer is involved! I can see their clever plan and it will not work."

I was confused and I looked from father to son. "I do not understand; Mortimer was taken prisoner does that not mean he is just a poor leader rather than a traitor?"

"Ha!" The King's snort spoke volumes.

Prince Henry said, "My father may well be right. The men of Hereford were slaughtered and yet Mortimer was taken prisoner. They now demand a huge ransom for him, from the crown!"

"And I will not pay! They killed Sir Robert Whitney, my Knight Marshal and the Welsh witches desecrated his body!" In the King's eyes, this made it personal.

Prince Henry appeared calmer and in more control of his emotions, "And that is another reason, Sir William, why Hotspur has returned home. He is angry with us for Mortimer is his brother in law and he is annoyed that we will not ransom him."

I shook my head. I was becoming more confused with each passing moment, "What has he to gain?"

The King was deep in thought and Hal explained, "The ransom could be paid but it would mean we could not pay the men and knights who fought for us. Hotspur has already objected to the fact that we have not paid him for defending the northern borders. The lack of money weakens the crown and Mortimer's nephew has a claim to the crown. He was young when my father was given the throne but now, he is manipulated by Hotspur and Mortimer. Mortimer gave himself to the Welsh. Hotspur is in collusion with Glendower although we cannot prove it and the man is too powerful."

King Henry rose and put his arm around me, "So, Will Strongstaff, once again the king of England and his heir have just one hope, and that is you. The Black Prince chose you well!"

I sat in a chair, stunned. Once more I would be at the heart of conspiracies, plots and knives in the night. The pleasant life of a lord of a manor was ended. I was going back to war. We left Caernarfon and headed for Chester.

Chapter 12

The King seemed quite happy to stay at Chester. London was too remote from both places of danger. With Percy in the north and Glendower in the west, he needed to be close enough to react to any threat from either of them. He allowed me and my men a day or two to recover and then sent for me. There was only Prince Henry with us. The young prince was a most thoughtful youth and while the King spoke, I saw him weighing every word. I am not certain that, if he had been king, he would have acted the same way but he knew that he was not the king and he would learn while he could.

"What think you of George Dunbarre? Can we trust him?"

I nodded, "For the moment yes, King Henry, for it is in his own interest to support England. Douglas is his enemy and Percy fights Douglas. He will continue to keep us safe but he is a good general, Your Majesty. He knows how to fight in the borders. If he should turn against us then I would fear him."

The King nodded, "And Neville?"

"I believe you can trust him. He has reason to both hate and fear Percy."

The King nodded, "Aye, there's the rub. We cannot trust Percy. This is the second time he has abandoned his position here and now he makes demands for money!"

I did not like to defend Henry Percy but the King wanted him to guard the northern border and he could not do both.

Prince Hal was Prince of Wales and he brought the King back to the matter at hand, "Your Majesty, this does not help us with the Welsh. Our ring of castles holds them here but now that Mortimer is captured then the door to the heart of England is open."

The King waved an airy hand as though to dismiss the words, "Fear not, the Earl of Stafford is mustering his men and the Earl can be trusted. He will not join the rebels. However, you are right, we need more intelligence. Strongstaff, I would have you take your men and find where this Welsh threat is. We watch the north. Ride to Powys. I give you until the middle of September to find out where Glendower and his men are gathering. I am reluctant to waste money paying men to fight until I have to. The Marcher Lords have had their chance. If Glendower ravages their lands then it is they who are responsible but I will not have my realm harmed."

It was a hard task but I had to obey. "Aye, lord." I left the hall immediately and went to my men and my squire who were in the outer ward, practising. I waved my arm to gather them. "Prepare your war gear for we ride on the morrow."

My two captains nodded and Alan of the Woods, who knew that if we were scouting, he would be at the fore, asked, "Where to, my lord?"

I sighed for the command the King had given to me was unfair and most difficult for we had not had any sighing of Glendower since the rebellion had begun. "We have to find Glendower and his army."

Only Harry reacted, "That is simple then. First, find the hidden haystack and the needle which is buried within it!"

My men laughed at his words.

"No one said that the road to knighthood was easy, Harry!" He nodded and began to flush. "We do not have long to do so. Owen, Geraint and David, you are all Welsh. You will take off my livery and adopt the garb of men for hire. You will ride two miles ahead of us and leave a marked trail."

David of Welshpool was a sergeant at arms. He knew he would be leading the two archers and he nodded, "And whence do we begin, my lord?"

"The battle was fought in Shropshire. The Shropshire hills would be a good place to start."

Just then the Prince appeared from behind my men. I guessed, from his words, that he had been listening. He was alone. "My lord, those who survived the battle said that the Welsh used the hills as a place to ambush our men. The battle has encouraged many Welshmen to return to Wales to fight. Students from the universities are leaving their studies to fight under Glendower's banner. Your men could pretend to be three such turncoats."

David nodded, "Thank you, Prince Henry, we can dissemble!"

The Prince, who was more intelligent than either his father or King Richard asked a question which struck to the heart of the matter, "And you three do not wish to join this rebellion against me and my father?"

My veterans all knew Prince Henry and they had helped to train him. When they spoke to him it was not as their future king but as a comrade in arms and he received that same honesty which they gave each other. "The rebels are wrong, Prince Henry. This Owen Glendower seeks to take advantage of a piss poor English knight." I saw Hal smile. He shared their opinion of Lord Grey. "Glendower farms poor land and he would rather own the richer land of England. Do not worry, Prince Henry, there are other Welshmen like us. True, there are young hotheads who will join the rabble-rousers. There always are. They will melt away when they face real warriors. The danger, as Owen and Geraint will tell you, will come from the archers."

"You do not need to tell me, David, for it was the archers who won the battle of Bryn Glas and I did not doubt, for an instant, your loyalty. I just wished to get inside the head of a Welshman. I am Prince of Wales and I need to find a way to rule these people." He turned to me, "A word, my lord?"

I nodded, "Prepare the horses and war gear. We will not need tents nor lances. We take spears. Harry, we need no banner and we can leave the horse armour here. If we have to fight a battle then we have failed."

My men disappeared and Prince Henry said, "I am not certain that my father employs the correct strategy here. I would have paid the ransom just to keep Percy on our side and then I would have watched Mortimer. Find Glendower but do so without risk to yourself. We need you and your men." He smiled and was the young lad who had come to Weedon to learn to fight, "I need you!"

"Do not fret, Prince Henry, I have no intention of being caught. I have brought twenty men and I would stack those against any other hundred men in any realm!"

"One thing more, Sir Thomas Fitzalan, the Earl of Arundel is a loyal man. King Richard abused him but he is a great friend of mine. His castle still holds against the enemy and he escaped from the battle. He will be someone who has knowledge of the enemy."

"Thank you for that information."

"Do not waste time seeking every answer. We need to know the whereabouts of Glendower. The information regarding Mortimer would be useful but it is not worth risking your life to obtain it. It will be easier for you and we have given you a hard enough task as it is."

We had sixty miles to go to reach the battlefield. We camped on a wooded and craggy hill just south of Criggion. We were now in Wales but there were no castles and lords to spy on us. Our three scouts had kept the road well-marked for us and we ate cold fare and drank from skins of ale.

Before we left, I spoke with my scouts who had rejoined us. "Clun Castle is still held by Sir Thomas Fitzalan. We will stay there tomorrow night and you three can scout ahead. We will leave and meet you on the battlefield. That will be as good a place as any to begin our search."

I hid the fact that I did not like Thomas Fitzalan. His family had opposed King Richard and he had helped to topple the King I had served. However, he was loyal to King Henry and, as a friend of Prince Henry, I would put aside my personal feelings. Of course, we might not be made welcome. The last time I had seen the lord had been in North Wales when we had returned from Ireland. I had faced down King Richard's enemies; that was when I angered the Percy family. The oath to the Black Prince had cost me dear.

We were, surprisingly, welcomed. I later discovered that Prince Henry had sent one of his pages, escorted by two men at arms to warn Fitzalan that I might be calling. Young Henry was a more thoughtful man than his father.

"Baron, you are most welcome."

I saw that he had suffered injury in the battle. His arm was in a sling and I saw men at arms with bandages on heads and arms.

I nodded at the sling, "You suffered that at the battle?"

His nostrils flared and his eyes widened, "Treachery! That was what it was, treachery! That traitor Mortimer brought

Welshmen who changed sides as soon as the battle began. Mortimer lowered the standard immediately. We still had enough men to defeat them!"

I now saw whence the King had heard the news and understood how he had reached his conclusion. "And where is Glendower now, my lord?"

He shrugged, "The man is as slippery as an eel and cowardly to boot. He was not on the battlefield but his army retreated into the vastness of a wild and mountainous Wales, taking Mortimer with them."

An idea began to form in my mind. This Welsh lord was clever and wished to avoid armies made up of knights who would defeat him in open battle. He would retreat to the higher ground. The castles around the periphery of his land would drive him to places with which he was familiar.

The Baron made us welcome in his lonely English outpost. It must have been a relief to see friendly faces. He seemed to have forgotten our first meeting or, perhaps, he had become more philosophical about our differences.

We left, the next day, for the battlefield. The Baron offered to send men with us but I declined as I was not sure we would return to the castle of Clun. I had a more circuitous route back to Chester planned. The battlefield, when we reached it, was a spectacle of horror. The English bodies lay where they had fallen although as carrion had feasted on them since the battle, they could have been Welsh for their features and garments were gnawed and ripped. My three scouts had remained hidden until we approached.

Owen shook his head, "A sorry sight it is and no mistake. They could have buried them."

Geraint looked angry, "They had their parts removed and put in their mouths. I am betting that it was the women who did that. A Welsh woman can be terrible cruel."

As much as I sympathised with the dead men, we had a job to do, "Did you find their trail?"

David of Welshpool nodded, "My dad could have found it and he was blind. The bulk of the army went to the south and west."

I heard a 'but' in his voice. "But?"

"The knights went north. They had no foot with them nor did they have wagons."

Alan and Edgar had joined me, "What are you thinking, lord?"
"That Glendower has gone north. He has gone home to hide."
"But, father, we burned his home at Glyndyfrdwy!"
"That was some time ago and he may have rebuilt it but he has another home less than forty miles from here at Sycharth. We try Sycharth first. Owen, does the trail head in that direction?" My Welshmen knew the land better than I did.

"Aye, lord, and I think you are right. Glyndyfrdwy was a finer home but Sycharth is a castle. If he has Edmund Mortimer that would be a good place to hold him."

"David and Geraint, follow the main army and let me know where they go. We will meet back at Chester."

We headed north and David was right; the trail was easy to see and to follow. They were not expecting pursuit. Animal and human dung marked their passage. It was clear to me that this was a column of mailed knights for where horses had left the road they had sunk into the ground. They were laden. It also became obvious that, although mounted, they had moved slowly. We were faster. We could have used a safer road which went through England but I wanted to ensure that we followed Glendower. If I had made a mistake and he was not with the knights then David and Geraint would bring us news of him. It was, however, a potentially dangerous action. We were heading for the heartland of Glendower's land and he would have with him the knights who would be the most loyal. For that reason, Alan rode ahead with Owen. He would be able to spot any danger and warn us.

We stopped just a mile and a half from the castle. Alan had ridden back to warn us that the castle was ahead. "We passed a stream up ahead and there is a heavily wooded area on both sides of the stream. It will be cosy but there are no houses close by and we can approach the castle without being seen."

"And where is Owen?"

"There is a village close by, Llansilyn. He has gone to buy food and ask questions."

"Good, then lead on."

It was not a river, in fact, it was barely a stream but the trees afforded good cover and we would only need to stay there one night. While my men made our camp, I went with Alan of the Woods towards the castle. It was an old-fashioned castle made of wood with a simple hall and a wooden palisade. We looked at it from the shelter of the trees by the road. Alan pointed out that the village lay on the far side of the castle.

"Were you seen as you rode north?"

"Probably, my lord, but I did not come back along the road. I took a circuitous route through fields."

It was a mistake. One armed rider might pass unnoticed but two would raise eyebrows. I said nothing to Alan. I should have been clearer in my instructions. Stephen the Tracker would have been a better choice for he knew how to disappear far better than any man I had ever known.

"No matter." I could hear noise from within the castle, even from a distance of over half a mile. There were horses within and many men. Smoke spiralled from ovens. If this was Glendower and his lords they would still be celebrating.

Alan had sharp ears, "Lord, I hear a horse."

The road bent around the castle and we saw Owen walking his horse down the road. As he neared the gate of the lower ward, I saw the gates open and men emerged. They stopped Owen and spoke to him. Had he alerted them or had they noticed that two riders rode north and only one came south? They seemed to speak for a long time. When I saw one of the guards laugh and clap Owen on the back, I breathed a sigh of relief.

We let him pass us and then mounted our horses and rode through the trees to intercept him at the road. He saw us and nudged his horse up the slope towards us.

"You had us worried, Owen."

He smiled, "They asked why two of us had ridden north and only one returned south. I told them that Alan was from Machynlleth and we had fallen out. I told them that I bought food and was returning to Newport and the family farm."

"Then why did they laugh?"

"I told them that my companion snored and his absence would be no loss."

"You were lucky."

"Aye, lord. Sorry, Captain."

"No matter, Owen, I should have allowed you to go on alone rather than riding before the castle. I was anxious to see if there was a village." Alan had obviously realised that I was disappointed in him.

I turned to Owen, "What did you learn?"

"That you were right, lord. Glendower is in the castle with his knights and with Edmund Mortimer."

"He is a prisoner?"

Owen shook his head, "If he is then he is the only prisoner I know who laughs and jokes with his captors. I saw him strolling with Welsh knights."

I smiled, "Then we have done what we were asked and can return to the King and the Prince."

"There is more, lord."

Owen was a reliable man and I nodded, "Go on."

"There are Breton horsemen and two French knights in the castle."

This was news indeed. The French were ever willing to foster discord in England and use it to increase their empire. They had done so with the Scots. Were they now using the Welsh?

"You have done well. We will return to the camp and eat. I think better with food in my belly."

Back in the camp all was well organised. Edgar and my men had fed and watered the horses and food was being prepared. I sat with Alan and Edgar while Harry brought me food. I told Edgar what I had learned. "This changes matters. We need to know numbers. It now becomes clear why Glendower headed back here. Mortimer is not a prisoner and the King is correct. The French involvement is worrying. Baron Fitzalan did not mention Frenchmen."

"To be fair, my lord, he was busy fighting for his life and might not have been able to differentiate." Edgar was a clever sergeant.

"Tomorrow I need to get as close to the castle as I can."

Harry said, "That is a risk, my lord."

"I know. Owen, Alan, is there another way to get to the village so that I could approach from the north?"

My captain of archers said, "I found a road which headed east and I found the river four hundred paces from it. That is a possibility."

"Then tomorrow we all ride up the river and I will walk into the village."

"Is that wise, you look like a lord!"

I laughed, "I know, Harry, but tomorrow I will not. We are close to the border with England and I will play a simpleton who is lost. You will all wait by the road and be ready to ride quickly if trouble comes."

"Lord, your son is right. You should not go alone. Two men stand a better chance than one."

I shook my head, "You attracted attention, Alan, when Owen returned alone. I will try to go when the road is busier. When you two went it was late afternoon. There may be wagons and the like. Knights require provender and wagons have to use this road."

The next morning, I took off my spurs and my sword. I kept a dagger in my belt. We dirtied my cloak and breeks in the mud of the river. None of us wore livery. I was not being foolhardy. I now had grey in my hair. I had not shaved and my stubble was also grey and made me look to be down on my luck. Older men drew less attention than younger ones. We headed up the stream. We walked in the centre which meant we left no tracks. I saw the rear of Sycharth for the stream bent to the east of the castle whilst the road turned to the west.

Alan stopped. "Here lord. There is a track which heads to the road. Follow the field boundary."

I nodded, "Give me time to reach the road and then walk the men and horses to hide close to the road." I was taking the chance I did because the stakes were so high. Glendower was elusive and slippery. If we could find him then that gave us an advantage.

I adopted a shamble and a stoop as I walked up the field boundary. I had the story I would use in my head. I had camped by the river and was seeking employment. I heard people moving towards the large village as I neared the road. There were wagons and therein lay my salvation. I waited until a wagon followed by two men had passed before I emerged and headed towards the village. I heard hooves behind me and a French voice shouted for us to beware. The two men who followed the wagon did not move. I assumed they did not understand and so I feigned ignorance. The riders shouldered their beasts into me and then the other two. I waved a hand but the two Welshmen were quite vociferous in their shouts.

"Foreigners!"

"Go back to France!" There was no love lost there. One turned to me. "Are you alright, old man?"

He spoke in Welsh but I gathered the gist from his expression and I nodded and then coughed as though I had an ailment. He said something to his friend which I did not understand. I could now see the edge of the village. The solicitous Welshman hurried to the back of the wagon and pulled an ale skin. He handed it to me so that I could drink.

I decided I could play dumb no longer and I took a chance, "Thank you, my friend."

He nodded, "English? I thought you were. What are you doing here? This is Wales you know?"

I nodded and pointed east, "I come from Kinnerley. My master was killed in the recent battle and I have no work. I thought there might be something here."

"Sorry about the job." He took back the skin. "You might have made a shrewd move. Owain Glyndŵr is on the rise. We have a wagon load of cheese and ham for him and his knights." He lowered his voice, "But he doesn't like the English. If you help us unload our wagon, I can give you some ham and a little cheese. You might hang around the village. Who knows, someone might like an old codger with a gammy leg like you."

This was better than I might have hoped and I nodded. "Food would be good and it is a start."

I saw, ahead of us, the castle. There appeared to be little scrutiny of those entering. A cart ahead of us was being hauled up the hardened path which led to the lower ward. When we reached the bottom, the friendly Welshman handed me a rope. "Here, pulling the wagon with us will get you ale too. The path is steeper than I expected."

The three of us tied our ropes to the wagon and walked up the ramp. The driver said something to the horses and cracked his whip over their heads. The three of us pulled and the wagon moved. I had to remember that I was supposed to be old and did not pull as hard as I might otherwise have done but we managed to reach the gate and the ground flattened out. A Welsh sentry

shouted something and pointed to our right. There was a long
wooden building and a stone built outdoor oven. I guessed it was
the kitchen. It was well away from the inner wall and the hall.
When the wagon stopped the driver began handing sacks of
cheeses and hams to us. I followed the other two into the wooden
kitchen. We just laid them on the table and returned for more. It
did not take the three of us long to empty it and the Welshman
appeared pleased, "You were more of a help than I thought. For
an old man, you are quite strong. You might get work here.
Come, we will sit in the wagon and eat."

Although I was desperate to escape, I knew it would look
suspicious if I left and so I ate and drank with them. It allowed me
to view the castle. It could easily be taken for it was made of
wood. I spied the stables and saw that there were many horses
grazing around it on the grass of the lower ward. The grazing
would not last long. There were men on the walls but not as many
as I had expected. However, from the upper ward, I could hear
much noise.

We had just about finished and were preparing to leave when I
saw a man I recognised, it was Edmund Mortimer. He was
chatting easily to a much older man and there were four other
knights with them. They were laughing and joking. He had, about
his waist, his sword. He did not look like he was a prisoner. The
friendly Welshman said, "And there he is, Wales' great hope,
Owain Glyndŵr." I now had confirmation of his presence. I kept
my face down as they rode past us but I was not noticed. They
rode out and headed south.

Once we had left the castle I said, "Thank you for the food
and ale. I will wait in the village to see what I can find."

"Good luck!"

They headed back out of the village. I would not be long
behind them. I heard the Welshmen in the village laughing and
saying how they would all be rich thanks to the Welsh lord who
had flouted England. These men might not take arms against
England but they would happily profit in its demise. I allowed
them a two hundred pace lead by pretending to go behind a wall
to make water and then walked after them. To any sentries on the
walls, it would not look odd. By the time I reached the track
which led to my men, the wagon had disappeared east. We would

be taking the road which led north at the crossroads. We would be heading for the Clwyd valley. My men were three hundred paces down the slope and hidden for they were dismounted. They looked relieved when they saw me, especially my son. I quickly changed into my riding gear and armed myself.

"Owen, take us home."

We rode up the track and, instead of riding to the crossroads, he led us across country to pick up the road when we were further away from the castle. My captains and Harry were keen to know what had happened. They would have to wait as we had plenty of danger ahead of us. We were alone and in Wales. The only English soldiers were safely ensconced inside their castles.

Part Two
The Road to Shrewsbury

Chapter 13

We only had twenty odd miles to go to reach Chester but they proved more dangerous than we had expected. We had ridden just five miles and were close to the border with England when trouble came. The border was a misnomer. It was an arbitrary line but there was something reassuring about it and, perhaps, that was why we relaxed a little. It was getting on for late afternoon when we neared the tiny hamlet of Y Galedryd which marked the border. It was a crossroads. The road turned north for Chester and Alan and Owen had turned and disappeared north as we entered the hamlet. We were just turning north when a column of Breton horsemen appeared from the east. They must have been raiding for I heard the noise of distressed animals. We were only saved by the fact that we wore our armour and we had quick reactions.

Edgar and I were the closest to them. As soon as they appeared, I drew my sword as did Edgar. Both of us had more experience than any other man in my company and we turned our horses to charge into them. We knew they were not English for all rode smaller horses than we did and they wore no mail, just a simple round helmet, in addition, they all carried a light spear. I had no idea of numbers when I swung my sword at the leading rider but I knew that offence was better than defence. Edgar and I caught the two leading riders by surprise. My sword tore across the Breton's chest and his arm. He tumbled or jumped from his horse. I could not tell. Edgar's war hammer drove into the other man's skull.

I heard Much Longbow shout, "Loose arrows!"

Harry urged his horse forward and he used his sword to slash at a Breton. His blade made the smaller horse flinch and the rider turned aside allowing my son to slash at his unprotected side. The blade came away bloody. A spear was hurled at my head. I wore no helmet; it was still on my cantle and I turned my shoulder. It struck the plate and mail protecting my arm. It was well thrown hitting the joint between plates and it broke the skin but there was no real wound to worry about. I spurred Hart and rode through the middle of them. Their spears were more dangerous when thrown. The closer we were to them the better. My men at arms and Harry had their swords out and were fighting for their lives. They were also fighting to protect me for I was deep in the centre of their column. Spears were thrust at me but they struck mail or plate. Their smaller horses meant that I was higher than they were and my sword struck down on arms and shoulders. When my archers' arrows fell on those further back it proved too much and the Bretons broke and headed south. That told me they were part of Glendower's army. They were running for his castle. It also meant that we would now be hunted.

As the last Breton fled, I shouted, "Secure the horses and put a Breton body on the back of one. We need evidence for the King."

Just then Alan of the Woods rode in, "How did we miss these?"

"It was not your fault. They came up the road after you had turned north. Now we need two of your archers as a rearguard. We are still close to Sycharth and Welsh knights might well fancy some sport. We will ride hard. We do not stop until we reach the Dee!"

Edgar had found a Breton who had died falling from his horse. We slung his body over his pony and led the other seven horses we had taken. I knew that the quicker thinking sergeants and archers would have taken coins and weapons from the dead but we did not have time for a thorough search. We galloped north as the sun began to dip in the west. In theory, there should have been no more enemies before us but the Bretons had surprised us and I stayed close to Owen and Alan of the Woods. I was lucky, Hart was a strong horse but I knew that some of the new men would be struggling. Their horses were not as good.

157

We had covered ten miles when I heard a shout from the rear, "My lord, Lol, son of Wilson says there are knights and they are chasing us."

I turned my head and shouted, "Tell them to close up. When they catch us, I would have us all together."

"Aye lord."

"Harry, you stay as close to me as you can. This is not the time for glory. We have news we need to deliver to the King and the Prince."

"Yes, my lord."

We passed the road to Wrecsam and still they closed with us. I could hear their hooves now but the twilight hid them from us. All sorts of ideas flashed through my mind. I thought to take a side turning and hide while they galloped past. I thought to find a bend and ambush them but the news we carried was so important that we had to reach Chester without any delay and that meant no tricks. In the end, they gave up as we rode across the crossroads between Buckley and Broughton. Perhaps they feared an ambush, I know not but Lol shouted, "They have stopped, lord. I can no longer hear their hooves."

We rode hard for another mile and then I slowed to a walk. There was little point in killing our animals for we had just ten miles to go. We would still be exhausted but we would deliver our news and then rest. I turned to Harry, "You did well, squire. That ride would have tested the mettle of many experienced riders."

He nodded and shifted uncomfortably in his saddle, "I am not sure that my body would agree with you, father!"

When the gates of Chester gaped open, I patted Hart, "You will rest for a week, my beauty! You have earned it!"

Neither the King nor his son were abed and were eager to know my news for I had arrived back sooner than they had expected. "Well, Strongstaff?"

The Prince went to the table and poured a goblet of wine, "Your Majesty, it is obvious that the Baron has ridden hard to get here and, from the blood spattered on his surcoat, he has had to fight. A few moments while he drinks some wine cannot hurt." He handed me the wine.

His father nodded, "It is a sad day, Strongstaff, when a man is reminded of his duties by his son. He is right but I am anxious to end this rebellion."

I drank all of the wine. I would have preferred ale as it would have quenched my thirst and the wine merely reminded me that I had not eaten since dawn. However, I could drive hunger from my thoughts, "We found Glendower and his knights. They were at Sycharth. I have men following his army but they went in a different direction."

The King's eyes lit up, "Then we have him. Sycharth is but a day of hard riding away. If he just has his knights then we can take him and end the rebellion."

"It is not just him, lord. There are French and Breton knights with him. The blood you see is Breton blood. We ran into them south of here and I brought a body back to be examined. I have to say that we were pursued by the knights from the castle and we only lost them close to Buckley."

The joy left his face and Prince Henry shook his head, "The French are ever ready to exploit threats to us. Were there many of them?"

"I counted a handful of knights and there were more than thirty Bretons but they are like fleas on a dog, Prince Henry, they will multiply."

The King nodded, "You have done well. We will speak again in the morning."

"I am not yet done, lord, there is more." Prince Henry poured some more wine for me and the King leaned forward in his chair. "I spoke with Fitzalan and he confirmed that Mortimer surrendered far too early in the battle. I saw Mortimer at Sycharth. He did not look like a prisoner to me. He and Glendower were riding with knights and he had a sword. I may be wrong but I do not believe he is Glendower's prisoner."

This time the King became more animated, "I knew it! You have done well, Strongstaff. I was right to withhold the ransom!"

I sipped the wine more slowly. My stomach rumbled and complained. It wanted food. I ventured a comment for it had troubled me on the ride north, "And that begs the question does it not, King Henry, what is Percy's involvement?"

"Aye, there's the rub. What are your thoughts, my son? Of late you seem to have seen that which was hidden in a fog to me."

"The Earl of Northumberland, Percy's father Henry, was partly responsible for giving us the throne. If he is against us then we are in trouble for his brother, Thomas, is Earl of Worcester and that city is the gateway to the west. We must tread carefully there. As for Hotspur? I agree with Sir William here; I think he seeks a crown. It may not be the crown of England but it is a goal of his." He poured himself a goblet of wine. "Perhaps we can play them at their own game. If the Earl of Northumberland wishes a crown why not tempt him with Scotland? It is closer to him than is London. You could make him Lord of the North and encourage him to strengthen the border. His son is a doughty fighter and the Scots are weak. With Dunbarre at his side, they could succeed."

The King shook his head, "That would make him a threat to us. King of the North? Would his eye not be drawn south?"

"You forget Mortimer. Mortimer may be Percy's brother in law but he is also the uncle of a potential claimant to the throne."

The King nodded, "I will think on this for we have not heard yet from the last of the scouts. When Sir William's men return then we will make a decision but I thank you both for your counsel. I know that you two are to be trusted." Almost as an afterthought, he said, "Did you lose any men, Strongstaff?"

I smiled, "No, Your Majesty, but thank you for your concern."

He laughed, "I know how you feel about them. Do you still have that fellow who risked his life in the snow for the boy?"

"Harold Four Fingers? Aye, he married Magda and the boy is now the squire of Sir Roger."

"You are like a family."

Prince Henry nodded, "I served with the family and they are a band of brothers. It is a model I seek to use. When I go to battle, I will surround myself with those whom I trust. They may be small in number but loyalty counts for more in battle than numbers."

I nodded, "You speak truly there, Prince Henry."

After a hurried few mouthfuls of bread and cheese I almost fell into my bed. Harry had prepared it and was eager to speak. I indulged him for he had acquitted himself well in the skirmish. I answered his questions honestly although I did not reveal the entire conversation. "Why does the King reward those who are his enemies? I do not understand it."

"So that he can take away what he has given when he is displeased. He did so with Conwy and Anglesey."

"But does that not make those men more likely to be enemies?"

My son had it aright but I tried to rationalize it, "He came to the throne with the help of the Percy brothers and he had to reward them, now those titles are a hostage to fortune. Now it is time for sleep. I am weary even if you are not."

As the candle was blown out, he said, "And it is the likes of us who pay the bill, eh father."

"Aye, son but keep those words for my ears only eh? I would not like to see you in the Tower for such comments. Prince Henry might understand them but King Henry would not!"

My two riders returned three days later. They looked weary and I think that they had broken their mounts. As soon as they entered the gates they were brought before King Henry and his son. As their lord, I was with them.

"We followed their trail, King Henry, to Machynlleth. There is a mighty army gathering there." David looked at me, "It is larger than the one we found when we raided, lord." I nodded and David looked again at the King, "There were French ships in the estuary. There were just three of them. We went into the town on foot and pretended to be seeking work as warriors. We were offered coin and places in the households of many lords. Men are flocking to Glendower's banner." He hesitated.

Prince Henry knew my sergeant at arms and he smiled, "Speak, David, for you will not be censured, that I can promise you."

David nodded, "Prince Henry, the people are angry. They do not like the laws which Parliament passed."

Those laws were contentious and had little to do with King Henry. They were draconian: Welshmen were barred from buying land in England, they could not hold any senior public office in Wales, they could not bear arms, either hold any castle nor defend any house, no Welsh child was to be educated or apprenticed to any trade, no Englishman could be convicted in any suit brought by a Welshman, Welshmen were to be severely penalised when

marrying an Englishwoman, any Englishman marrying a
Welshwoman was disenfranchised and all public assembly was
forbidden. Now the King saw the effect his Parliament had
created.

The Prince nodded and I saw the King reflecting on the
problem. The Prince said, "And the land through which you
passed to reach us, how lies it?"

He was emboldened by the words of the Prince and he was
honest, "Prince Henry we hold the castles all else lies in the hands
of the rebels. This is the first time we have spoken English since
we parted from Sir William."

The Prince took a purse of coins and handed it to David,
"Here is payment for the two of you. You have earned it, for now
we can see the picture more clearly. The fog has cleared has it
not, Your Majesty?"

The King roused himself and smiled, "Aye, you have and now
if you would leave my son and me, we need to have conference
about this matter. I will send for my senior lords and bishops."

As we left, I knew not what they could do. It was now
September. They could not begin a campaign before winter. The
vastness that was Wales would be protected by a blanket of snow
and ice. It would be Spring before they could muster an army and
Glendower would merely grow stronger. We went to the stables
to look at the two horses my scouts had ridden. They would need
the winter to recover. I spoke with the horse master. I was in a
privileged position for I was known to be close to the King and
his son. I procured two replacements for my men. Who knew
when we would need them again?

It was the seventeenth of the month when the rider from the
north rode in. He was from Sir George. Henry Percy had had a
great victory over the Scots at the Battle of Homildon Hill.
Douglas and five earls had been captured. Many hundreds of
Scots had been slain. The north was safe and perhaps my
pessimism was misplaced. Two days later I was summoned to the
King and his son. Sometimes a stone is thrown into a pond and
the ripples travel further than one can imagine. So it was that day.
The stone was the battle but the effect could not even be
imagined!

I was excluded from the discussions but the King, the Prince and his advisers were closeted together in the Great Hall. Nobles arrived each day. I was summoned after they had spent a day hidden in the Great Hall. This was not a private meeting. There were senior lords and bishops making it a formal court. The King sat on a throne and his son just behind him, flanking them were the senior lords and bishops. I knew them all and all knew me. I saw that the Earl of Stafford had been summoned as well as the Dukes of York, Surrey and Kent. This was partly due to the problems with the Welsh rebellion but I also suspected that the news of Hotspur's victory was on the agenda. I wondered at the great conclave. We had had a victory against the old enemy but this gathering seemed to have a hidden meaning.

"Sir William Strongstaff, let all present know that you are held in high esteem by ourselves and the crown. There is no knight in the realm who has shown himself to be braver or more loyal than you. It is for that reason that we entrust you to deliver this missive to our lords in the north." The Bishop of Chester stepped forward and handed me a parchment with the King's seal upon it. "You are to deliver this to Sir Henry Percy who has recently defeated the Scots. Although we are most pleased that the foul barbarians have been repulsed, we forbid our lords from asking for ransom without we know. The letter makes it clear, Sir William, that any such act would be considered an act of treason and would be punished accordingly."

I saw, in that moment, that the formal court was deliberate. All had been party to the letter but by speaking it aloud to me, it became public knowledge. Someone would tell Percy before I reached him. I wondered if I was to be the sacrificial goat for I knew that Henry Percy would live up to his name and he would not sit idly by and allow the greatest ransom since Richard the Lionheart's to go to a King who had done nothing to gain it. I had more questions than an inquisitive five-year-old but the setting precluded them. King Henry was a very clever man.

I bowed and said, "I will do all that I am bid and when I am done, Your Majesty?"

"Then you may return to your manor having served us well." He nodded and Prince Henry handed me a leather pouch. "Here is a reward for the service you have done us thus far. We will need you again, of that, I am in no doubt. And now we will retire to our chambers. This gathering is ended and you may all retire to your homes. I will now leave Chester and return to Northampton."

Thus dismissed, there would be little opportunity for the dukes and earls to discuss the events. Prince Henry bowed and stayed close by me. When we had space around us and could speak, I said, "Is this well done, Prince Henry?"

"Perhaps it is not well done but it is necessary. In this, I agree with my father. We need the coin from the ransom although I doubt that we will be given any but if Percy gets it then he will be rich enough to fund a second rebellion in the north. He is related to Mortimer. Your news was most disturbing, Sir William. When you speak with Percy do all that you can to rein him in. I would not have us fight the most powerful leader in the north. It would be a war which would tear apart this land. The French are already seeking to widen our divisions. Help to heal them, Sir William,"

I knew that I could be honest with Prince Hal and say that which would upset King Henry. "Am I a sacrifice, Prince? It is well known that Percy does not like me and that he has a temper. I could end up as a hostage."

He tapped the parchment, "This makes you a royal herald. To injure you would be treasonous."

He was right; a formal attack would be treasonous, but the miles from Warkworth to Weedon afforded many places for an ambush by men who might not wear a livery but would be acting under the orders of Hotspur.

"Then I will take my leave of you, Prince Henry."

"Sir William, come March I will need you and all of your knights for I intend to move against Glendower. You will fight under my banner and I will guarantee scutage."

I nodded, "You know we will be there."

"Aye, with or without the coin. You are a true knight and a model I try to emulate. I am still learning."

"That is true and you have a heavier burden upon your shoulders than a couple of manors. You have Wales and England to carry!"

He smiled, "Do not forget France and Normandy for I have not!"

164

It took two days to reach Weedon. I was not disobeying the King for the better road passed close by my home. The royal warrant meant we could stay at royal residences. I would avoid York and stay at Middleham which was closer to the northern road in any case. My men and Harry knew my mission and they were all intelligent enough to know the dangers.

Edgar said, "So we take these men and the rest with us, lord?"

"No, Captain; you and Alan will stay at Weedon. We go to war again in April and we need more men. I have coin from the King. I will take Harry, four sergeants and four archers only. Any more might constitute a threat to Sir Henry and I know that my presence will anger him enough as it is. Such a small number means it is a bodyguard only."

Edgar shook his head, "The men of Northumberland are both tricky and cunning, lord. They have to be to fight the Scots. I do not like it."

"Nor do I but it is a royal command and I will obey it."

My wife was also unhappy. "Husband you have been away from your family for so long of late. Our daughter is due to give birth any day. Can this not wait?"

I shook my head, "As much as I wish to see my first grandchild this is an instruction from the King. When this is done then I will be at home. You have me all winter!"

She gave me a sharp look, "Which means you will be gone again in spring!"

I would not lie and I nodded, "I fear so."

We left before dawn the next day. I slipped from my bed and dressed without waking my wife. Harry was already up. He now knew the import of what we did and was a more serious squire than when he had helped his brother Thomas. My four sergeants were in the stables with James the horse master. Geoffrey of Gisburn, Stephen of Morpeth, Richard son of Richard and Oliver the Bastard were all from the North. Indeed, Stephen of Morpeth had served the Percy family. My four archers were also experienced and all but Gurth were single: Simon the Traveller, Gurth Garthson, Harry Fletcher and Walter of Sheffield. We took one sumpter with spare arrows, cloaks and emergency food. We would be housed in castles but who knew what lay ahead for us?

Chapter 14

We called at Middleham, because Mary had written a letter to her mother which she asked us to deliver. We were treated well in all of the castles but the place we enjoyed our rest was Middleham where we were treated like family. After that, we knew we would be in Percy land. We crossed the Tees and headed up through Durham. The Palatinate was ruled by the Prince Bishop and as the Scots had raided his land, I thought that we should speak. Walter Skirlaw was a good man but he had to tread a fine line as he dared not offend the Percy family for they guarded his northern borders and he was a churchman. He had been Bishop of Coventry. I enjoyed speaking with him for he liked to build; he was a creative Prince Bishop and not a plotter. I knew that, in the past, many had been men who preferred to scheme. Bishop Skirlaw was not such a cleric. He had built bridges at Yarm and Bishop Auckland. He was not a warrior but what he did was for the Palatinate and I admired him for that.

He gave me information about Henry Percy which I did not know. "He is very popular in Chester, my lord. He has many friends there. Often riders come from Cheshire to speak to his lordship and they often stay here."

This was neither gossip nor tittle-tattle; the Bishop was giving me a message. The King had been at Chester when he had held his meeting. Who were the spies and did Percy already know of the King's decision? I had expected that someone would take him the news but I had hoped that I would reach him before that. My mission suddenly became even more dangerous. The next day we crossed the Tyne and headed for Warkworth. Once the castle had been so poorly built and defended that when William the Lion attacked it the garrison fled and the villagers were slaughtered. Henry Percy had turned it into a fortress upon which any attacker would bleed trying to assault it. A huge mound was surrounded on two sides by water and the design of the gatehouse and keep were spectacular. It marked the start of what Stephen of Morpeth called 'real Percy Country'. We had passed through Morpeth and felt the animosity of the people there for those, like us, who came from the south, but when we stopped at the tiny hamlet of Amble, we were keenly aware that we were not just unwelcome, we were despised. Word of the King's messenger had preceded us and the people of Northumberland regarded Henry Percy as a favoured son. We were close to his heartland and, as we were not his knights, we were regarded as enemies. We looked north to the castle.

"There it is, my lord, and as hard a place to take as the Tower, I would wager."

I nodded, "You may be right, Stephen, and it is fortunate that we don't have to take it merely enter it and then leave!"

That sobering thought silenced them all but Harry, "And if they do not allow us to leave?"

"Then we will be hostages and King Henry will have a war but the difference is he will have right on his side for we will be the victims."

Simon the Traveller sniffed, "It won't make much of a difference to us though, will it, my lord? We will still be prisoners."

I shook my head, "No, just Harry and I. I am sorry Simon but you have no worth to Lord Percy. He will let you go and you will ride and tell Lady Eleanor and my son that we are taken."

I had said the words to reassure them but they had the opposite effect. They became angry, swearing that they would die rather than let me be taken.

"Listen to me, even if I am taken prisoner I will come to no harm. I am a pawn which would be captured by the enemy. If I am incarcerated you will do as I command and return to my home with the news. Do you understand?"

"Aye, lord."

"And when you are in the castle, smile but keep your ears open. Do not be drawn into arguments for I know the men of the north will try to provoke you into a fight. Do not entertain them.

We need to know as much about these people as we can, for one day we may have to fight them."

We rode the last mile to the increasingly impressive castle. Its design meant that it rose higher and higher before your eyes as you approached. I knew from the reception we had received in Morpeth and Amble that they knew we were coming. Perhaps they had known from the moment we had left Chester. It mattered not. We crossed over the drawbridge and under the barbican. We were not stopped and that confirmed my belief that we were expected.

Once inside a young knight greeted me, "Sir William, if you and your squire would come with me, Sir Henry is anxious to speak with you."

"And my men and animals?"

There were two pages with him, "Ralph and William will take them to their quarters. They are next to the stables in the outer ward."

I nodded to my men, "You will be well looked after."

Stephen of Morpeth said, "And we will be ready, my lord, whenever you need us!"

The knight must have recognised his accent for, as we headed towards the Great Tower he said, "You have local men who serve you, my lord?"

"I have men from all over England and Wales. All of my men are good men." I think I had him worried by my words. Was I suggesting that I had men close by or that my men might take action if I was threatened? I had brought a very few men and that might make them suspect me; I had not thought of that. I meant neither but confusion amongst my hosts could only help me. I had no doubt that Henry Percy would question his knight before he spoke with me. We climbed the steps to the porter's lodge and thence up a narrow stairway to the Great Hall. As we climbed, I pictured myself fighting my way in and I knew it would not be easy. At the top of the stairs, we entered a lobby. There were two chairs and a table. A couple of servants waited.

"If you and your squire would wait here, my lord, I will tell Sir Henry that you are here."

We sat and I winked at Harry to put him at his ease. The servants poured us a goblet of wine each, handed them to us and then stepped back. Both looked to be old soldiers. I would take nothing for granted. These were Percy's men and had not been chosen for their skills in pouring wine; they were there to watch us and if they had to, stop us from leaving. As I had predicted we were kept a while. The knight was being questioned. Hotspur would put on a face to greet me and I doubted that I would see him lose his temper. He was still Hotspur but he was now older and I could see that he was within touching distance of power. It was not yet a crown but it was a throne, the throne of the north. With his arch-rival in these lands, Douglas, in his hands and Sir George as his ally, he ruled the land from coast to coast. He ruled from the Firth and the Forth in the north to the Tyne and the Eden to the south. It was a vast land.

We were summoned and I nodded, reassuringly to Harry. We had spoken, on the road north, of the attitude he should adopt. He knew what he had to do. The Great Hall was not as large as some I had known. I saw Sir Henry and his household knights. They ranged from young men, like himself, to knights like me with grey in their beards and hair. There was no Sir George; he must have returned to Dunbarre. I also saw Lord Douglas. He looked, surprisingly, relatively happy. Was this another Mortimer situation?

"Welcome, Baron William. I believe that you have something for me?"

I now knew that there were spies in Chester. The letter had been beneath my cloak. Whilst the people of Morpeth and Amble knew we were English and from the court of King Henry, none knew that I carried a letter. I stored that useful information in my head and I took out the parchment, "King Henry sends you his greetings, Sir Henry, and his thanks for keeping his borders safe."

Sir Henry nodded and broke the seal. He scanned the parchment. That he knew the contents was clearly obvious when he spoke before he could have read every word. "So, the King wishes to steal the money from the ransom I am due for having defeated the Scots in battle?"

"I believe he wishes to be involved in the negotiation, my lord, and as such the King seeks that which he is due."

"And you are to negotiate for him?"

I shook my head, "The King will be in Northampton and if you rode there, with me, then all discord could be ended." I did not think for one moment that he would agree but Prince Henry had asked me to do all in my power to bring Sir Henry back into the fold. I knew it was a quest which was doomed to failure.

He stood and threw the parchment to the floor. It was a deliberate act which he wished me to see. He was telling me that he cared not for the King's commands. He stood before me and tried to intimidate me. He was a powerful warrior and most men were smaller than he was. I was not and I looked back into his eyes. I would not fight with him but my eyes let him know that I was not afraid of him either. As he spoke, he used his right hand to tap the fingers of his left, "First, he refuses to ransom my brother in law, Mortimer. Then he fails to negotiate a peace with Glendower. He promotes a child to rule Wales and favours those who have raided me. He does not pay me for my defence of his land nor the prosecution of the siege at Conwy and now, when I have defeated a brave and noble earl on the battlefield while he squatted like a toad in Chester, he seeks to profit from my victory! Has the King lost all of his senses? Has the crown made reason depart his body? I reject his demands! He is being a tyrant!"

I nodded, "My lord, will you put this answer in writing?"

My calm and reasonable voice surprised him, "Why should I? You are his lickspittle and you can bear the message to him."

I smiled, "Then I need to be clear about the exact wording of the message. The King forbids you to ransom Lord Douglas and the other prisoners without his permission. Do you intend to seek ransom for them?"

I saw his eyes flicker towards Sir Archibald. His answer was evasive, "I have not yet asked for ransom, however, when I do, then the ransom will be for me and my men for we earned it through force of arms."

I nodded, "So I will tell my King, the King of England and your liege lord, that you refuse to obey his lawful command but that, as you have not yet asked for ransom, you have not stepped on the rocky road to rebellion."

I had chosen my words carefully. I was buying the King time as he needed to be able to raise money with which to fight

England's enemies. I sensed that Henry Percy was waiting for a better reason to announce his total opposition to royal authority. His answer confirmed my deductions.

"You are a clever man for one dragged up by camp followers." He thought to insult me but I did not rise to the bait. "That is the message you may deliver to King Henry." I nodded. "It is a pity that we never met in the lists, my lord. I have heard that you are a great warrior and served England since the time of the Black Prince. As the greatest knight of my age, I should have liked to test my mettle against you in your prime. Now you are past your prime it would be no contest."

Once more he was insulting me and hoping that I would react. I smiled, "Oh, I still use my sword and have yet to be bested, my lord, but I have never bothered with the lists or tourneys. To me, fighting has always been about winning the fight, anyway I can. The only way we would have fought would have been had you opposed the King of England. The oath I swore, all those years ago, was to protect the King of England, whoever he was and I still keep my oath." My eyes told him that I would fight him despite his prowess.

He nodded, "The King does not deserve such a brave knight who enters the den of the lion and beards him. We will entertain you this night. You leave for Northampton on the morrow?"

"Aye, my lord."

"It is a dangerous road. My men will escort you to the borders of my land. I would not have any harm come to you or your message whilst you are within Northumberland's borders." He was giving me a message. Once I left his land, I was fair game. I had no doubt that his killers were already heading south to waylay me. That was why he had not committed the message to parchment.

Harry and I were taken back to the outer ward. We had a chamber in the Carrickfergus Tower. It was close to the wooden hall my men were using. We passed them and I nodded to them. Harry made to speak as the door was closed but I shook my head and put my finger to my lips. I spoke loud enough for the men who had escorted us to be able to hear, "That was more cordial than I expected. Perhaps Sir Henry is becoming wiser and less hot-headed now that he is older."

Harry was quick-witted and he nodded as he poured water from the jug into the bowl. "Aye, he seemed reasonable."

I kept my voice loud so that the listeners could hear, "We will ride hard tomorrow. First Durham and thence to York. We can change horses in York. The King will be anxious to receive our news."

The grin on Harry's face told me that he knew what we were doing. I would no more visit Archbishop Scrope in York than I would lie down in a bed of vipers! As we ate that evening, I was aware that orders had been given. Sir Henry's household were playing a part to lull me and make me think that all was well. They were pleasant and the conversation was light. Despite their efforts, I learned much. The King's letter, the contents of which were already known to Hotspur, had driven Douglas and Henry Percy closer together. I had suspicions about Percy and Glendower. Was he now lying in bed with another of England's enemies? The knight did appear to have a genuine interest in the Black Prince as he questioned me closely. His questions showed that he had studied the Prince. The man who had defeated the French with knights was a legend and Henry Percy sought to be a legend. It became obvious that he wished to win a great battle like the battle of Crécy or Poitiers, not against Scots but against serried ranks of heavily armoured knights. I answered his questions honestly for there was nothing to be gained by lying.

As we left, to be escorted back to our chamber, he clasped my arm, "I can see that you are a brave man and, I think, an honest one. We have had our differences but I can see now that you have a true heart. It is a pity that you now follow such a venal king."

I nodded, "Aye, lord, for we fell out when I supported the former King and this, as you call him, venal king, was put on the throne by you and your father. It just proves that we should be careful what we wish for."

The moment of reconciliation was gone. I had angered him and I regretted my words immediately. I should have nodded and smiled. I should have continued to play a part. He did not like to be reminded of his actions. "Good night, Sir William. I shall not see you again. Have a safe journey!"

As the door closed on our chamber I said to Harry, who had served me all night and heard all that had been spoken, "Well, we have an interesting journey ahead. I am glad we brought our mail!"

The escort south was the young knight who had greeted me and ten men at arms. They were not a threat; they were the surety that, when we were attacked it would not be on the land of the Percy family. I already had an idea where the attack would take place but I kept that to myself. The young knight, Sir Edward Blakemore, was a pleasant companion. His family came from Whitley Bay on the coast and he was the one, from the family, who had chosen a martial future.

He had taken part in the raids of the previous year and the battle of Homildon Hill but he, like Henry Percy, was keen to know of wars and battles beyond our shore. I think he was a frustrated crusader. All thoughts of reclaiming Jerusalem had ended despite the Popes who still urged knights to throw their lives away in a useless and flawed gesture.

"You must be assured of a place in heaven, Sir William, for you have fought the heretic Cathars and the Lithuanians."

I shook my head, "I did not fight in the Cathar wars and as for the Lithuanians? They have their own beliefs and live far away. One of those who was a so-called barbarian now lives with us and has married one of my sergeants."

He looked disappointed, "I thought there would have been glory in such a war."

"The men we fought, by and large, were ill-armed and without mail yet they fought and died for their families. There was neither honour nor glory in that war."

I could tell that I had disappointed him, "Then where is the glory?"

I turned to look at him. He reminded me of Thomas and Richard. He was young and he had ideals. The difference was that Thomas and Richard had both seen treachery and falsehood in knights. Sir Edward had not, "You know my story?" He nodded. "Then know that I learned war through men like your sergeants. I fought for pay and for booty. Knights do the same except that they call it ransom. I learned that if any of our company was captured then they would not be ransomed and the best that they could hope for was imprisonment. Death was a more likely outcome. When you fought the Scots, the ones you killed were men such as that. They were men who had little in their lives save the comradeship of arms and when they died, their families, if they had any, would be left without any means of support. Is that glorious?"

He was silent for a while and then said to Harry, "Your father does not paint a pretty picture of knighthood, Master Henry."

My son nodded, "Aye my lord, but it is a truthful one."

We parted with our escort at the bridge over the Tyne close to the New Castle. I knew, from his words and his attitude that the young knight knew nothing of the ambush which had been laid. "Farewell, Sir William. You have given me food for thought and I am honoured that you were so honest with me. Not all those who are my superiors do the same. I hope we meet again under more pleasant circumstances."

"As do I."

We crossed the bridge by the Gates' Head and took the road south. I waited until we had cleared the ridge of the Tyne Valley and dropped towards Durham before I spoke to my men. "Our foes mean to ambush us. My guess is that it will be in York or after York."

Harry said, "But we will not be travelling to York!"

"I know, for I laid a false trail but Percy has fallen out with the Earl of Westmoreland, despite the fact that they are related by marriage. He will try to implicate the Neville family in our deaths. We ride first to Durham. I need to speak with the Bishop and apprise him of the situation. Then we ride hard for Middleham. I will speak to Sir William. He can pass a message to his uncle. We will be vigilant all the way home but once we have passed Middleham then we travel as though we are creeping around Warkworth Castle in the depths of night. Archers, once we are south of Middleham then you keep your bows strung. Better a wasted string than a dead man."

They chorused, "Aye lord."

I knew they had taken strings from the Welsh we had slain when we had campaigned. There was an irony in the fact that we would be using the strings taken from rebels to slay potential rebels.

I gave the Bishop enough information to prepare him for a potential rebellion in the spring. He must have realised my danger for he offered me an escort south to the Tees. I declined for I did not wish to alert the Percy family to the fact that the Bishop was an ally of the King. We were nearing the bridge at Piercebridge when Simon the Traveller said, "Lord we are followed."

I nodded, "We were picked up as we left Durham. There are two of them and they are good."

Simon laughed, "Why am I not surprised that our lord is as good a tracker as Stephen the Tracker."

"Let us say I learned to acquire such senses when I was barely able to walk. They have kept me alive. When we have crossed the Tees, I want the four of you to ambush them where the road divides. I want them to think that we take the York road."

"If we ambush them then they will be dead."

"I think that Percy has sent his best men. Your ambush may hurt them but I do not think that it will end the threat. I just want them confused and to lose us, albeit briefly."

Oliver the Bastard nodded, "Aye lord, for once we are south of York there is but one road home and that will be where they spring the real ambush."

The road rose after Piercebridge and twisted through trees. It was Roman but they had had to cope with a steep ascent and the road twisted and turned. As we reached a bend where we would be unseen, I waved to my archers and they disappeared. We clip-clopped south towards the fork in the road. I was relying upon the skill of my archers and I was justified. We reached the crossroads and waited. It was some half an hour later that I heard hooves. I turned when I saw them riding down the road. They had a horse with a body slung over its back.

Simon reined in, "You were right, lord, they were good and there were three of them. One has an arrow in his leg and the other will be thanking his weaponsmith for the arrow was stopped by his mail. We recovered the body and the horse."

I nodded. "Ride down the York Road and bury his body a mile down that thoroughfare. Make the grave easy to see and then join us at Middleham. You can come across the fields and through the woods. I am counting on the fact that if they find the body then they will assume that we carried on to York."

We separated. The road to Richmond and Middleham undulated, twisted and turned. It was easy for us to see if we were followed. I had a man at arms wait at each bend to watch for those pursuing us and when a suitable time had elapsed, he rejoined us. It slowed us down but it kept us secure and we did not end up with a crick in the neck. It was late when we rode into the farm. Our archers were already there and enjoying Mary's ale.

"We were not followed, lord. Your ruse may have worked."

"And that merely buys us time. Mistress Mary, I will go to the castle to speak with Sir William. Harry and I will not be long."

"The food will be ready when you return, my lord. I have made a rabbit pie!"

We walked to the castle. It was not far and Hart had done me great service already. I was recognised and admitted, "This is late for you to call, Baron William. Is there trouble?"

"If I could speak with you in private?"

"Of course."

Once we were in a small room which acted as a guard chamber for the Great Hall and with our squires guarding the door, I told him of my mission. "Your uncle will know of the King's letter. All of the land must know it now but he will not know my suspicions that Hotspur will act in collusion with Douglas and, perhaps, even Glendower. As Sir George Dunbarre is Douglas' enemy then that means any attack or danger from the north will come through Westmoreland."

"Do you think it is likely?"

"Not soon, for winter will be upon us and the battle that was fought took place at the end of September. Men and horses will need to recover but, come the new grass, I would advise your uncle to be alert." I spread my hands, "I am just a humble knight and my advice can be ignored. I do this for the kindnesses you have shown Mistress Mary and for your uncle's loyalty to the King."

"And that is reciprocated. Will you be safe?"

I laughed, "I doubt it but I am prepared and any who wishes me harm will have to get up early in the morning to do so."

Although we had arrived at the farm late, we left before dawn. I wished to steal a march on the men who would attack us. They would search York for us. Archbishop Scrope would be complicit in that search and then they would take the road south. I wanted them on the wrong foot and following rather than waiting for us.

Our first stop was Wetherby. It had been a Templar manor but a raid by the Scots in the wake of the battle of Bannockburn had left the town devastated. There was an inn and we stayed there. Many Tyne men had joined the Scots after Bannockburn and the residents were suspicious of any who had a northern accent. It was one reason why I chose the town as a place to rest. The landlord confirmed that we were the first visitors for some time. We slept well.

The danger would come after Doncaster where the York Road met the road from the north. We reached Doncaster after dark. I had hoped to reach it in daylight and spy out any enemies but our horses had gone as far as they could. We stayed, not in the castle but at an inn. After unstringing the archers' bows and seeing to the horses we dined together. The unusual occurrence that a lord would eat with common warriors raised eyebrows. I did not mind such curiosity. However, that attention also brought us intelligence. Tom Davison had been a sword for hire. I had come across him when I was a gentleman with just Stoney Stratford to my name. He had fought under the banner of the Constable of Lincoln and was a King's man. He had been lamed in one of the battles fought for King Richard and he recognised me.

He waited until the inn was filled to capacity and we were finishing our meal before he sidled over to us. He leaned over, "Sir William, do you remember me, Tom Davison?"

I smiled and wondered if he sought an ale from an old comrade. "Aye, Tom, I do. You are faring well?"

He nodded, "My lord, might I have a word in your ear?"

He sounded serious, "Of course. Harry, go and buy Tom an ale and give him your seat."

Tom sat next to me, "Lord, there were men in town this day and they were seeking the Baron of Weedon. They said he travelled with nine men. None had seen you and so they left."

"How many were there?"

"I saw four but there were others for when I reached my home, my son, who knows that I served with you, described other men asking for you at the bakery where he works. When I heard that you had ridden through the gates, I came to speak with you and warn you."

"And for that I thank you. Are they still in the town?"

"If they are then they are stuck here for the gates are closed now and none will be allowed in or out until daylight."

The ale arrived. "Stephen, take the archers and see if you can find these men. Seek their horses."

"Why do they seek you, lord?"

"Let us say, Tom, that I am still on the King's business and these men are the King's enemies." I took five silver pennies and slid them across the table to him.

"No, lord, I could not take them for you are on the King's service."

"Take them or I will be offended."

He stayed with us until my archers returned. "They have left, lord. There were ten of them and they took the road south."

I nodded, "They know that we have not reached here. They will seek to ambush us further south. Tom, where would you ambush riders on the road?"

He drank his ale and considered my question, "A few miles south of here is Old Edlington. It is a handful of houses. After you leave the village the road climbs and enters a wood. Many men walk their horses up the slope for it is steep. After that there are many other places where you can be ambushed for the forest becomes increasingly close to the road but that is the first place of danger and they would wait there."

"Then we prepare for an ambush there!"

Chapter 15

Knowing the site of the ambush and thwarting it were two entirely different matters. We rose and ate well, leaving later in the day. There was a temptation to use the road when it was busy with other travellers upon it but I decided against that they were innocent people and did not deserve to be embroiled in our problems. I also decided against dividing our forces. I needed all of us to be together. We still passed travellers heading north and passed others who were heading south but the main traffic had already used the road by the time we were upon it. The men who would be ambushing us would have to be quick because it was a busy road and they would not wish to be observed. If we were quicker, we would win.

Simon the Traveller took charge of the archers, "We use bodkins; one of the bastards escaped because he had mail!"

Stephen of Morpeth had organised the four sergeants so that he rode next to me, Richard son of Richard next to Harry and the other two had the two spare horses next to them. As we neared the village, my archers each nocked an arrow. Loosing from the back of a horse was never accurate and the bows in their hands would tell an ambusher that we were wary, but my archers would be our first response and any time they might buy for us could make the difference. The six of us rode with swords drawn.

We reached Old Edlington shortly after noon when the villagers were going about their business. They looked up in surprise at the armed men riding through. One greybeard saw our swords and said, "Get the bairns, indoors!" He must have been the head man for all obeyed. They would await the sounds of combat. If none came then they would emerge. Places like Old Edlington were filled with cautious men!

I saw the spot Tom had told us of just up the road. It was a perfect place for an ambush with cover on both sides of the road and a slope which began gently and then became steeper as it twisted and turned. We had taken it steadily since Doncaster and our horses were not yet tired and I decided we would ride up. I sought signs of men in the woods. These attackers would be good but there were signs to look for. Simon had told me that they wore mail. I looked for reflections from metal in the greens and browns of the woods. The men were good but my eyes were still sharp and something glinted four hundred paces ahead.

Harry Fletcher said, "Have you seen it, lord?"

"Aye, I have. Simon, be ready!"

I spurred Hart a little for when the action began the sooner I could reach those trying to harm us the better were the chances of our survival and I did not wish to move Hart from a standing start. My archers won the battle of being the first to draw their bows. Two of the ambushers were hit but the waiting warriors also had crossbows and a bolt slammed into Gurth Garthson's leg, pinning it to his saddle. I was already peeling off to the left to hit those in the woods there. Stephen of Morpeth rode right. A bolt smashed into my chest. My plate held although it was dented and the bolt hurt. That told me how close the crossbowman was to me. In fighting such as this you needed quick reactions and hesitation could kill. I knew that all before me were enemies and when I saw flesh I swung. A spear hit the plate on my leg and slid up. Potentially it might have hurt me but my blind swing had hacked across the man's face. He dropped his spear and held his hands to his damaged face.

I heard shouts and cries as my archers duelled with theirs and I urged Hart on. Two warriors stepped out with axes as I heard a scream from behind as Harry slew the half-blinded man. I slowed my horse for I needed help to take on two axemen. Hart had no mail, not even a caparison. It was Oliver the Bastard who forced his horse next to mine. The two axemen shouted to someone and I saw two men running towards us. They had obviously had a longer line of men to ambush us and we had set it off prematurely. Suddenly one of the axemen fell with a bodkin tipped arrow sticking from his chest. As the second swung his axe at me Oliver the Bastard hacked off the man's arm and I jumped the body of the man slain by the arrow. The two men who had been summoned were now at a disadvantage. They were running and they were not steady. My horse would reach them quicker than they anticipated. One thrust his spear at my left side. Fearful that the spearhead might catch Hart, I jinked the reins to the left and the spear slid down Hart's right side and struck my leg. I ignored the pain as I leaned forward and slid my sword into the man's throat. Harry made his horse rear as the second spearman tried to stick his spear in Hart's side. The attacker's head was smashed open.

I looked around for more danger. There was none for any survivors had fled.

"Is anyone hurt?"

"Gurth has a bad wound to the leg, lord. I am dealing with him." That upset me for the only married man I had brought had been Gurth. He knew the north well and that was why I had chosen him. That we had not needed that knowledge now came back to haunt me.

Stephen of Morpeth appeared from the other side. "There are four dead on the other side of the road, lord. I think seven of them escaped."

I nodded, "Thank you, Oliver, that was a timely blow. You had better see to the man."

"He is dead, lord. He has bled to death."

I saw that the man had tried to staunch the bleeding and failed. "We had better search the bodies. The King will want evidence of who has sent them."

"Do we bury them, father?"

I shook my head, "We need to put as much space between us and the north as we can. The survivors may go to York and we know that the Archbishop is an ally of the Percy family. Put them in the ditches by the side of the road."

The bolt had nicked Gurth's bone. He would walk with a limp for the rest of his life and his recovery would be slow but he would be able to draw a bow. In the time it took to tend to his wound we had found all that the men had. The coins told us nothing except that there were two French coins and five Welsh ones amongst them. What was more telling were the three adornments we found on the horses. They were the Percy lion.

They were evidence enough of Percy's involvement. We had three more horses as booty and we hurried south. We rode hard and reached Nottingham which was a royal castle. My warrant gained us chambers and a healer for Gurth. The Constable was keen to know what had caused the wound. Although it was a royal castle, as we had discovered at Chester, that did not mean there were not spies there. I told him that we had been ambushed by bandits.

"In the present clime of rebellion and unrest, my lord, I would be more likely to believe that they were sent by the King's enemies. You are known to be close to the King and all the land knew that you had been sent on an errand dear to his heart." The very public announcement of my mission had almost cost us our lives.

We rode hard the next day and reached Weedon after dark. Poor Gurth was in a bad way and I felt guilty for having forced the ride upon him. My wife and my daughter were pleased to see us. Harry was still young and his mother feared for him. I saw her examining him for wounds.

I smiled, "Only Gurth was wounded and it will heal. We were lucky for we were attacked but your son is a warrior. I did not worry about him!"

I saw the pride in my son's eyes. "And do we ride to Northampton tomorrow, father?"

"We do. It will mean I can discharge my duty to the King and come back to the bosom of my family!"

As I lay in bed with my wife, she asked me about the journey. "You were in danger the whole time, were you not?"

I would not lie to her and I said, "For most of the journey home, aye."

"The King is wrong to put you in such danger."

"Some would argue that he is the King and can do no wrong."

She laughed, "And you of all people know that is not true. You served poor King Richard and saw his flaws and weaknesses." I said nothing. "Will there be war?"

"I fear so."

"And that means that Richard, Thomas and Harry will be in danger."

"They are warriors."

"I know but for me, I would that you try to keep them out of it."

"I will try but Richard and Thomas are the King's men and if he calls them to arms then they cannot refuse."

"And you will ride to the aid of Prince Henry in Spring."

"I will for he asked me to go and, to be truthful, wife, I see hope for England when his hands are on the reins of the realm. His father plots too much!"

She snorted, "That I know and he sees you as a chess piece! You are the knight he uses to dazzle his enemies. I know enough of the game to warn you that you may be the knight sacrifice."

"I will try to avoid that. When I return from Northampton, I will have a better idea of my position. I hope that the King will have no need of me for some time."

I used my best mount, Hawk, and dressed well for the visit. I took only Harry but my wife had sent me with a list of things she needed. This year we would not have a ceremony of knighthood and we could enjoy Christmas. She sent me for spices and aqua vitae. Thomas and Mary would share our celebration and my wife intended it to be joyful. She also sent me to buy some lace for Alice's child would be born in the next days and once she knew the sex, she would have a garment made for the christening.

We arrived early but the King was out hunting. I used his absence to buy that which I needed. He did not return until after noon. By then I was waiting in the antechamber to the Great Hall. "Had I known you had returned I would have cut short the hunt! What news?"

I gestured to the Great Hall, "Perhaps, King Henry, we could speak in there. The fire is warming and this may take some time."

"I am duly chastised. You are right." We went inside where he sat and then waved me to a seat. He had advisers and lords with him but an imperious wave of his arm moved them out of earshot. "Tell me all. Begin with his reaction."

"I expected more anger but I think he was calm because he had already heard the news. There is a spy in Chester."

His face screwed up in irritation rather than anger, "I should have known. They were always Richard's men. What were his exact words for I see you come without parchment?"

"He would not commit to writing. Let me think." I closed my eyes so that I could hear them again, "*I have not yet asked for ransom, however, when I do, then the ransom will be for me and my men for we earned it through force of arms.*"

"He is being clever. He does not disobey me nor does he obey me, but I can see from your face that there is more."

"It seemed to me, King Henry, that Earl Douglas was content to be in Warkworth. He might not have been as easy as Mortimer with Glendower but he did not seem to me like a beaten man."

"Then this is a conspiracy. They think to trap us between two stones; Wales and Scotland. And now the French are involved, I am surrounded by enemies." He stared at the fire and then suddenly turned, his hawk-like eyes fixed on me. "He let you go?"

"He sent men to kill us, twice."

The King laughed so loudly that the lords all turned to stare at him. "I knew you were the right man to send." I thought it a little cold. It suggested that he expected me to die. He must have realised that. "I am sorry, Strongstaff, but I knew that you had enough men to escape any trap he set."

"I took but eight men and a squire, Your Majesty."

He looked genuinely shocked, "Then I am sorry. I assumed you would take all of your men."

"I did not go to start a war, Your Majesty, unless that was your intention."

He shifted uncomfortably, "No, of course not. Was there more?"

"He laid the trap so that the blame would be at the doorstep of the Earl of Westmoreland."

"You have proof it was Percy's men?"

I took out the three pieces of horse furniture. "These were on their horses and they had French and Welsh coins in their purses. It is not conclusive but…"

"You are right. So, I need to do something to drive a wedge between the Percy family and the Douglas clan."

"They seemed very close, Your Majesty."

"Not the son, the hothead. He is lost to us now. It is just the manner of his death which is to be decided, no I speak of his father the Earl. I have a mind to give him the lands of Douglas in Scotland."

"Are they yours to give, King Henry?

"Enough of them are and the simple act will drive a wedge between them. Keep this to yourself Strongstaff. I am thinking aloud and I may not do this yet." I nodded. "I value your opinion. You knew more than I did in Lithuania. How do you see this situation?"

"I think Your Majesty has it aright. There is a conspiracy. There is too much coincidence here for it to be other. The question is the timing. This seems to me like the time Simon de Montfort and his son had two armies and thought to crush Prince Edward."

He leaned forward, eagerly, "Aye and the Prince turned the tables on them defeating first one and then the other." He leaned back again and I saw him planning and plotting. I said nothing. He turned to me after a while and said, "My son has asked for you to go to him in March." I nodded, "Just take your men. I would have your knights await my pleasure for I will use Northampton as my base. My son will be bait but I am neither callous nor heartless. I know with that defender of kings at his side, you, Strongstaff, he will not come to harm. It has taken me a long time to realise this but I know it now. When this is all over and England is at peace then I will reward you properly. I have not done so yet but you deserve more."

"You need not, King Henry, for everything I do is for England and its King. I have done it my whole life and I cannot change now."

"And that is why I will reward you for you do not ask when others do less and demand! Enjoy the time with your family!"

Christmas was joyous. I had my first grandson, William, for he was born while I spoke with the King. Sir Richard and Alice joined Thomas and Mary at my home. I had not had many Christmas celebrations but this one made me wish to enjoy such a one every year. It was perfect. My children were all at home and I was accorded honour, love and laughter. What more could a man wish for? I had something I had never had while growing up. I had a family. My extended family, my men at arms and archers also enjoyed the celebration. My wife had an old cow butchered and we feasted as we had never feasted before. The twelve days of Christmas were celebrated in every way possible. When it was over and my daughter, grandson and Sir Richard returned home, I felt an emptiness inside. Of course, it was soon replaced with anticipation for Mary was also with child. I would have a second grandchild! God was smiling on me.

We also received news, when Sir Richard came, that Sir Edmund Mortimer had shown his true colours. He had joined the rebels of Wales and married Glendower's daughter. It had come as a surprise to Sir Richard and his father but not to me. The battle where he had surrendered had been part of a clever plot. King Henry and his son had been proved right.

It was January when God ceased to be so benign. He sent me an ailment which brought me close to death. Had I been abroad I might have suspected poison. At first, I brought forth the food I had eaten the night before and that was replaced by shaking and shivering. I grew hot and feverous. My wife put me to bed and watched me herself. She waited two days to see if I would improve but I did not. I spent more time asleep than awake and that sleep was troubled. I saw the faces of all those I had killed in battle. Worse, I watched those I had loved die before my eyes again. Then I had a dream of a battle so terrible that I had never seen the like before. I saw the Prince, wounded and many men surrounding the King and hacking at him. I woke in the dark shivering. A hand stroked my head and I fell into a troubled sleep once more.

On one of the occasions I woke I saw, above me, the doctor from Northampton Castle. In my delirious state, I wondered if he had come to tend my wounds as he had often tended the wounds of my men. Then I realised that I could not hear his words, nor those of my tearful wife who clutched at his arm. Was I dying? I saw no priest and then thought that this was all a dream. The next I knew I was cold and clammy but my head felt as though men were hammering with war hammers on my helmet. I found I could barely breathe. It was as though a sea was washing over me and then all went black. I woke and all was dark but I knew, somehow, that I had not left my bedchamber. I tried to move my arms and move the bed covers but I had no strength in them. I tried to sit up and I did not have the strength but I did hear a voice. It was Harry's.

"Mother, he stirs, I will fetch a light."

I felt a warm hand on my hand, "Lord, but he is still cold!"

The room was bathed in light as the candle was lit and I saw my wife's face above me and that of Harry. I tried to speak but it came out as a croak.

"Here, father, have some boiled water. The doctor said you would be thirsty."

"You live husband! You live!" She leaned down and kissed my forehead.

Harry raised my head and poured some water into my mouth. I drank heavily and then Harry laid down my head. "What happened? How long…."

"Ssh, speak not, husband, and I will be the teller of the tale. Harry, go and have the cook warm the broth and send riders to Thomas and Alice. Tell them that their father lives! Tell the priest we do not need him but he should give thanks to God for bringing back our lord." Harry went and I wondered at my wife's words. "You were struck down with some pestilence. The doctor from the castle came and gave you a potion." She buried her head in my chest and began to sob, "I am sorry, husband, I have failed you. I dallied and delayed instead of sending for him when you first fell ill. I thought it was a winter chill and I could heal you."

"All is well."

She raised her head and mopped my brow with a cloth. "You have lain between life and death these seven days. The doctor said that the ague would leave you in eight days or you would be dead."

I closed my eyes. Seven days. I had not been inactive for seven days my whole life.

I felt my wife's hand stroking my head, "I thought I had lost you and that made me realise just how much I would miss you if you died. You go to war and death is part of war but, somehow, no matter how perilous the position, I always believe that you will return. I have not prepared myself for your death and I see now how wrong that is. Each time you return I am pleased to see you but I just look at the profit you have returned." She made the sign of the cross. "God has punished me for my greed! We have money enough and it is people who are more important and none is more important to me than you! We have stewards and reeves who are good people. We have a grandchild and that is what we will focus upon. We have had an epiphany, husband and God has sent us a sign. We will not ignore his warning."

I gave my wife a wan smile which she took to be a sign of my illness but I knew that I had at least one more battle to fight. I had promised Prince Henry that I would be at his side when he rooted out Glendower and I would keep my word. I had less than two months to recover my health for I could not even rise from my bed! I prayed to God that he would help me to recover in time.

Chapter 16

I was not allowed to leave my bed, save to make water, for a week. Thomas and Mary, Alice and Sir Richard all visited with me. The bairn was kept from me for fear that some part of the pestilence remained. I assured them all that I was well and on the mend. Thomas had taken over my duties as lord and that pleased me. He had ensured that all of the men of the manor had practised each Sunday. He had worked with my archers and men at arms. Although he had heard of my illness the King had not bothered to ask after me and that had angered my son and wife.

Thomas had shaken his head, angrily, "You probably picked up whatever ailment it was while on his service. He uses you like a hunting dog and it is not right!"

"No, son, he is the King and above such things. I know that I am used and it is my choice. I could refuse service for I am asked to do more than my title and duty demands but I choose to do what I do for the King. It is my choice, always remember that."

I told him, while his mother was absent, that I would be going to Wales in March but that he and the others would not have to.

"So, we will sit safely behind our walls, as will the King, while you and Harry risk your lives with Prince Henry?"

"No, for I think the King will be heading north." I had worked that out over Christmas. My words about Prince Edward and the machinations of de Montfort had stirred an idea in his mind.

"You are too weak at the moment to stir from this hall let alone mount a horse."

"Let me worry about that. We have food aplenty and I know how to recover. I watched men recover from such ailments in Spain. They did not hide under their blankets; they got to their feet and fought the ailment as they would an enemy armed with a sword. My problem is your mother. She will not understand. I need your help with her. You have shown that you are prepared to take over the manor and that is good. Now you need to help me become Baron Strongstaff once more."

He shook his head, "We will never change you, father, I can see that and the best that we can do is to keep you alive as long as we can despite your efforts, the King's and, it appears, God's to end your life as quickly as possible!"

When I rose, my wife tried to contain me in the bedchamber but I persuaded her to allow me the run of the hall. I ate all that was put before me. I became the child of seven summers who was always hungry and gnawed a bone through to the marrow! When my wife was absent, I took my sword and went through the strokes and moves I had had as my daily routine when I had been King Richard's guard. At first, I was pathetically weak but a combination of determination and good food made me stronger.

God sent us good weather as Spring approached and I used that as an opportunity to leave the hall. I waited until my wife went with Mary, my daughter, to visit Alice and my grandson. I had James the horse master fetch Hart. Harold of Lincoln, now firmly established as one of my men, fetched Harry's horse too.

"You do not think I would let you ride alone did you?" My squire grinned at me.

I confess that I was grateful. The weather had improved but after such a long time in a warm hall, the cold hit me like a slap in the face. Hart seemed to sense my condition and she picked her way on the smoothest path possible. I used the ride to speak with my son. "We will need to ride to Shrewsbury at the start of March. Your mother will not be happy and so you shall have to organise this. Call it part of your training as a knight."

The happy go lucky boy who had helped Thomas had now become a serious young man who had almost lost his father. "Your ailment has made me realise that we all take you for granted too much. Do not fear, father, you now have a second cloak upon your back. When you ride into battle I will be as close to you as your backplate."

I patted Hart and smiled at my son, "Hopefully, it will not come to that. Prince Henry has learned much and I am confident that together we can end Glendower and his threat."

"I have already spoken with Edgar and Alan. All will be ready. They have a great number of arrows. The only problem is Gurth Garthson. He is eager to ride with us. Alan is reluctant to take him for his leg, while healing, does not allow him to move as quickly as he ought."

"Then when we return, I will speak with him. I take it his wife does not share his opinion?"

He laughed, "You read minds now, eh, father? Aye, you are right. She is with child again and she wishes her husband to stay closer to home."

Gurth and his wife had three children. Taking him north had almost robbed his family of their father. When we returned from the ride I called in at his smallholding. He farmed half an acre and had a few animals. His wife made cheese. He limped out to see us when he heard the horses approach. "My lord, it is good to see you well. We were worried."

I dismounted and found myself chafed; the illness had taken my edge away. I would have to ride daily to truly recover. "And you too, Gurth. May we come in?"

"Of course, lord." He stood aside to allow us to enter.

His wife, Anne, heavily pregnant, was trying to tidy. I waved her sit, "Mistress Anne, sit for you are with child and what I need to say concerns you too." She looked at me. "It is a command." She sat and the three children all stared at me. I smiled at them, "You know your father is a brave man?" They nodded. "Gurth, I saw that your wound troubles you still."

"It will get better, lord. We ride to war and I do not have to run."

"Yet, in battle, we cannot predict what will happen, can we? What if you fell behind and could not run? We both know that your comrades would not leave you and your lameness might be the cause of their death!"

"That will not happen, lord."

I laughed. "It seems that illness makes us all fortune tellers. Gurth, you have a family as I do. I would have you as guardian of my hall. Your home is attached to the hall and when I am absent I would have you command the men of the hall and guard my family and my manor. They all use the bow and you would be their captain. I would pay you for the task."

I saw gratitude in his wife's eyes. Proud Gurth said, "You need not pay me, lord. If you wish me to do this then I will."

"And a bodyguard is worthy of his hire. I should know for I was the King's bodyguard. You accept?"

"Aye, lord, I do."

"Then you will take over the Sunday training and when I go to war you will organise the watch."

Mistress Anne rushed over and kissed my hand, "My lord, thank you. I will pray for your recovery in church."

We left and I told Alan of the Woods of the arrangement. He was pleased for he knew the risk a lame warrior brought to a company. "And you know we will need all of the archers." He nodded. "Allow them all the time you can with their families for I know not how long it will take to quell the Welsh."

"Aye, lord, they are expecting a long campaign. And it is good to see you up and about. We all prayed for you.".

I was touched by the affection shown to me by my men. It contrasted with the way men felt about our King. His son, in contrast, was a Prince men would die for.

I had to broach the subject of my departure towards the end of February. I had expected a storm but I endured a hurricane from my wife. She wondered if I had lost my senses. She swore that the illness had affected my mind and that I should be locked up for my own safety. I allowed her to bluster as I suffered the torrent of tears and arguments.

When she had cried herself out, I said, "Wife, you told me that you did not fear my death in battle. It was an ailment which hurt me. I have given money to the church to thank God for my salvation. I go to war and there, I believe, I will survive. Tell me truly, wife, when was the last time we lost a man?" She could not think of an answer. "There you have it. I promise that I will return and I leave Thomas at home, along with my other knights. He will see his child born."

She was slightly mollified but still upset, "And will this be your last war?"

"How do I know that? I am a Baron and I have a great responsibility. Should I have refused the honour? Would you rather I was just a gentleman?"

She shook her head. We would not have enjoyed the life we had if I had remained a knight or gentleman. She took my hands in hers, "I do not wish to lose you. I know I have taken you for granted and worried too much about crops and coin. That is over. When you return from Wales you will see a new Eleanor."

We left on the last day of February. I had both Hawk and Hart. Harry had a new courser which James and Harold had schooled for him. We took a wagon with arrows, spears and spare mail. We had four servants. All of them had been soldiers. We headed for Shrewsbury. It was a bastion against the Welsh. The Prince had realised that Chester was too remote and Shrewsbury allowed him access to both the heart of Wales as well as the north. I hoped that my men would be accommodated in the castle but we took tents in case they had to make do with the fields. The journey took four days. When we began the journey, I was not fully recovered but the ride and the routine of a route march completed it. I knew that my arms still needed to recover their strength but that would come. I was aware of the concern of Harry and my men. They watched me constantly as though they expected a relapse.

The castle had a superb position. It was in a loop of the River Severn and had the river's protection on all but one side. The neck of land close to the barbican was at its narrowest point. It meant an assault had to try to take the formidable barbican. I saw that other companies had arrived and were accommodated to the west of the castle where the loop of the river afforded more land and yet the camp was well protected by the castle. I saw the white swan standard flying from the castle. The Prince was at home.

I pointed to the field beyond the castle. "I am guessing we camp there. Take the men and make our camp. I will go with Harry and speak with the Prince.

We were expected and as we dismounted in the outer ward and ostlers took my horse a page arrived and said, "Sir John is awaiting you in the Great Hall. Prince Henry is in the camp speaking with the men who have recently arrived."

Sir John Stanley was the Prince's steward. He was a valiant knight and I liked him. Marginally older than I was, he was a Cheshire knight but a loyal one. He had done well marrying into a rich family, the Lathoms, and was now a rich man. He fought for the Prince and sought no recompense for doing so.

"Sir William, it is good that you came. We all heard of your illness and the attempts on your life. The Prince was most concerned."

"Aye well, all is well that ends well. God spared me and I am now whole and we can root out the Prince's enemies."

"They have grown, my lord. You heard about Mortimer?" I nodded. "It brought Glendower that which he lacked, knights."

I nodded, "And how stand our castles?"

"The ones in the north, Beaumaris to Conwy are secure but Harlech and Aberystwyth, which we recovered in November, are besieged. We learned from last year and the Prince keeps them supplied by sea but the cost is exorbitant. Holding on to Wales costs the Prince more than fourteen hundred pounds a year! Every lord who is able to, withholds his taxes. They are either rebels or cite the threat from the rebels as the reason they cannot pay. It is too bad."

"And the Prince has a plan?"

"He does but he holds you in such high regard that he wished to wait until you arrived to formalise it."

"And the forces at our disposal?"

"Twenty-four knights and barons, five hundred men at arms and two and a half thousand archers." He shrugged, "Of course most of this is in the form of promises. We have less than half of that as yet."

I was not downhearted. The fact that we had so many archers meant we could match the Welshmen and the land over which we would be campaigning did not suit large numbers of mailed men. I might not even need my war horse! When Harry arrived with our bags we were shown to our quarters. I was a senior lord and would be accommodated in the castle. I had come far since I had served in Spain.

I did not see the Prince until it was time to eat. I was the only baron present and so I was seated at his right hand. There were twelve knights present too. Harry was now used to his duties and he moved easily between the table and the kitchens. As in most castles, the kitchens were on a different floor. Negotiating the narrow stairs was never easy. Harry had learned from his brother.

"Well, Prince Henry, are we well prepared?"

"I hope so Baron, but we do not have enough men. I went around the camp today; I learned that from you and my peregrinations taught me much. The men are confident, especially yours. They told me how serious your illness was. You should have let me know."

I shook my head, "Prince Henry, I knew nothing until I recovered. It was my family suffered."

"And that seems to be your lot in life."

I nodded, "When the threat of Glendower and Hotspur is over then I can enjoy some time with my children and grandson."

"Your men seem to think that you believe they are linked."

I nodded, "It is the Mortimer connection which tells me that. When I delivered your father's letter Hotspur was too calm. It was as though he was unconcerned with the loss of ransom. Oh, he blustered and he expressed anger but it was for show. He now has an excuse for rebellion but he wishes to draw your father's eye south. So, I have spoken to Sir John but I do not know your strategy."

"That is simple. The Welsh have raided at will. English farmers have been slaughtered and their animals were taken." I did not point out that I had been ordered to do the same to the Welsh. "We hit Glendower where it hurts him. Sycharth and Glyndyfrdwy."

"We burned Glyndyfrdwy, Prince."

"He rebuilt it. It is not as grand as it once was but it is a gesture to show us that he is resilient. When we have destroyed them, we make his homeland of Cynllaith, a wasteland. I will be ruthless. Mortimer's defection has shown me that we cannot play this as though it is a tourney with men applauding clever strokes with a sword. The people who look to me as their prince are suffering."

I was seeing a Prince reborn. He was now a man. Just approaching sixteen summers he had spent the last three years learning how to be a leader and now he had made his decision. He would be a ruthless one. As we ate, he told me about his plans in detail. His father had been to war but Hal was a true warrior!

"My father is using his cunning to defeat our enemies. He has granted the Earl of Northumberland the earldom of Douglas and large parts of Scotland. It is a clever ruse and may buy us time to defeat the Welsh before Hotspur is ready to attack us." I was not so sure but it seemed to me that the King had given away that which was not his and so it cost him nothing. It was a ploy which might succeed.

Over the next days, more contingents arrived. The knights were young ones. I was with the Prince when he greeted them and I saw a different approach to that of his father, the King. The Prince spoke to the men and not just the lords. He showed what appeared to be, to me, genuine interest. We were not a large army but we would be a closely knit one. A letter also arrived from his father confirming him as Lieutenant of Wales. It was he who would lead the army. He could be advised but he was in command. There would be no senior lord countermanding him. I hoped his father was showing confidence in his son and not distancing himself from any potential disaster. Then I remembered our last conversation in Northampton. His father had specifically asked for me. I was there as insurance.

The night before we left, he held a council of war with his barons and knights. He told them what he had told me the night I had arrived. He had a small army but it was all mounted and we would move quickly. "First, we ride to Sycharth. Sir William has already scouted it out and we know its strengths and weaknesses. It is made of wood and it is small. We surround it and we use our arrows to destroy all within. If we have to then we fire it and burn all those within. They have rebelled against me and they will pay the price."

I was witnessing a butterfly which had emerged from its cocoon. Gone was the awkward caterpillar and in its place was a powerful beast which moved with grace and purpose. He was decisive and his words inspired the knights. These were not the lords like Hotspur and the Earl of Northumberland who sought power. These wished to serve a young lord who seemed to care about them. I now saw why King Henry had asked me to join this campaign. He could trust me and knew that Prince Henry could rely on my judgement. I suppose it was the mark of a good leader. Despite the fact that there were three thousand of us we were hardly ponderous for only the knights, less than thirty of us, needed a baggage train. The archers carried their spare shafts on horses while the men at arms just rode palfreys; we were not going into war horse country. As we had been at Sycharth most recently my men led. Alan of the Woods and my archers led the way as we headed towards the castle on the border.

We had less than twenty-four miles to go and the Welsh were not expecting an attack this early in the season. My archers rode hard. Behind them came my men at arms and, as we neared the castle, I sent Alan of the Woods to ride to the far side of the castle and ensure that none escaped. I rode, with my men at arms into Llansilyn. Behind me rode the Prince and he planted himself before the gates. Leaving Captain Edgar to secure the village I rode back to the gates and the Prince. He bravely placed himself within bow range and he took off his helmet. It bordered upon the reckless.

"I am Henry, Prince of Wales and Lord Lieutenant of Wales. This is the castle of the rebel Owain Glyndŵr. I demand that you surrender the castle to me to save useless loss of life for you are surrounded and this castle will fall!"

A Welshman peered over the top of the gatehouse and shouted, "This is not England, this is Wales and we bow the knee to the English invader no longer. Soon you will not have a throne Prince Henry so, be a good boy and go home!"

It was deliberately insulting to the Prince but I also picked up that there would be an attempt to take the English throne. I stored that information for later. The Prince did not react angrily. His voice was calm as was he, "I ignore your insults and I offer, once again, the olive branch of peace. Surrender to me and you shall leave here unharmed. Swear not to fight me again and you shall keep your swords. It is a reasonable offer and I make it once only. Reject it and the consequences will be dire."

"We reject it!"

An arrow was sent from within the walls. It was poorly aimed for it struck the breastplate of the Prince but it caused outrage amongst our men who began baying at the walls. They were like a pack of dogs who wished to be unleashed. Prince Henry showed his class when he held up his hand and shouted, "Peace! They have made their decision and many men will rue that decision."

Our men all banged their swords and spears and chanted, "Prince Harry! Prince Harry!" If there was one thing the common soldier liked it was when his leader showed he was not afraid of an enemy.

He turned his horse and rode back to me. "You were lucky, Prince Henry!"

He nodded, "Aye, but we now have the right of it and that helps. We will surround their walls and let them stew this night. We will stay in the village. Have your men evict the rebels."

I looked at the young man who had grown up so much in the past year. "Yes, my Prince." I turned my horse and galloped towards Captain Edgar. "Tell the people to leave. The garrison has annoyed the Prince and they must pay the price."

"Aye, lord. You heard Sir William."

As the people were moved out one man spoke out. I recognised him having seen him when I was playing an old man in the village, "This is not right, sir. We are just innocent people who go about our business."

"Really? Then you did not profit when Glendower brought Mortimer here and you rubbed your hands at the profit you made?" He made the sign of the cross for how could I have known? "Leave and take just what you can carry on your backs. Go into Wales and ask your would be King for help! Let us see what he can do!"

Shoulders slumped, the villagers headed west. They had not had time to dig up their treasure. They took clothes and food and that was all. Glendower would know that the Prince was coming but, for once, we had the advantage of surprise. He would not know which direction we would take. We used the houses for accommodation and our campfires ringed the walls of the castle. We butchered and cooked the animals we found and we ate well.

The next morning the castle was ringed by two and a half thousand archers. They did not have bodkins nocked but war and hunting arrows; we would not waste the valuable bodkins. The Prince waited until every archer was in position and the walls were manned. For some reason, the Welsh did not send their arrows as soon as they saw our men. Perhaps they were waiting for some formal beginning. The Prince gave it to them. He had the horn sounded three times and two and a half thousand arrows descended into the castle. Many, in fact, most, would be wasted but it mattered not. Flight after flight was sent over and the Welsh responded. Eight of our archers were hit, three fatally. The Prince ordered the horn to be sounded once and the archers fell back. It was not generosity. He had served with my archers and knew that rest between flights increased their ability to rain death. The archers drank and some, like my men, changed their bows and strings.

Prince Henry waved his arm and the horn sounded twice. The archers returned and when the horn sounded thrice, they resumed their attack. A white flag was waved and the Prince had the horn sounded once. "Do you surrender?"

It was not the knight who had spoken before, it was another and he shouted, "Aye, we surrender. You have slain half of our men!"

"Then open the gates and throw down your weapons."

The gates opened and we saw the devastation the arrows had caused. The men who had been wounded on the walls were being tended to by healers. As the Prince and I stepped in through the gate I saw bodies littering the walls. None were knights or men at arms. The Prince turned to Sir John, "I want all the knights gathered in the hall. Take the weapons from the rest. Each archer will lose three fingers from their right hand. The mail will be taken from the men at arms and then they will be taken back to Shrewsbury where they will be made to work."

The steward nodded, "And the knights?"

"I will deal with those." I went with the Prince and our squires to the hall where the knights were being herded. They stood in a disconsolate line. There were eight of them. "Where is the man who insulted me?"

They pointed to a body on the gate of the inner ward.

"Then he has cheated the hangman. Have you ransom?"

One knight said, "It will take me two weeks to raise the coin."

The Prince turned to his squire, "Have my men at arms hang this one!"

The knight dropped to his knees, "But Prince Henry…"

"You are a rebel and I will not wait one day for ransom. The rest of you, take heed of this man's death for it presages yours! Send your squires for ransom. If it is not here by dusk tomorrow, then you hang. We have no time to dally here! I have a country to win back."

He was the only knight we hanged. We left a week later having burned the village and the castle. The ditch was filled with the Welsh bodies. It was a grisly sight and I did not think the Welsh would rebuild. We headed north for Glendower's main home.

Part Three
The Battle of Shrewsbury

Chapter 17

The prisoners and the treasure had been taken to Shrewsbury and so, for Glyndyfrdwy, we had fewer men. This time it was the men at arms and knights who reduced the hall. Glendower had rebuilt it. There were men guarding its walls but we rode in at dawn, having scouted it out at night and we swept through the grounds sweeping all before us. This time there were no knights. The garrison were all slaughtered and we scattered the women and servants. The men were taken as prisoners to Shrewsbury. As we searched the hall for treasure I asked, "What will you do with the prisoners, Prince Henry?"

"It is simple, Sir William, when we catch up with Glendower, they become bargaining pieces. Let us see how he views the damage we do his own people?"

We left three days later leaving the hall and grounds burned and ruined. Glendower's recently restored home was no more. We headed for Machynlleth and the heartland of Wales for that way we would pass close to the great mountain of Snowdon. There was a religious significance to the mountain in the centre of North Wales and the Prince was making a statement. The Prince decided that as the Welsh had been gathered at Machynlleth we would raid that too. There was no resistance as we moved into the higher ground and through the narrow valleys. Any potential ambush was negated by our mounted archers who were able to ride as a screen before us. We found deserted villages devoid of people and animals. It was fortunate that we had eaten well at Sycharth and Glyndyfrdwy for there was little food to be had. It should have made our men resentful towards the Prince but as he endured the same privations that anger was turned towards the Welsh. The odd Welshman that was found died! Our archers were in no mood for prisoners.

The other problem we had was grazing. Three thousand horses need a great deal of grass. My men and I were lucky. We had brought oats from home. The Prince commented upon it, "Very clever Sir William yet you are the only knight who has done so."

I nodded, "Perhaps I am the only knight who had to care for the horses of the Blue Company in the dry and desiccated land of Spain. If a man went afoot there then he had signed his own death warrant. I learned to husband horses." I saw him taking that in. When he became King and led campaigns in France, the lessons he learned in Wales were well used.

When we reached Machynlleth we found a deserted town and so the Prince had it fired. We spent a couple of weeks ensuring that there were no more rebels and then we headed back to Shrewsbury. We had tightened our belts and they now rested on clearly visible ribs. We were in no condition to relieve the sieges of Aberystwyth and Harlech. The Prince was wise enough to know that we had hurt the Welsh but any further action would result in irreplaceable losses to us. As we headed back, I heard the frustration in his voice that the Welsh, and Glendower in particular, had not faced us. He was angry about Mortimer who had defected and yet not had the courage to use his own knights to fight us.

"Prince Henry, you are making the correct decision. The Welsh will just draw us deeper and deeper into their mountains. You chose the balance of this army wisely and our archers now outnumber anything the Welsh can field. They seek to weaken us and our horses by making us chase shadows. There is a plot and a plan to the enemy. I still believe that Hotspur is part of that plot. He has done nothing about the ransom for Douglas and his armies still sit in the north. I fear that Glendower seeks to draw us away from the heart of England."

The Prince heard my words but was not convinced. Once back in Shrewsbury he set about feeding our men. The horses gorged on the new grass and I was privy to the letters he and Sir John wrote to his father. The men we had led had not been paid. An army the size of ours was expensive. His letters to his father begged for money to prosecute the war against the rebels. Parliament would not consider negotiation nor would they fund a war. The supporters of Richard saw this as a way of hurting King Henry. I had seen the fickle nature of Parliament when I had served King Richard. They were petty men using the power they had for their own advantage. They cared not a jot for the common man yet their rhetoric suggested that everything they did was for them.

As we sat, one evening in May, the Prince began to plan what he would do next. "I have some monies of my own left to me by my grandfather, John of Gaunt, I will use those. How much is the shortfall and the pay for the army, Sir John?"

The steward scanned his documents, "A little short of nineteen hundred pounds, sire."

I saw the Prince considering. He nodded, "I will pay that from my own coffers. When Glendower is defeated, I will reclaim it from him! Pay the men and prepare to leave. We head directly for Harlech. We know that the land will be scorched and there will be nought to eat. Each man will carry his own provisions. We will move quickly. We leave in two days." He smiled at me, "I know that the first thing the men will do when they are paid is to spend a great portion of it on ale and whores. I would not ride with men who have thick heads. This way they go to war with two of their appetites satisfied!" He had wisdom beyond his years. His father would not have thought of that. He would just have left and not considered his men.

We did not head for Machynlleth instead we made directly for Harlech. The Welsh had spies and scouts out and they knew we were coming. The castles of Aberystwyth and Harlech were important to the Welsh for they were the southernmost castles of the northern ring. If the Welsh were able to reduce them then the greater part of Wales could be protected from the English. If they could take Shrewsbury then Glendower would have a secure kingdom.

The Welsh met us north of the castle. Whoever led them, and I did not recognise the standards, was clever enough to keep his men far enough away from the castle to eliminate the possibility of a sortie into their rear whilst giving them the opportunity to flee south to Aberystwyth. The Welsh arrayed themselves before us. They used the standard formation which most armies used at that time. There were groups of archers in long, narrow blocks and between them were dismounted men with spears and shields. They had two groups of mounted men and they lined up on the flanks.

The Prince looked at his steward and then me, "They expect us to line up in the same way as they do."

I nodded, "It is like the chess games you and I played, Prince Henry. He moves a pawn and we counter it."

"And that plays into his hands for he has superior numbers of men on foot. Sir William, I would have you lead half of the men at arms and place them on the right. I will lead the rest and the knights on the left. Sir John, I would have you form the archers into three long lines across our front."

He looked surprised, "But if the enemy horse attack them then they will be slaughtered!"

"Aye, but we will prevent that, eh Sir William? Have the archers on the extreme left and right leave a gap between their files so that our men at arms and knights can pass through. I will sound the horn three times when we are to attack, Sir William."

"Aye, Prince Henry." It was a good plan but not without risks. As I waved my arm for my men to follow me, I turned to Harry. "I will ride Hawk this day and you will ride Hart. You will need to be close behind me with a spare spear. Watch yourself."

"Do not fear, I am not the child who first went to war and watched you and my brother fight. Now I know what I must do."

Once in position and mounted on my warhorse I turned to the men I would be leading. There were almost two hundred men. The better part was my own men. "When the horn sounds, we pass between the archers. For that reason, we form up now in those lines. The men of Weedon will lead. That is not because they are better but they know me and the way I fight. Our aim is to destroy their horsemen and then turn and destroy the rest. Do not worry about their archers. Our archers will duel with them and today the Welsh will see who is better! Do not worry about forming lines because speed is of the essence. Hit them and hit them hard!"

As I donned my helmet, they cheered and banged their spears and lances against their mailed hands. They roared my name.

Some of them had shields. They were the ones who wore no plate. All of my men had greaves and breastplates. The Welsh archers would not be wasting bodkins for when they loosed their arrows, they would be loosing them at archers!

Sir John Stanley had the men formed. I saw that Alan of the Woods and my men were in the centre. The Prince's standard was lowered and then raised. I heard Sir John shout, "Loose!" and two and a half thousand arrows flew towards the enemy. They had fewer archers but the cloud which came towards us was heavy enough. The long thin columns of archers meant that their arrows did not land, as ours did, on the same spot, some were shorter and some were longer. Two arrows struck me behind the rear rank of archers, they bounced from my plate. They were wasting war arrows. The duel lasted for ten flights and I saw that both sides had losses. I prayed that there were none amongst my men.

Then the horn sounded and I spurred Hawk, "For God, England, and Prince Harry!" The men all cheered and we rode through the narrow gaps left by the archers. They were only three men deep and we burst before the archers. They would concentrate their arrows on the centre of the Welsh line as soon as we had cleared their front. The Welsh knights and mounted men at arms were less than a hundred and fifty paces from us. They had been caught unawares for they must have thought the three lines of archers precluded a mounted attack. They began to charge but, from a standing start, they would hit us at the walk whilst we, although not in a line of riders boot to boot, would hit them at the gallop for already Hawk's legs had opened and he was eating up the ground.

As was my practice I looked for a knight who looked to be a leader. He would have a Welsh dragon somewhere on his surcoat. I spied one who had a blue dragon. He also had a lance but he rode a courser and not a warhorse. A war horse would be wasted at a siege. It meant my horse was bigger and would be far more aggressive. We also had the advantage that we were slightly uphill from them. I would use every advantage I had. He came at me so that it would be lance to lance. He was trying to negate my warhorse. He wore a full face, boar's snout, basinet. I had the better vision but I risked splinters in the eyes. It was a risk worth taking. I had more experience in a charge than any knight I knew, for I had been doing it longer. I allowed the Welsh knight to think he had chosen the correct side to attack. Although we were at the gallop Hawk had a little more speed left in him and when we were ten paces apart, I pricked his side and, as he leapt forward, I stood in my stirrups and lunged forward with my lance. My sudden burst of speed took the Welshman by surprise. He had intended to strike a few heartbeats later. My lance smashed into his chest. I had put all of my force behind the strike and the lance head splintered and shattered. Pieces of wood flew from it. He had a cantle but that merely held him more firmly against the strike of the lance. He threw his arms up and the spear fell.

I shouted, "Harry, take him, prisoner! He is hurt!" I knew that Harry would be close for he had seen me shatter my spear and he would be fetching me another. I drew my sword and did not wait for the response. Hawk had, quite literally, the bit between his teeth. He was under control but only just and, for once, I was glad that I did not have a shield to worry about. His snapping jaws made the horse of the Welsh man at arms flinch as he struck at me with his spear. It grazed along my side but my swinging sword connected with his helmet. It was an open sallet basinet like mine and the edge drove through his nose and into his skull. He tumbled to the ground.

And then I was through the mounted men at arms and knights. I looked around and saw that I still had ten men with me. Raising my sword, I pointed to the left and shouted, "Follow me!"

I turned Hawk who had finally begun to tire and charged towards the dismounted men at arms who guarded the flanks of the archers. I saw that our archers had won the duel of the archers and more Welsh archers lay dead than alive. The arrows had also thinned the men at arms and our sudden flank attack took them by surprise. Spears came around to defend the flank but Hawk had a mail hood on his head. The first spear slid along the links and I swung my sword upwards. The Welshman had a mail hauberk but my long sword swept up, under the split and into his groin. As Hawk rode into the mass of men at arms my sword slice upwards into unprotected flesh. The spear fell as he dropped to the ground in an attempt to hold in his guts. I reined in and pulled back on the reins as I stood Hawk on his hind legs. It was a terrifying sight for the men at arms and archers. They began to run even before his mighty hooves smashed into their bodies. One archer and a man at arms were a little slower than the others and they paid with their lives. I saw that we had turned this flank and, ahead of me, I saw that the Prince and his knights had also driven deep into the enemy ranks.

My men at arms and I worked our way through the archers and men at arms who fled our archers. Almost two thousand men were now charging them. I struck flesh and metal. My sword soon became an iron bar but that still cracked open skulls and broke arms. The fleeing mob flooded across the river. Armour was discarded along with weapons. No matter what happened at Aberystwyth one army was destroyed. It was noon by the time the slaughter had ended. There were ten knights and their squires captured. I wondered if Prince Henry would be so draconian this time.

The gates of the castle were opened and we entered. I saw a new side to the Prince that day. The constable of the castle had been at his wit's end for they had almost run out of food and his men were at the point of mutiny. The Prince addressed all of them in the inner ward, "You have all served England well and you shall be rewarded. We have ten knights for ransom. The garrison of Aberystwyth will each receive half of that ransom and you will be paid for the time you have served without pay. England does not forget!"

Cries of, "Prince Harry! And "England!" rang out.

My men at arms had all survived but we had losses amongst my archers. Matthew the Millerson and Christopher White Arrow both died of their wounds. We had been shriven before the battle but they had lived long enough for the priests we had with us to give them absolution. Both were single men. I would not have to explain to families how two brave men had died.

We waited a sennight at Harlech. Men and animals needed to recover. The Prince also waited for the ships bringing the supplies to arrive. We had captured not only weapons but animals and food. The Welsh had stopped us taking them from their farms but they had obligingly brought them to Harlech and we benefitted. We then headed down the coast to Aberystwyth. Once again, the Welsh took all that they had and headed into the mountains. The men besieging Aberystwyth also heard of our approach. Perhaps news of the victory we had enjoyed reached them for they broke the siege before we arrived. By the last week in June the north of Wales was, once again, surrounded by English castles and all that the Welsh held were the mountains. The Prince was happy about that and we headed back to Shrewsbury. We had our ransom and we had our victory. More importantly, the Prince had learned to lead men on the battlefield. It was a good lesson and soon his leadership skills would be put to a more severe test.

We reached Shrewsbury and I believe that the Prince would have released my men and me, had we not heard disquieting news from the south. Glendower was marching down the Tywi valley. He had begun to take English castles. We had taken the north from him and, perhaps, he saw the south as a better opportunity to defeat the English. We sent the news to King Henry who was at Northampton gathering men to go to the aid of Hotspur in the north. The Scots were gathering another army.

That evening some of Prince Henry's earlier doubts returned. "Perhaps I should take this army and head south to defeat Glendower. This might be our opportunity to end the rebellion."

I looked at Sir John who nodded for me to speak. He was a good steward but it was I who knew warfare. "That would be a grave error, lord. We would leave Shrewsbury unprotected. Your father is in the east and if an enemy could take Shrewsbury then they would, effectively, cut Wales off from England. We know that Chester supports any who oppose your father."

"But the men of South Wales; do I abandon them?"

Sir John shook his head, "Lord Carew is there and we have good castles. The ones they have taken are of little importance. Carmarthen, Pembroke and Kidwelly can hold out and we have to trust to the men there. They have not yet been called to battle. It is their time, my Prince."

Prince Harry looked from me to Sir John and then nodded, "And you believe, Sir William, that there will be a threat to us here?"

"I do."

"Then we prepare for a siege. My father will come soon enough but until then we wait behind our walls, for I do not have enough knights yet to face another army."

On the ninth of July, we heard the news that I had been expecting but which came as a surprise to the rest of the country. Hotspur evaded the Earl of Westmoreland and, taking a small army, reached Chester where he raised the standard of rebellion. He had finally shown his true colours and he was within a day's march of Shrewsbury. War had come and he had managed to split the forces of King Henry and his son. The Prince sent to the Earl of Worcester and asked him to bring his men to our aid. We had to find as many men as we could to defend the walls. War had come and we were unready!

Chapter 18

The King sent a messenger to tell us that he was moving towards us and that Hotspur had moved to Sandiway in Cheshire where the men of Cheshire were flocking to his standard. Prince Henry summoned me on the eighteenth of July when the Earl of Worcester arrived with the men of Worcester. With the extra men, the Prince felt more confident. I did not for I did not trust Worcester. He was a Percy!

The Prince sent for me as soon as the news and the Earl of Worcester arrived. While the Earl settled in the Prince spoke to me in private. "I know your opinion of the Earl, that he is a Percy, but we can no longer choose with whom we fight. He commands the men of Worcester and I wish you to put aside your feelings about the Percy family. I know you were correct about his uncle and about Glendower and for that I am deeply indebted but I will not have dissension amongst my lords. The Earl has not shown any traits which would suggest he is disloyal. When he lived in my home in London, he was a good friend and guide."

I did not trust him but I had no evidence, this time, to back up my feelings. "Of course, Prince Henry!"

"Good. I would have you and your men seek Hotspur at Sandiway. I need to know when they march south. Do not risk yourself, or your men for we will need you in this battle but I would have warning of the arrival of the enemy."

"Aye, lord." As I turned to leave, I saw the Earl of Worcester as he entered the Great Hall. He smiled with his mouth but in his eyes, I saw enmity. I merely nodded as I passed him. He brought with him many men from Worcester but I, for one, would have preferred to fight with fewer of his men but soldiers that we could rely upon.

I took Hart this time. We would, at worst, be skirmishing and I would not need my warhorse. We headed north with my scouts in a screen before us. Sandiway was not a large town but it was well positioned and just fifty miles from Shrewsbury. We made a camp in the forest of Delamere just five miles from the rebels. We had seen the smoke from their fires as we neared them. Knowing where they were was not good enough. We needed numbers and we needed the names of the lords who led them. There was little point in sending my men to ascertain that information. I would have to go with them. I selected the men I would take and none of my men were happy with the situation but I would not be deflected from my purpose. Harry was annoyed that I left him behind.

We had taken spare horses for the ride and the eight of us rode them. I took Stephen the Tracker and archers with me. We would be watching the camp under the cover of the night and none were better than my archers at hiding. I also took archers for there were many Cheshire archers and I hoped that we could mingle with the ones already there. I wore a plain surcoat and cloak. If I was seen by Percy or Sir Edward then I was undone for they knew my face. July meant very long days and although our horses were tired, we reached the camp just after the sun had set. I hoped that the night's cloak would hide me. We left the horses, with Alf the Grim to watch them, and headed across the fields to the camp. The fires made it almost like daylight in parts. We would avoid those areas which were lit by them.

We were half a mile from the camp when Stephen the Tracker and Much Longbow stopped. There were other men in the forest. I hid my face and moved away from the others. I listened to the conversation.

Much had an easy way about him, "Well met, friend. Why are you leaving the camp? Does the food not please?"

I heard a grim laugh, "What does not please is the fact that many of our friends came to see what was this gathering and they have been forced to join Hotspur's army. We are no rebels. King Henry may not be the best of kings but he is our king."

"Thank you for your advice, whence go you?"

"We head for Lincoln and you?"

"We were going to the camp to see if the pay was better than that of the King but we will now head for Chester."

"Farewell."

I waited until they had departed before joining Stephen and Much, "You heard, lord?"

"I heard. We will not enter the camp. String your bows and we will examine it from a distance."

It had been fortunate that we had met the archers or else we could have been forced into Hotspur's army. We were helped by the fact that we had to pass one of the horse herds There were more than two thousand horses and they were constantly moving. We slipped amongst them. They had been gathered in a walled field with just one gate and we avoided that one for it would be guarded. The number of horses suggested a large number of mounted men. When we reached the wall, I found that we could see into the camp. The light from the campfires would limit the view those in the camp had of the land beyond the camp. We would be hidden but they would be seen. I realised that there was no way that we would be able to examine the whole camp and any numbers we came up with would be an estimate only. I sent my men left and right so that we could share our findings when we returned to Shrewsbury.

I peered over the wall. I was lucky in that I could see some standards. I recognised the banners of Sir Richard Venables and Sir Richard Vernon. I knew how many knights they commanded. I also spied Archibald, Earl of Douglas. He was laughing with some knights whose livery I could not see. The prisoner had become the ally! This was true treachery! There appeared to be many archers. When the battle came it would not be easily won. Gradually my archers returned to me and tapped me on the shoulder. The last to return was Stephen the Tracker. I nodded and followed him. We had gone but four hundred paces for I was counting when horsemen suddenly burst out of the undergrowth. Perhaps we had been seen, I did not know, but any horseman was an enemy.

Instinct took over and I drew my sword and, as I turned to the sound of the hooves, slashed blindly. Luck was on my side and my blade bit into the side of the horse's head. It reared and fell, crushing its rider. My archers were quick and their bows were strung. Stephen the Tracker nocked an arrow and released it into the chest of a second horseman. The fallen horse and rider, along with the dead man at arms meant that the other horses had to avoid them and my archers, at almost point-blank range could not miss. The longer we stayed the more chance there was that more men would come and overwhelm us.

"Run!"

I stood and waited on the path. Sure enough, a rider loomed up out the dark. He had expected me to join the others and run. His instincts made him swerve and I slashed across his leg. I cut through his leg, stirrup and into his horse. He fell from the saddle and was dragged a few paces. When it stopped, I ran and, tearing the left leg from the stirrup, clambered on the horse. I felt a thump in the back as an arrow hit me but it was a war arrow and I was unhurt. I reached my men at the same time as Stephen the Tracker. The archers who had not accompanied us had bows at the ready and the four horsemen who thought they had me met a sudden and speedy death. I dismounted the horse and mounted Hart. "Let us ride. We have done all that we can here!"

We rode hard until dawn and then stopped. There was no sound of pursuit and our horses were done in. While we watered them at a stream, I spoke with the archers who had accompanied me. From them, I worked out that we faced an army of over ten thousand men. With the garrison in Shrewsbury and the men we led, the Prince had no more than a little shy of three thousand men. Unless his father reached us, we would be in trouble.

Our exertions and the need to conserve our animals meant that we did not reach the castle until dark. While my men saw to our horses I went to the Prince. He was with Sir John and he was keen to speak with me. I gave him the news and he nodded, "My father and the Earl of Stafford are bringing twelve thousand men. God willing, they will reach us and we will outnumber the enemy."

"Prince Henry, they have many archers. From what we learned they are forcibly making all archers serve them."

"Then I am glad that we have the Earl of Worcester and his men." I nodded. "Eat and get some rest. Tomorrow we prepare the defences."

I did not get a full night's sleep. I was woken by Captain Edgar, "Lord, wake! The Earl of Worcester, Thomas Percy, has fled the castle to join his nephew." I jumped to my feet. I took little pleasure that I had been right. The Earl knew of our preparations and our defences. We ran to the gatehouse. There were dead sentries and the gates gaped wide.

The Prince had them closed and then sent Sir John to discover what had happened. His face was ashen when he returned, "Prince, we are undone. The Earl has taken with him: five knights, ninety-six men at arms and over eight hundred archers. Worse, I have discovered that he has robbed your house in London and used the money to pay for this treachery! You have just twelve hundred men left to face Hotspur and his army!"

It was a disaster and Hotspur now greatly outnumbered us! I turned to Harry who had followed me, "Dress and rouse our men!"

The Prince did not panic. "We have food for a siege and my father is coming. We know that and I am guessing that Hotspur does not." He turned to me, "And Glendower? Is this a clever plan to allow him to attack us from the Welsh side?"

I considered the matter and then shook my head, "I think that might have been the original plan, but our chevauchée into Wales may have made him change his ideas. He was supposed to draw us away from Shrewsbury to allow Hotspur to sneak south and surprise the garrison at Shrewsbury. We did what we did too quickly and your wise decision to return here and not head down the Tywi might have saved the realm! Glendower may be coming but from the Tywi valley, it will take him at least a sennight to fetch an army hither. We face Hotspur and the men he has gathered."

The Prince nodded and turned to his steward, "Have the people of Shrewsbury fetched into the castle and tear down all of the houses which abut the walls."

As he hurried off, I said, "I will set sentries to watch the horses and then have the walls manned. The enemy knows we have scouted their camp and Hotspur will act quickly. With Worcester at his side and knowledge of our paltry numbers, he will seek to take us first. You would make a valuable hostage."

The Prince laughed, "First he would have to defeat us and then take me alive!"

For one so young Hal had great courage. All now counted on his father doing that which he had promised and coming to our aid. We had walls to man for the initial assault would be on the town and then the curtain wall. It would take some days for Hotspur to build war machines to take the castle. We had fewer than a thousand archers left to us and our knights numbered just thirty. More than fourteen thousand men would be attacking our walls. As I hurried to the camp I wondered if my knights were with the King. I had thought them safe but they would now be in as much danger as Harry and I. I saw the clever machinations which had brought us to this pass. It was no wonder that Hotspur had been so calm when I had told him of the King's decision for he must already have put in place the plans for Glendower and Mortimer to do that which they did.

My men had acted quickly. "Captain Edgar, I want two of your men to remain here and guard our horses. Sir John will arrange for others but I want our mounts secure."

"Aye lord."

"Alan, get our men to the town wall. We will not be able to hold it long but we can slow up the enemy. I will follow with the men at arms."

Mailed and ready I led my men through the castle and the town to the walls which surrounded Shrewsbury. Sir John and his men were tearing down buildings which were close enough to the curtain wall of the castle. If they were not destroyed, they could be fired and the castle would fall. My archers were already on duty at the town gate. The castle was so strong that the town walls were a hindrance to an enemy rather than an obstacle but if we could slow down an attacker and make them bleed it would help us in the long run and archers could slow any enemy down. There would be protection from the walls and height. Until they gained the walls an attacker would be in the open and we could kill them. Thomas Percy, Earl of Worcester, would have told his nephew that there were buildings he could fire and he would live up to his name and race to get to us.

"Edgar, intersperse our sergeants amongst the archers. Harry, have you the horn?"

"Aye, my lord."

I shouted, "Men of Weedon, when Harry sounds three blasts we retire to the castle but we do so facing the enemy. We know the streets of Shrewsbury and they do not. Use that knowledge to our advantage."

"Aye, lord!"

It was early afternoon when the Prince arrived on the walls. Since noon he had sent men to join us. Almost half of his archers were on the curtain wall. He and Sir John stood next to us. I pointed to his surcoat, the lions and the fleur de lys marked him as the Prince. "That will draw men to you, Prince Henry. It would be safer to wear a plainer surcoat."

"I am Prince of Wales and I would not hide behind another man's coat. If I am marked to die then so be it but I have Sir William Strongstaff at my side and members of my family are ever safe when you fight at our side. I am content to be so marked."

Sir John said, "If they come after dark then our archers will have no targets."

"I know but if darkness does fall then I shall send the archers back to the castle and we will watch this night."

The advance of the enemy host was marked by a few villagers who lived at Harlescott, a mile north of the castle and town, rushing down the road to avoid the advancing rebels. They were admitted and the wooden gates slammed shut. "They come!" The Prince looked at me and nodded. He lowered the snout visor on his helmet.

"Archers, nock! When you see an enemy do not wait upon the command but loose! These are rebels and traitors; the order is, kill them!"

Hotspur had done as I would have done and sent archers on horseback guarded by sergeants to take the gates. They rode, not in a column but in a loose line across the fields and past the smallholdings which lay to the north of us. Alan of the Woods and my archers knew the range. They had had most of the day to inspect the killing fields before us. I saw as I looked down the wall, that he had commanded some archers to change arrows. There were men in plate and mail. They needed bodkins. The enemy were confident, perhaps overconfident. The defection of almost half of the garrison might have led them to believe that we would surrender as soon as we saw them. Whatever the reason they did not stop when they should have and arrows plucked them from their saddles. Barely six men managed to escape the killing zone and gallop back out of range. Horses wandered disconsolately towards the river. Water was always a lure for horses and their masters lay dead or dying. I saw one sergeant try to raise himself. A single bodkin slammed into his back and he lay dead.

The Prince nodded and lifted his visor to speak with me, "I see Alan of the Woods has not lost his skill."

"Aye, Prince Henry. If he has an arrow aimed at you then you are a dead man!"

The enemy were now warned and they halted short of the line of bodies. I heard horns as whoever commanded the vanguard organised their men. This time the archers came on foot. They had bows strung and arrows nocked. Sergeants bearing shields preceded them. The thirty odd dead men had been a warning. Our archers still had a slight advantage. The fighting platform was just three paces high but it meant our arrows could strike theirs before they could reply. We would not send our arrows at their sergeants. It was their archers who were the threat. Cheshire archers had a good reputation!

The shields helped the enemy but Alan and our archers still managed to hit archers who exposed an arm, a leg and even a head. Twenty more men were hit before they were within range and they began to release their arrows. More than half of the garrison archers had defected and they now outnumbered us. Ironically, the Prince and the sergeants on the walls were safe for the archers who attacked used war arrows to try to clear our archers from the walls. The duel went on until I saw the sun begin to dip in the west. We were losing too many men. I was about to mention that to the Prince when he said, "As soon as it is dark, they will breach the walls. Now is the time to retire to the castle walls."

"Harry, sound the horn." As the notes rang out and men departed, I said, "Edgar, our sergeants will be the rearguard. Prince Henry get inside the gates as quickly as you can!"

He laughed, "Still commanding the future King of England! Some things never change and I, for one, am glad! I will obey Will Strongstaff!"

I waited until he had descended and then turned to leave. The enemy had realised that we had quit the walls and were racing to the gates. They had no ladders and they would have to break down the gates with the poleaxes wielded by the sergeants. We had time but it would take some time for the five hundred men who had guarded our walls to get through Shrewsbury's gate. We formed a block of warriors six men wide and five men deep. We walked backwards through Shrewsbury's deserted streets. Doors gaped open and there were items scattered around the houses showing the speed the burgesses had shown when leaving their homes. I could hear the crack of metal on wood and then there was a cheer as the gate was splintered open. The sun had dropped behind the hills and a gloom had settled upon Shrewsbury. Arrows flew and struck our helmets, plate and mail. None did damage. Then the first of the sergeants hurtled down the road. They had long weapons and we had swords, axes and daggers but this was not an open battlefield. There were houses to the side and the only swing the enemy could make was overhead. With men behind it would be a restricted swing and the first five men who ran at us discovered that to their cost. A knight tried to swing his poleaxe overhand. He caught the helmet of a man behind. It slowed his swing and as the axe came down, I blocked it with my sword and rammed my dagger under his right arm. Blood spurted across my hand and he fell. The other four met similar deaths and the enemy now had a barrier of bodies.

We used the hiatus to take another forty steps and found ourselves in the place where buildings had been cleared. I heard, from the walls, Alan of the Woods shout, "The gate is clear, lord! You can turn and run!"

I trusted my archers and I said, "You heard the Captain! We have done all that we needed. Now run."

As we turned, I heard a double whoosh of arrows. Alan of the Woods and my archers sent theirs towards the enemy and a blindly loosed shower struck us in the back and heads. Natty Longjack fell. An arrow had pierced his left shoulder and the force of the arrow had knocked him from his feet. Harry and I sheathed our swords and picked him up. I felt a thump on my back as an arrow hit me there and then Harry and I half dragged and half carried the wounded sergeant. We made the gates and they were slammed behind us. We were now truly besieged.

Natty smiled wanly in the fading light, "I owe you a life, lord and you too Master Henry!"

"Before this is over, Natty, there will be many lives lost. Get to the healer!"

Chapter 19

The enemy set fire to the rest of Shrewsbury. Perhaps they hoped that the wind would come to their aid and spread to the castle. It did not and dawn found us facing each other across a blackened field of charred and burned buildings. The men of Cheshire and Northumberland then made the mistake of taunting our men. We had lost archers on the walls and we had not had time to recover their bodies. Their heads, complete with right hands stuffed in the dead mouths were embedded in the ground just beyond bow range. Or so they thought. One of their men decided to drop his breeks and bare his arse at us. Alan of the Woods could send an arrow further than any man I knew and he carefully chose a war arrow, nocked it and sent it into the buttocks of the Northumbrian. He fell screaming and blood spurted.

Much Longbow nodded in satisfaction, "Unless they have a healer close at hand that is a dead man!"

He was proved correct. Within a few moments, the man stopped twitching as the widening pool of blood spread. I heard a command given and the archers pulled back. Hotspur thought he had all the time in the world to break us down without too great a loss of men. Once again, he was proved wrong. In the late afternoon, one of the camp guards ran up to the gatehouse where the Prince, his steward and I had spent the day. He pointed to the south-east, "Lord, there are outriders from your father. He and the army are crossing the river at Alcham. He will be here by dawn. He has the Earl of Stafford with him!"

The word spread and men cheered. The same news must have reached Hotspur for, as darkness fell, his army headed up the north-west road to the village of Berwick.

Prince Henry nodded, "He has not let me down and now we have a chance."

By dawn, the King's army was marching along the loop in the river. The Prince and his father had hailed each other across the river. I saw the banners of my son and knights amongst the host of knights who followed King Henry. I also saw that along with the Earl of Stafford, the Earl of March was with them. "Let us march to Haughmond Abbey. We will camp there and seek battle with Hotspur."

"Aye, and I will send scouts to find where he has fled."

We chose four of my archers and they headed north and west after the rebel army. We headed up the road to the Abbey. The Prince left a garrison at the castle for we had men who were not mounted and then we rode to the Abbey. By nightfall, father and son were reunited. While the two Henrys spoke, I joined my son and my knights. I saw the relief on Thomas's face, "My mother feared that your illness would have weakened you!"

I laughed, "That was months ago but it is good to see my knights."

"And I also bring news, you have another grandson, Henry."

I was overjoyed, "And mother and child are well?"

Thomas laughed, "Mary was made for bearing children!"

I now had even more reason to return home. All that was needed was to defeat Hotspur, no easy task, and then Glendower! When my scouts returned, they said that the enemy was in Berwick which lay a few miles west of us on the other side of the Whitchurch Road. The King held a council of war. I was not invited. I was satisfied that Sir George Dunbarre was there. He had an old and wise head upon his shoulders for I had seen, in the borders, his skill. They did not need me. I did not mind for I was able to spend the time with my knights and sons. Their company was preferable. I was about to turn in when I was sent for by Geoffrey, one of King Henry's pages, "His Majesty would like to speak with you, Sir William."

I went alone to speak with him. The Prince was there and the Earl of Stafford as well as his standard bearer Sir Walter Blount. The King began without preamble, "Sir William, I thank you again for all that you have done for my son. We did not invite you to our council for it was a council of peace and not war."

222

I was shocked that the King could even consider peace talks. "Peace, King Henry? Percy and his uncle are rebels and traitors! You do not negotiate with them!"

He laughed, "Ever telling a King what he may and may not do. His father, the Earl of Northumberland is bringing men from the north even as we speak. Glendower has had his nose bloodied but he may march to aid Hotspur. The men I have are all that there is. I am not certain that we can beat them for they have a greater number of archers."

"We can beat them, King Henry, give us a chance."

He looked at his son, "And those were the exact words my son used. We may well have to fight but we try peace first. We leave at dawn towards the Whitchurch Road. The abbots of Haughmond and Shrewsbury will ride to the rebels and negotiate with them. I have asked them to discover what are the grievances and demands of the rebels."

"Surely you do not give in to demands?" I shook my head and remembered a brave young King Richard, younger than Henry was now, facing down Wat Tyler and his mob. He had not given in to demands. I did not mention that. His son also had affection for the dead King.

"Do not lecture me. That is not the reason I summoned you!" His face was angry; no doubt he had remembered King Richard and Wat Tyler. I saw Prince Henry shake his head. He would be a different king from his father. "If we have to fight tomorrow then you and your knights will be in the centre with me. My son will lead the left and the Earl of Stafford the right."

I was torn for as much as I wished to fight with my son, I wanted to be there to protect England's hope, Prince Henry!

"I also wish you to act in the role you performed so admirably for my cousin. I wish you to be my bodyguard." He nodded and Sir Walter handed me a surcoat. "Tomorrow, you will wear my spare surcoat. I have another knight, Sir James of Stockton, who will also wear my surcoat. If we have to fight then I wish to confuse my enemies." He smiled, "I understand that Sir James has done well in tourneys and none can best you in battle. It would be better if you wore a boar's snout helmet too!"

I shook my head, "I will happily play the King but I fight in my own helmet."

The King nodded, "So long as you fight to protect the royal person then I am happy. The number of archers which Percy commands means that we fight on foot. Have your squire use one of my shields." He smiled, "Hopefully, we will be able to negotiate a peace and you will not have to draw a sword."

I shook my head, "Hotspur will fight. You can put money on that, King Henry!"

The Prince left with me, "I confess Sir William, that I would have you at my side if I could but this may be for the best. There is much anger in the Percys. They will wish blood. We both know that arrows do not choose their victims. They cannot ask for ransom. Tomorrow will either be peaceful or a bloody day. I pray you to take care and live. If God allows me to live and to become King of England then I will need you by my side."

When I told my knights of the King's decision, they were angry both with the negotiations and the deception. Sir John said, "He expects Hotspur to try to kill the King! You will find the best of his knights trying to slay you!"

I nodded, "If that is my lot then so be it but you will not need to risk your lives."

Sir Roger snorted, "Lord, I have spent half of my life fighting for you! No matter what surcoat you wear I will be protecting your back!"

My men chorused their agreement. I felt proud although I also felt dread. This could be the end of my family for despite my words I knew that Hotspur was a good general and even if we won there would be many good men who would die. After I had prayed that night and as I lay in my cot, I reflected that this could be my last night on earth. I would not see my new grandson and then I took heart. This would not be the end of my family! I had two grandsons. Even if Thomas and Harry died along with me my title was hereditary and Henry would inherit it! For some reason that made sleep come a little easier.

We left early in the morning and set up our baggage camp just half a mile north of Harlescott. It felt strange to be wearing a royal surcoat. I had a cloak about the surcoat so that I was hidden from the eyes of the enemy. Harry took Hawk to the baggage camp. I had left most of my valuables in Shrewsbury and did not have to use the tents erected for the purpose. The churchmen and their escorts left for Hotspur's camp which was to the north of us. We were negotiating but we arrayed for war. Hotspur had set up his lines beyond the range of bows. Our archers would face the rebel archers. Prince Henry commanded our left and the Earl of Stafford our right. The two abbots returned and told the King that Hotspur was aggrieved that he had taken the crown illegally and that it should have gone to the son of the Earl of March. He also claimed that the King had sworn before he was crowned that he had no intention of claiming the throne. The letter the King had sent was also cited as a cause for the rebellion.

I was close to the King when he gave his reply, "My lords, ride back to Sir Henry and tell him that if he sends someone to negotiate, I will try to answer these charges for I am loath to spill English blood this close to Wales."

The King was hopeful about the outcome and he laughed and joked with us while we awaited the return of his emissary. "We can settle this amicably and then head for the Tywi valley where Lord Carew has just defeated seven hundred Welshmen. This day may see the start of a time of peace in the realm."

I knew when the emissary arrived that a battle was inevitable. It was Thomas Percy, the Earl of Worcester who came to deliver the rebels' answer. His face showed the enmity he felt towards the King as he listened to the King's answer to the charges the rebels had laid. "I will return to London and summon Parliament. We will ask Parliament if I have the right to be King. If they decide against me then I will abdicate in favour of whichever man they choose to take the crown. As for the ransoms then, to save bloodshed, I will allow Sir Henry to collect the ransoms from the Scots although, as I see the banner of the Earl of Douglas on the field, I think that there will be no ransom."

Sir Thomas stood and said, "I will deliver your words!"

He was away so long that I thought we might have to camp a second night. Eventually, Thomas Knayton and Roger Salvayn, two of Hotspur's esquires brought us his answer. "Sir Henry rejects your proposals for you lied to get the crown. You are perjured and false. Prepare to die at Sir Henry's hands!"

All of us were shocked at the answer Hotspur had sent for King Henry's words had been most reasonable. The reason for the battle appeared to be the past and I wondered why they had bothered to negotiate. We later learned that Sir Thomas had lied to his nephew. That lie cost almost four thousand men their lives. The King nodded, "Go to your battles. We fight this day!"

I looked west to the setting sun. We had just two hours before dark. We might be fighting at night and that was a hard thing to do when you were fighting your countrymen. I took off my cloak as Sir Walter gave the signal for us to move up. Once we were in range of arrows then the killing would begin on both sides. I turned to my sons and my knights. I held my hand out and each of them laid their right hand on top, "May God be with us and I pray that when this day is done, we are all here to meet again. If today is my turn to die then it has been a privilege and an honour to fight alongside each of you, your squires and your men!"

None wore helmets yet and I saw that each of them was too full to speak so they nodded. Sir Roger and Sir Wilfred had fought with me since I had served King Richard. Sir John had been my squire and my sons were dearer to me than my own life. We moved to the north. Our men at arms followed us. Captain Edgar was behind us but Captain Alan was with the other archers.

Bizarrely there was no formal command to fight. As soon as the archers were within bowshot they loosed as did the men of Cheshire. Harry had one of the King's shields and he held it before us. Arrows rattled and smacked off it. Some hit my arms and my helmet but did no harm for I had plate and the arrows, in the main, were war arrows and then men began to die. I saw our archers' ranks thinned. I knew that the archers of Cheshire would also be suffering but some of those who were dying were my men. Both sets of archers were the best at what they did and they fought without even thinking about fleeing. Both sides began the battle with more than four thousand archers. Forty thousand arrows descending from the sky would kill and wound many men and kill they did. I was ten men from the King and Sir James of Stockton was ten men the other side of him. I was close enough, therefore, to hear the news when it was delivered to him, "Your Majesty, your son has been struck in the head by an arrow!" The King nodded. I could not see his face for he wore a boar's snout basinet but I think he would have been upset and it might have sucked the heart from him.

More men fell and then I heard a wail. "The right has broken!" I turned and saw that the men on the right of us, under the command of the Earl of Stafford, had suffered many casualties and could bear no more. They ran. When Sir Edmund, the Earl of Stafford and his knights joined us I knew that disaster had struck us. With the Prince dead or out of the battle at least and our right wing in tatters then Percy could focus all of his attention on us. I heard his horns sound as he led his men to attack. The arrow storm would end and the butchery begin.

With Sir George and the Earl of Stafford close by the King he had the greatest knights in the land to protect him but it soon became obvious that he would be the focus of the rebel attack. Night would fall soon and having come so close to victory Hotspur and Douglas would want the battle ended before the King could escape. Although the arrow storm had ended, Cheshire archers still advanced with the knights and esquires. The arrows would be more deadly for they would be sent horizontally and with a bodkin tip could force their way into the visor of a helmet. I was a rarity. I used a sword and dagger while the rest used longer weapons such as pikes and poleaxes. Perhaps I was a relic of the past but it was the way I had been taught to fight and I felt more comfortable with a sword in my hand. My open helmet helped me too. It put me at risk of an arrow but allowed me better judgement to deflect pole weapons.

As soon as our flank was unprotected then Hotspur and his men ran at us. Already men were falling before us. The rebels were desperate to get to the King. I saw Hotspur as he hacked his way towards Sir James of Stockton. Now the winner of many tournaments would be tested for Henry Percy was a killer. I had to force my attention to the battle before me. I could not see the knights behind me but I had the King, Sir Walter, Sir George and Sir Robert Gousehill to my right. Between us were half a dozen knights I did not know save that they were young and keen to protect the King.

A half a dozen men launched themselves at me. A knight led his men at arms to garner the glory of killing the King. It was my son, Thomas, who took on the knight. We later learned that it was Harold's tormentor, Richard de Ros and behind him came a man I recognised. It was Jean de Caen, the many who had almost ruined

Gilles' life. The mercenary recognised me and began to shout, "This is not the…"

He got no further for I could not allow the deception to be revealed. I shouted, "Killer of women! Today you pay for your crimes!"

The man had a double-handed axe and he swung it at me. He knew I was old and perhaps he thought I would be slow. I moved too quickly for him and I stepped inside the swing so that we were face to face and only the haft hit my arm. I slid my sword into his surcoat and it found the bottom of his breastplate. I sliced the sword through the mail and saw his mouth widen in pain. I stabbed upwards with my dagger and managed to find a gap so that the bodkin tip of the dagger went through his mail and into his elbow. He was hurt but he could still shout and reveal that I was not the King. I pulled my sword and pushed it up between our two bodies. He dropped his axe and grabbed the sword with his left hand for I had hurt his right arm. He was a strong man and he tried to stop the blade. I found a strength from I know not where and when the tip found his coif, I saw his eyes widen and he shook his head. I rammed it upwards and it went through his lower jaw and into his skull. I saw the light leave his eyes and when I stepped back, his body slid from my sword.

I saw that Thomas had despatched the knight he had been fighting and I shouted, "Back in line!" Sir Roger and Sir Wilfred had also moved forward and now they rejoined me.

It was Sir Archibald Douglas and his men who next came at me. The canny Scot allowed his younger knights to come at me and my men first. I saw a long spear, held by a young knight, hurtling towards my face. The young Scottish lord thought he had the King. I could see, for he had an open helmet, his mouth forming the cry of victory. It was premature. I flicked the head of the spear to slice through the borrowed surcoat as I brought my sword down on the weak part of his armour between his shoulder and his helmet. It broke the links, ripped through the jupon and then sliced through muscle, sinew, tendons and arteries. His head was shaking as he tried to lift an arm which would not obey his orders. He fell at my feet.

I had no time for self-congratulation for as Sir Archibald hacked into Sir Walter Blount, a second Scottish knight swung his poleaxe at my head. It was a powerful blow and neither my sword nor my dagger would slow it. I did the unexpected and dropped to my right knee. As the axe head slid over my head to hit my backplate I lunged upwards with my dagger. The bodkin tip tore through the mail and into his thigh. He too dropped to a knee and as I rose, I brought my sword down on his helmet. He still did not fall and I rammed my dagger through the eyehole of his visor. He still refused to die and so I swung my sword hard at the side of his head. This time he fell but, to make certain he was dead I placed my sword on his throat and put all of my weight on it.

A voice from behind warned me of danger. Sir Roger shouted, "Lord, ware right!"

I barely had time to block the blow from the pike which was thrust at my side. Sir Roger brought his war axe down on the man's head but the Earl Douglas took advantage of Sir Roger's distraction and hacked his poleaxe into his neck. As my knight and former captain of my sergeants died, a red mist descended over my eyes. I brought my sword around so hard into the side of the Earl of Douglas' surcoat covered plate armour that I severed the leather straps holding it. As the plate began to come apart, I smashed my sword into the side of his head. He was stunned and he dropped his poleaxe and fell to his knees. I saw nothing but my dead knight and I raised my sword to end his life. He lifted his visor and shouted, "Quarter! Quarter! I yield!"

It was the King who saved his life. Even though King Henry was fighting for his life he still had the wit to shout, "Sir William! He has yielded!"

I nodded and it was in that instant that Hotspur slew Sir James of Stockton and, as he fell, a cry rang out, "The King is dead!"

The King did not answer and so I shouted, "The King lives! The King lives!" Harry grabbed the Earl and pulled him behind us. It was brave for others around the Earl had yet to surrender.

Hotspur saw not me but my surcoat and he tried to get at me. Sir George Dunbarre pulled the King away to safety. I heard him shout, "Come, Your Majesty! You must not be taken!"

We were losing the battle and we had to hang on until dark when night's cloak would enable us to slip away. Until then we had to fight for our lives and I would be facing the most feared knight in England, Henry Percy. I was tired and I was much older than he was. It would be a foregone conclusion that he would win but I had to buy time for Sir George to get the King to safety.

Arrows still flew. One clanged off my armour and then I saw a second hit the Earl of Stafford full in the face as he raised his visor to see better in the increasingly gloomy twilight. He fell and lay still. Another brave knight had perished.

Sir Walter Blount was losing his battle with Hotspur. Sir Henry had already hacked into Sir Walter's body three or four times and his last blow ended the matter. His pole axe found the gap between plate and helmet. As he died his grip on the standard slipped and the standard began to fall. If it fell then the remnants of our army would flee. My son, Thomas, ran forward and caught it before it fell. Hotspur raised his bloody poleaxe to end my son's life.

"No!" I threw myself between the poleaxe and Thomas. I was able to use my sword to block the haft of the axe. Thomas pulled the standard behind me.

Sir Henry shouted, "I have you!" Then he looked into my face and shouted, "Deceit! You are not the King!"

He was so shocked that I was able to swing my sword into his side. All of my anger, as well as the fear of losing my son, went into the strike and he reeled. I had not broken the skin but I hoped to have cracked a rib or two. I went into the offensive and brought over my sword to hit his head. He managed, somehow, to block the blow but he was on the back foot and I kept driving him backwards. It was a confused mêlée all around us. No quarter was sought or given. My son was, for the time being, safe. He had followed the King with the standard but once I died then Sir Henry would pursue him. I had to keep going as long as I could and pray that darkness came to save us.

Sir Henry had experience and to buy himself time to recover his balance he swung the end of his poleaxe at my legs. I jumped in the air but landed awkwardly on the leg of the body of Sir Walter Blount. I almost toppled and Sir Henry jabbed at me with the spike at the top of the poleaxe. It came for my eye. My reactions saved me and I flicked up my dagger to divert the spike which merely scraped along the side of my helmet. I regained my balance, as did Hotspur. My first blow must have cracked a rib for I could hear his laboured breathing. He lifted the visor on his helmet and I took advantage for he held his pole axe with one hand. I hacked into his side again. This time it was the opposite side and I saw his face as it contorted. I had hurt him.

I was aware, to my left, of a cheer and a cry of, "Prince Harry! Prince Harry!" Was it possible that he was alive? I had hope once more and often that can make all the difference. I prayed that Sir George had taken the King to safety. We could always find more men and fight another time.

Hotspur had two hands on his poleaxe but I could see that his movements were awkward. I balanced myself. My sword was now blunted and was like an iron bar but I could wield it one-handed. Sir Henry needed two hands for his poleaxe and I still had my bodkin dagger. I feinted with my sword to test his reactions. He brought up his poleaxe but it was slower than it had been. When my blow failed to strike, he lunged at my chest and I turned as the blade came towards me. The spike tore through the surcoat revealing my plate beneath. I rammed my dagger at his back and found the gap between his back plate and breastplate. The dagger slipped through the mail links as though they were not even there and they came away bloody.

In anger, he swung his poleaxe and I danced out of its reach. "Trickster! You are a commoner who has neither honour nor skill!"

"Yet I will be the man who kills you and kill you I will. Do not ask for quarter. I shall not grant it. Only one of us leaves this field and it will not be you!"

I was deliberately provoking him to make him lose his famous temper. He roared at me and put all of his force behind a sweep. I saw it coming and dropped to my knee. The blade slid over the top of my helmet. Had I had an adornment as some knights affected then the helmet would have been torn from my head. I stabbed him behind his poleyn with my dagger and cut into the tendons behind the knee. His scream was feral. The light was now so bad that all around us were shadows. Surely the King had got to safety by now. I stepped back as he threw his poleaxe at me. It hit me in the chest and I tripped over a dead squire. He drew his own sword and held it in two hands. It would be sharp and I lay almost helpless on the ground. I used the only weapon I had left which could reach him; I swung my right leg and the rowel on my spur rang across the greave on his leg. He fell but had the wit to hold the sword in two hands to drive it into my body as he fell. I made a cross of my dagger and sword. Hotspur's blade was slowed but not stopped. It clanged into my helmet. Had I not blocked it then it would have split open my skull. He lay on top of me and I felt his left arm move to pull his own dagger. When I was a boy I had wrestled and now those bouts came to my aid. I shifted my weight as he tried to reach his second weapon and threw him from me. I used my dagger to lift my weary body up and I placed the tip of my sword beneath the bottom of his breastplate. I was tired beyond words and darkness was almost upon us. If I was to escape this defeat, I had to kill him quickly and get Harry to safety! Hotspur swung his sword at my leg. It hurt as it smacked into the plate but I gritted my teeth and leaned on my own sword. The tip went into the mail and through it. It tore into his jupon and then I saw his eyes widen as it entered his body. I leaned harder and blood spurted from his mouth. I twisted and turned the blade and when I saw his sword fall from his lifeless fingers, I pulled out my bloody blade.

I turned and, in the gloom, I saw Sir John and Sir Wilfred. Of my sons, there was no sign. All around us men were engaged in mortal combat. I shouted, "Hotspur is down! Hotspur is dead!"

I was answered with cries of, "You lie!"

"Hotspur lives!"

"Speak, Sir Henry! Tell us he lies!"

I shouted, "God, St George and victory! Let us end the lives of these despicable rebels."

From my left, I heard the Prince shout, "Aye for I am with you, Sir William!"

He ran towards me and I saw, sticking from his helmet, an arrow. Even in the dark, I could see the blood on his surcoat which made it look black. At that moment he could have been the Black Prince himself. It was that single action which ended the battle for a Northumbrian voice shouted, "It is true! We are undone and the flower of Northumberland has been plucked!"

While others cheered and chased the fleeing rebels I sank to my knees and said a prayer of thanks to God. I had survived. Now I prayed that my sons lived too!

Epilogue

The battle was a bloody one and many men had died. I had not just lost Sir Roger: Egbert Longbow, Robin Longarrow, Lol son of Wilson, Walter Longridge, Natty Longjack and Geoffrey of Gisburn had all died. Others, including Alan of the Woods and Edgar of Derby, were also wounded. Many hundreds had died. Numbers were hard to estimate for even as Sir Thomas Percy, Sir Richard Vernon and Sir Henry Boynton were being executed in Shrewsbury, men were being hunted down and slain.

Once I had found my sons and we had retired to the castle, I was more concerned with Prince Henry. He had been hit in his head by an arrow. He had raised his visor, the better to see the battle. Much Longbow suggested that the bow had not been fully drawn or it was at the end of its flight or else he would have been killed. The arrow missed his brain and his spinal cord but the first healers were little more than leeches and they broke the arrow. It took a good surgeon, John Bradmore, to remove the arrow. The castle was being used as a hospital and I was there with my two sons to watch the operation. King Henry was dealing with the aftermath of the battle.

I watched as the surgeon spent some time gradually removing the shaft of the arrow. Through it all the Prince never uttered a complaint, He bore it stoically. Harry was used as an assistant to constantly apply wine to the wound to purify it. I think that might have helped to numb the Prince's pain. After six hours, and as dawn was breaking, the arrow shaft was finally removed from the broken shaft. King Henry entered within moments of the operation ending. I suspect that he had waited outside and was unable to bear the sight of his son suffering.

"You will take my son to Kenilworth Castle and stay with him there until he is healed. You shall be rewarded, surgeon. Now, all leave us while I speak with my son."

Outside the three of us, Thomas, Harry and I, all spoke of the battle. "Are all battles as terrible as that, father?"

I shook my head, "Even in Spain I never saw one fought so desperately but then again this was Englishman against Englishman. Men fought, not for money, but for their leaders."

"And you defeated one of their leaders and slew the man they say was the greatest knight of his age."

Thomas shook his head, "No, little brother, that honour belongs to our father."

"Do not give me that title, son, for the last thing I need is to have men trying to take it from me."

"Harry, how do you feel about knighthood? You were behind me all the time in the battle. You stopped men from attacking me in the rear. You deserve it."

"When I see men like Sir Walter and Sir Roger dying, I wonder if I am good enough. I will think on it and give you an answer by the time the Prince is healed."

"And that shows that you have grown and you are ready." I turned to Sir John, "And I think we make it a double knighting. Ralph shall be knighted for he fought as hard as any."

The Prince was carried to a wagon. The surgeon and Prince Henry's household knights would go with him to Kenilworth where the surgeon would have to make special tools to help him take the arrowhead from the skull. The Prince was, mercifully, asleep as he was carried. away and was not there to see justice performed on the men who would be executed. The King showed mercy and was more generous than I expected. Fewer men were executed than was expected. However, the rebels who were captured were heavily punished financially. Some had estates taken from them. The Tudur brothers were found and they were also executed. Justice had been done.

After Worcester and the others were hanged, drawn and quartered, the King took Sir George and me apart where we could talk. "I owe both of you my life. Had you not pulled me away, Sir George then I would have perished and, you, Strongstaff, took my place and killed my enemy. More you captured Douglas and I will not make the same mistake as I did before. We will share the ransom. I intend to bankrupt the Scots! They joined Hotspur and they will share his pain! To you, Sir George, I confirm that you are Earl of the March of Scotland and to you, I give Percy's estates, Kyme and Croftes in Lincolnshire, and a house and chattels in Bishopsgate, City of London for life. To you, Sir William, I make you Sherriff of Northampton and give you an annuity of five hundred pounds a year."

We both nodded our thanks.

The King smiled, "You deserve more but that is all that I have to give you. This rebellion is not over. We have the Welsh to defeat. I do not doubt that the Scots and the French will try to take advantage of the rebellion and finally there is the Earl of Northumberland. I cannot let either of you go home yet. I have lost Sir Walter and the Earl of Stafford. My son cannot join us. I need you until Percy is brought to heel! This is not the end of the war but it might be the beginning of the end."

As he left us, I realised that my new grandson might be walking and talking before I saw him for the first time. Then I realised I was being selfish. My son Thomas would be apart from his wife and his child. What we had to do was end this rebellion quickly and then we could all go back to our lives. King Henry had shown me that he was a King. He had been merciful when others expected him to be ruthless. He had defeated a dangerous enemy who sought to rule England. I was still doing that which the Black Prince had asked of me, I was protecting England and the Plantagenet family. It would be a task which would take a lifetime and, I now realised, quite possibly my life. That was my lot but who would have thought that the child of a camp follower would become a Sherriff? The stars had plotted my course and I would have to sail it.

The End

Glossary

Abermaw-Barmouth
Ballock dagger or knife- a blade with two swellings next to the blade
Begawan- a metal plate to protect the armpit
Chevauchée- a raid by mounted men
Cuisse- metal greave
Dauentre-Daventry
Dunbarre- Dunbar
Familia – the bodyguard of a knight (in the case of a king these may well be knights themselves)
Galoches- Clogs
Hovel- a simple bivouac used when no tents were available
Medeltone Mowbray -Melton Mowbray
Mêlée- a medieval fight between knights
Poleyn- a metal plate to protect the knee
Pursuivant- the rank below a herald
Rondel dagger- a narrow-bladed dagger with a disc at the end of the hilt to protect the hand
Sallet basinet- medieval helmet of the simplest type: round with a neck protector
Sennight- Seven nights (a week)
The Pale- the land around Dublin. It belonged to the King of England.

Historical Notes

The Welsh rebellion and the actions of the Tudur brothers are well documented. Percy's involvement was a rumour, a rumour I have used. While researching the book I discovered documents which spell the Earl of March's name as Dunbarre. Most modern books use Dunbar but I have used the contemporary spelling. The raid of 1401 did take place and led to a retaliation by the Scots in 1402. It was while the Earl of March was defeating the Scots at Nesbit Moor that Glendower captured Edward Mortimer.

Henry Percy did defeat the Scots at a famous battle: Homildon Hill where the Earl of March fought alongside him. Although a victory, the battle laid the seeds for the Battle of Shrewsbury for a cash strapped King Henry demanded the ransoms for the Douglas knights.

The battle at the Blackadder Water was called the battle of Nesbit Moor (June 22nd 1402) which lies south-east of Duns. The Earl of March caught many hundred Scots returning from a raid in Northumberland. The Scottish knights I used were at the battle. The earl and his men did not lose any and the Scots were all either captured or slain.

The French did involve themselves in the Welsh rebellion from as early as 1402 and Bretons were at the battle of Bryn Glas. King Henry sent a letter to Henry Percy which forbade him to ransom the prisoners he took. It was like pouring petrol on fire for the King had already refused to ransom Percy's brother in law. King Henry, as I hope I have shown, was a most complicated king.

Warkworth Castle (Author's Photographs)

Prince Henry's wound

An arrow penetrated on the left side below the eye and beside the nose of the young prince. When surgeons tried to remove the arrow, the shaft broke, leaving the bodkin head embedded in his skull some five to six inches deep, narrowly missing the brain stem and surrounding arteries. Several other physicians had already been called on to resolve the problem but were unable to help. Bradmore instructed honey to be poured into the wound and invented an instrument to be used in the extraction. Two threaded tongs held a centre threaded tong, which could be inserted into the wound: the shape was not unlike a corkscrew inside a split cylinder. The centre rod, once it located the shaft of the arrowhead, could be inserted into the socket and it, along with the device, could be extracted. The instrument was quickly made, either by Bradmore or by a blacksmith to Bradmore's specifications. Bradmore himself guided it into the wound to extract the arrowhead successfully. The wound was then filled with wine to cleanse it. I find it remarkable that a sixteen-year-old could fight the whole battle with an arrow embedded in his head and then be awake when it was removed. It took six hours to do so!

The Battle of Shrewsbury

The Battle of Shrewsbury was an unusual battle. Not until Towton would so many Englishmen slaughter so many of their countrymen. There were no horses used. When the men of the Earl of Stafford fled, they raided the baggage train and many hundreds of horses and much treasure was taken. King Henry did, indeed, have knights dressed as him. The battle was fought at such a pace because of the negotiations which took place and meant they had only two hours to fight the battle. The Earl of Worcester did not report back the King's message. He also stole money from Prince Henry's house in London. Although a peripheral figure in my novel he had much to do with the battle. Hotspur's death was a mystery. In fact, as few had seen him die, because of the dark, there was a rumour that he was still alive. King Henry had his body disinterred and his head placed on a pike so that all would know that he was dead. The two bloodiest battles fought in the mediaeval period in England were this one and Towton. Both were fought by two sides made up of Englishmen!

This was an interesting book to write for there is much we do not know. Were Glendower and Percy colluding together? Certainly, Hotspur had a Welsh squire who came from Glendower's land. Mortimer, too, had his own agenda. This saga is not over yet. There is a northern rebellion to come and the Glendower uprising is not quashed until 1412, the year before Henry IV died.

I have tried to show the complex nature of Henry IV but he was an enigma.

Sir William, now a Sherriff, will return with his sons and Prince Henry. When I began the series, I envisaged it ending at Agincourt....

...we shall see!

For the English maps, I have used the original Ordnance survey maps. Produced by the army in the 19th century they show England before modern developments and, in most cases, are pre-industrial revolution. Produced by Cassini they are a useful tool for a historian. I also discovered a good website http: orbis.stanford.edu. This allows a reader to plot any two places in the Roman world and if you input the mode of transport you wish to use and the time of year it will calculate how long it would take you to travel the route. I have used it for all of my books up to the eighteenth century as the transportation system was roughly the same. The Romans would have travelled more quickly!

Books used in the research:

- The Tower of London -Lapper and Parnell (Osprey)
- English Medieval Knight 1300-1400-Gravett
- The Castles of Edward 1 in Wales- Gravett
- Norman Stone Castles- Gravett
- The Armies of Crécy and Poitiers- Rothero
- The Armies of Agincourt- Rothero
- The Scottish and Welsh Wars 1250-1400
- Henry V and the conquest of France- Knight and Turner

- Chronicles in the Age of Chivalry-Ed. Eliz Hallam
- English Longbowman 1330-1515- Bartlett
- Northumberland at War-Derek Dodds
- Henry V -Teresa Cole
- The Longbow- Mike Loades
- The Scandinavian Baltic Crusades 1100-1500
- Crusader Castles of the Teutonic Knights (1)- Turnbull and Dennis
- Crusader Castles of the Teutonic Knights (2)- Turnbull and Dennis
- Teutonic Knight 1190-1561- Nicolle and Turner
- Warkworth Castle and Hermitage- John Goodall
- Shrewsbury 1403- Dickon Whitehead

For more information on all of the books then please visit the author's web site at http://www.griffhosker.com where there is a link to contact him.

Griff Hosker
June 2019

Other books
by
Griff Hosker

If you enjoyed reading this book, then why not read another one by the author?
Ancient History

The Sword of Cartimandua Series (Germania and Britannia 50 A.D. – 128 A.D.)
Ulpius Felix- Roman Warrior (prequel)
Book 1 The Sword of Cartimandua
Book 2 The Horse Warriors
Book 3 Invasion Caledonia
Book 4 Roman Retreat
Book 5 Revolt of the Red Witch
Book 6 Druid's Gold
Book 7 Trajan's Hunters
Book 8 The Last Frontier
Book 9 Hero of Rome
Book 10 Roman Hawk
Book 11 Roman Treachery
Book 12 Roman Wall
Book 13 Roman Courage

The Aelfraed Series
(Britain and Byzantium 1050 A.D. - 1085 A.D.)
Book 1 Housecarl
Book 2 Outlaw
Book 3 Varangian

The Wolf Warrior series
(Britain in the late 6th Century)
Book 1 Saxon Dawn
Book 2 Saxon Revenge
Book 3 Saxon England
Book 4 Saxon Blood

Book 5 Saxon Slayer
Book 6 Saxon Slaughter
Book 7 Saxon Bane
Book 8 Saxon Fall: Rise of the Warlord
Book 9 Saxon Throne
Book 10 Saxon Sword

The Dragon Heart Series
Book 1 Viking Slave
Book 2 Viking Warrior
Book 3 Viking Jarl
Book 4 Viking Kingdom
Book 5 Viking Wolf
Book 6 Viking War
Book 7 Viking Sword
Book 8 Viking Wrath
Book 9 Viking Raid
Book 10 Viking Legend
Book 11 Viking Vengeance
Book 12 Viking Dragon
Book 13 Viking Treasure
Book 14 Viking Enemy
Book 15 Viking Witch
Book 16 Viking Blood
Book 17 Viking Weregeld
Book 18 Viking Storm
Book 19 Viking Warband
Book 20 Viking Shadow
Book 21 Viking Legacy
Book 22 Viking Clan
Book 23 Viking Bravery

The Norman Genesis Series
Hrolf the Viking
Horseman
The Battle for a Home
Revenge of the Franks
The Land of the Northmen
Ragnvald Hrolfsson

Brothers in Blood
Lord of Rouen
Drekar in the Seine
Duke of Normandy
The Duke and the King

New World Series
Blood on the Blade
Across the Seas

**The Anarchy Series England
1120-1180**
English Knight
Knight of the Empress
Northern Knight
Baron of the North
Earl
King Henry's Champion
The King is Dead
Warlord of the North
Enemy at the Gate
The Fallen Crown
Warlord's War
Kingmaker
Henry II
Crusader
The Welsh Marches
Irish War
Poisonous Plots
The Princes' Revolt
Earl Marshal

**Border Knight
1182-1300**
Sword for Hire
Return of the Knight
Baron's War
Magna Carta
Welsh Wars

Henry III
The Bloody Border

Lord Edward's Archer
Lord Edward's Archer

Struggle for a Crown
1360- 1485
Blood on the Crown
To Murder A King
The Throne
King Henry IV

Modern History

The Napoleonic Horseman Series
Book 1 Chasseur a Cheval
Book 2 Napoleon's Guard
Book 3 British Light Dragoon
Book 4 Soldier Spy
Book 5 1808: The Road to Coruña
Book 6 Talavera
Waterloo

The Lucky Jack American Civil War series
Rebel Raiders
Confederate Rangers
The Road to Gettysburg

The British Ace Series
1914
1915 Fokker Scourge
1916 Angels over the Somme
1917 Eagles Fall
1918 We will remember them
From Arctic Snow to Desert Sand
Wings over Persia

Combined Operations series

1940-1945
Commando
Raider
Behind Enemy Lines
Dieppe
Toehold in Europe
Sword Beach
Breakout
The Battle for Antwerp
King Tiger
Beyond the Rhine
Korea
Korean Winter

Other Books
Carnage at Cannes (a thriller)
Great Granny's Ghost (Aimed at 9-14-year-old young people)
Adventure at 63-Backpacking to Istanbul

For more information on all of the books then please visit the author's web site at www.griffhosker.com where there is a link to contact him.

Printed in Great Britain
by Amazon